Paladin

Book Four in the Serendipity Series

Brieanna Robertson

Whimsical Publications, LLC

Florida

Paladin is a work of fiction. Names, characters, and incidents are the products of the author's imagination and are either fictitious or are used fictitiously. Any resemblance to actual events or persons, living or dead, is entirely coincidental.

To purchase the authorized electronic edition of *Paladin*, visit
www.whimsicalpublications.com

Cover art by Traci Markou
Editing by John McAllister

Published in the United States by
Whimsical Publications, LLC
Florida

ISBN-13: 978-1-936167-13-5

Printed in the United States of America

Acknowledgements

This one's for Shawn, one of the only real Paladin left in the world.

And to all of the Vikings who made several years of my life like a trip back in time-
Agnarr, Dragnar, Kali, Grim, Erik, Larla, Yrsa, Nick, Kadlin and all the others.
Hail Hammerstorm!

Also, a special thank you to the Gateway salesman, Brandon Whitelaw. I stole your name for my favorite family and you never even knew it. I named Traveyn's first son after you.

"Cade!" Tawny called with a sigh. "Wait a sec!"

"Shut up!" Cadence spat. "I have nothing more to say to you."

"Cade, listen to me—"

Cadence whirled. "No, you listen to me! I am sick to death of having people tell me what I am and what I'm not. You, of all people, know how much I hate that and yet you label me anyway." Angry tears burned behind her eyes. "How in the world am I supposed to prove to anyone that I'm not a screw up if nobody ever gives me any room to breathe? I can't even think with all of the restrictions people try to place on me! I am not seventeen years old! I am a grown woman! I can make my own decisions, and if I mess up my life, it's my business! So lay off!" She shoved random things into her duffle bag with vehemence.

Tawny heaved an exasperated sigh. "Why can't you just find somewhere to breathe around here? Why do you have to go gallivanting off across the country with a stranger?"

"What am I supposed to do, Tawny? You work every single day. I don't have a job until the band goes on tour again. At least this would kind of be like a job! Or would you rather me just wander around Wal-Mart for eight hours every day while you're at the hospital? How many quarter pounders at McDonald's do you think I can eat in a day? Or maybe you think I should take up knitting, or needlepoint, or something equally as dull and boring. Maybe then you will all get off my back!" She crammed one more thing into the duffle and zipped it up, then shoved past Tawny and strode angrily back into the living room.

Talis' eyes followed Cadence as she re-entered the room. She opened up the storage closet and yanked out a sleeping bag.

"Oh, no way!" Tawny cried, flying back into the room as well. "You are not taking my sleeping bag!"

Cadence glowered, flung the sleeping bag back into the closet and slammed the door. She flopped her stuff down by Talis' feet and pulled on a sweatshirt. It was going to be dark soon and she knew that, even though the days had been hot, the desert nights were still chilly. It would be even worse in the mountains.

Talis glanced between the two women. Tawny was standing with her arms folded and she looked extremely irate. He shot Cadence a small smile and went over to her. "Tawny, I can understand your apprehension and your skepticism," he said. "You're right, I am a stranger. You do, however, know my name and the name of my friend. Do you think I would have given you any information about me at all if I was planning on hurting Cadence?" He spotted a small pad of paper and pen on the kitchen counter and he went over to it. "Here is my cell number," he said. "As well as the numbers of all of my friends. Most of us usually get a signal up there. We're camping on this side of the Pinals, so, if you need to find us, just keep driving on up your road until you find our campground." He looked up at her. "Would you like my social security number too so you can track me?"

She rolled her eyes and snorted, obviously trying to ignore his small, teasing smile. His grin was too sexy for words. "Don't be stupid."

"Look, I promise you Cadence will be safe. My friends are nothing but honorable." He handed the list of phone numbers to her.

Tawny looked down at the list and frowned. "Tempyst? Draco? Raven? What, are all of your friends from a fantasy novel or something?"

"Ash, Raven and I are very skilled with blades of any kind. Raven is the champion in armored combat, Ash is the best jouster known to man, and I took first in knife and axe throwing this year. Devlyn is a champion archer, as well."

Tawny stared at him for a moment before she folded her arms and fixed him with an expression that would have withered any less of a man. "Well at least I know that if my friend gets attacked by a bunch of angry, medieval Celts, she'll be protected," she said, her voice saturated in sarcasm.

Talis sighed. "Look, if it makes any difference, Traevyn Whitelaw is my brother."

"Traevyn Whitelaw? The famous artist?"

Cadence's eyes widened at this new information.

He nodded. "The one and only."

Tawny gave a thoughtful frown. "Oh..."

Chapter One

Talis' laughter echoed through the backstage corridor as he made his way toward the dressing room the band was in. "Evie, you are not going to deliver anally," he said to his sister-in-law, who had called him on the phone a few minutes ago.

"I really think I am," her despondent voice replied. "My butt has never been this huge. I swear, this baby's gonna pop out the size of Seth."

Talis shook his head as he pictured his pint-sized sister-in-law delivering her twenty-two-year-old brother. "Well, the Whitelaw men tend to be a little on the tall side. Like father, like son."

Evie groaned. "I just want it out."

Talis opened up the dressing room door, flashed his VIP pass to the band and raised his hand in greeting as he set his bag of supplies down.

"So, you're coming in a few weeks, right?" Evie asked.

"Yeah, I just finished up the renfaire down here. I'm going camping for a few days and then I'm heading up to Julian's for a bit. After that, you guys are stuck with me for awhile." He glanced around the room and spotted his client—the tall, lean, Gothic front man of the metal band, Bleeding Passion. Van Marshall.

"You're such a nomad," Evie teased.

"Hey Evie, hold on a sec, okay?" He held the cell phone against his shoulder and reached his hand out to Van. "I'm Talis," he introduced. "The tattoo artist you requested."

Van smiled warmly and shook his hand. "Van. It's good to meet you. Sorry we have to do this here. I wanted to do it as an anniversary present for my wife and, with the tour being so hectic, I couldn't squeeze it in anywhere. This is the last show so I thought it would be easiest to get it done afterward. That way I can just go on vacation and relax." He made a slashing gesture with his hands and shook his head.

"It's fine. My partner, Jerry, has done a lot of work for your band before."

"I know. That's why I requested your business. Why don't you watch the show? We go on in a few. Just come back here afterward."

Talis nodded his agreement just as the door opened and two women came in. One was Kat, Van's wife and head of security. She was one woman Talis would never want to mess with. She was beautiful, but with her martial arts training, he had a feeling she could probably kick him into the next century. The other woman made him stop dead in his tracks. She was gorgeous. Slender and regal-looking with platinum hair that was pulled up into a messy ponytail. Random red and black streaks peeked out and he could tell it was hacked into all different lengths. She shared a laugh with Kat and walked right past him. He watched her continue into the room, his eyes immediately catching the tattoo across her shoulders. He couldn't see what it was because most of it was hidden beneath her black tank, but the color was beautiful.

"Dang," he murmured.

"What?" Evie questioned. "Talis, are you there? What's going on?"

Talis started, remembering Evie was on the phone. He turned his back on the goddess and tried to regain his bearings. "I, uh..." His sentence disintegrated as his eyes meandered back to the woman. She was talking to Van and he let his gaze travel over her shapely body and creamy skin.

"Talis!"

He jumped and snapped back to reality at his sister-in-law's shout. "Sorry, I think I just saw the most beautiful girl on the planet."

"Are you working?" she asked. "What's all that noise?"

"Yeah, I'm working," he replied. "I'll call you later, okay?"

"Okay, take care, Tal."

He smiled. "You too, Evie. Hang in there. Tell my big brother hello." He hung up and put his cell phone back in his pocket.

"Cadence, what are you doing?" Lance Lawson, the bass player's voice called.

The beautiful woman turned in her progress toward the door. She fixed the blond rock star with a vicious glower. "I'm going to watch the show, your majesty," she grumbled.

"From the wings, right?"

Her eyes narrowed as if in warning. "I'm going into the crowd tonight." She turned back toward the door.

"Cadence, I don't think—"

She whirled. "Cram it, Lance! I don't remember asking you what you thought! I work here. I have clearance." She waved her laminate in annoyance. "And in case you forgot, I'm twenty-two years old." She spun again and barreled out the door, practically mowing over a roadie who was trying to get in.

Talis raised his eyebrows and exchanged a look with the bewildered crew member. The roadie shrugged and rolled his eyes. With a smirk, Talis followed after the girl. He did, after all, want to see the show too. He would just...casually make sure he was standing somewhere near where she was. That would make everything so much better.

The crowd was already frenzied from the opening band and it was difficult for him to get off of the stage and down into the crowd without being mauled. People caught sight of his VIP pass and immediately thought he could get them backstage. He saw more girls in the five minutes it took him to get from the stage to the floor than he had in his entire life, along with a lot more sets of double Ds. The girl who had come out after him didn't seem to have that problem, but then again, she was female. He briefly thought Lance's idea of watching the show from the wings might not have been so bad.

He managed to wedge himself in between a really enormous guy all in leather and a super model wannabe who looked very displeased that he had pushed in front of her. He ignored the dirty looks she kept shooting him and scanned the crowd for the beautiful woman who had seemingly disappeared. He heaved a sigh. She had been right in front of him. How could she have just vanished?

The crowd started to shout and scream as a roadie came out to do a quick sound check, and Talis chuckled. He loved rock concerts. They were so full of life and energy. He let out a yell or two of his own and grinned when the lights dimmed and everyone started to go crazy.

It amazed him that he was standing in the front at a Bleeding Passion concert wearing a VIP pass. Bleeding Passion was one of the hottest metal bands out there. All of their albums had gone double platinum, and Van Marshall was the most sought after rock god Talis had ever seen.

He loved the band's music and had always thought it was cool that his partner Jerry had done so much work for them, but he had never figured he would get the opportunity to meet them himself, let alone tattoo Van Marshall. Evie's brother, Seth, would kill him when he found out. He idolized Bleeding Passion, and Talis was pretty sure that he wanted to *be* Van Marshall.

The decibel with which the crowd managed to scream when Bleeding Passion actually emerged onto the stage made Talis' ears feel like they were going to explode, and the band launched immediately into one of their newest songs. He was jostled and tossed around like he was in a blender. He grinned, throwing his arm up in the air and screaming along with the rest of them.

Five songs in, Talis had to skirt away from the growing mosh pit, certain that he didn't want to have to tattoo Van Marshall while he was bleeding and battered.

Two people were currently crowd surfing and one of them landed right on top of him. Some flailing appendage, he wasn't sure which one, walloped him in the head and he stumbled as the surfer came tumbling down. He reached out on instinct and wrapped his arms around the person to keep him from hitting the ground and being trampled by the crazed fans. The person slid down his body, gripping onto him for dear life.

He looked down into blue eyes and his heart stopped. Holy crap, it was that girl from backstage. He stared at her, his arm still holding tight around her waist. Her hair was a mess, sticking out all over, and she was sweating from exertion and the horrendous, saunalike body heat the fans were generating. But her eyes... He felt like there was no bottom to them. They were large, clear, and gorgeous.

She stared up at him for a long moment and something silent passed between them like a sizzling electrical current. It seemed to take her by surprise, and she broke their eye contact to reach up to try and smooth her hair.

"Thanks!" she shouted, looking back up at him. "I thought I was a goner!"

Talis smiled and slowly released his grip on her. Fortunately, the band had just launched into one of their chart toppers and the fans were pressing in like rabid dogs, forcing her body to remain close up against his. She searched his eyes briefly, then managed to turn around. Paying him next to no attention, she went back to rocking out with the band.

He sighed and continued to watch, content to have her close to him at all.

After the show had ended and people started to file out of the auditorium, the woman in front of Talis wiped the damp strands of hair out of her face and turned to look at him with a smile. "Thanks again for rescuing me," she said. "I thought for sure I was going straight down on my head."

He gave a soft chuckle and basked in the beauty of her gorgeous smile.

"I see you have a VIP pass. Did you win a contest or something?"

He frowned. "A contest?"

"Yeah. Did you win a backstage pass?"

"No, I was hired to be here. I'm a tattoo artist. Van wanted some work done."

She nodded, then immediately frowned. "Wait...were you backstage before the show?"

He felt his face light up. So she *had* noticed him! "Yeah, I was just getting situated. Van told me to come watch the show." He pointed to her laminate. "You part of the crew?"

"Yeah, one of the roadies. I like to watch the shows, though."

She started toward the backstage door and Talis followed, trying not to stare too badly at the graceful way her hips swayed. His cell phone blared, startling him out of his appreciative trance, and he pulled it out of his pocket. "Hello?" He smiled at the voice of his longtime friend, Raven. "Yes, the trip is still on," he said as he grabbed the stage door and opened it for the woman. "Why are you even asking? We do this every year." He meandered through the corridor toward the dressing room as his friend rambled on. "Ash and I are taking vacation a day early, though. I think Tempyst might come, too. We want to spend one night at the river. He really wants to go fishing or something... Okay, see ya then. Bye." He hung up and returned his phone to his pocket.

The woman turned and gave Talis a smirk. "Male bonding?" she teased.

He grinned. "Yeah. Every year my five best friends and I go on a camping trip to kick off the renfaire season."

She frowned. "Renfaire?"

"Renaissance faire. We travel them every summer."

She stopped in her progress toward the dressing room and turned to face him. "Wait a sec, you mean you actually work at those silly things?"

He arched an eyebrow. "Well...yeah. They happen all over California during the summer. My friends and I go from faire to faire—"

"And do what?" She laughed, obviously amused by this conversation. "Pretend to be knights in shining armor?"

He frowned at the mocking tone of her voice. "We compete. We entertain. Several of my friends are craftsmen."

She folded her arms, unable to keep herself from giggling. "And what do you do?"

He stared at her for a minute. She was not giggling because she thought it was fascinating. She was laughing right at him. Right to his face! Now that was just rude. He crossed his arms as well. "I joust and—"

She burst into laughter.

His eyes narrowed. "—and I play guitar for the belly dancers. I compete in hand-to-hand combat, as well." He ran a hand through his hair and sighed, disappointed that she obviously did not have the personality to match her beauty. It was just his luck.

She kept giggling and shook her head.

"Katydid!" A blonde woman ran up to her suddenly and grasped her by the arm. "Your friend Tawny is out back waiting for you. Hurry up! And if you breathe one word of me helping you to anybody, I will never do anything for you again. Do you understand me?"

Cadence's eyes widened and she stood straight. "Where's Lance?"

"He's in the dressing room. I managed to get your duffle bag out to Tawny, so go before he finds out that it's me who conspired against him and divorces me!"

Cadence gave the blonde woman a squeeze on the arm and flew down the hall toward the back door.

"Nice talking to you!" Talis called after her. "Glad I could amuse you!"

The blonde woman raised her eyebrows and looked up at Talis with a perplexed expression. "Who are you?"

He looked at her. "Oh, I'm Talis. I'm the tattoo artist Van hired."

"Oh!" She grinned and held her hand out. "I'm Rochelle, Lance's wife and the band stylist. Come with me. I'll show you to the dressing room."

He started walking behind her, neglecting to tell her that he'd already been in the dressing room. He sighed and entered, going straight to his bag of supplies and getting down to the business at hand. He didn't know why he was so bothered by the fact that the woman had laughed at him. He'd been laughed at before. His occupation was unconventional and not everyone appreciated or understood it. But still...

For some reason, he had expected more from her than just irritating mockery and a shallow attitude. He didn't know why. He had no evidence on which to base that assumption. It had just seemed to him that, when he had looked into her eyes, he had seen more depth than that.

He shook his head to clear his thoughts. Oh well. It wasn't the first time he had been wrong about a girl, and he was positive it wouldn't be the last. Right now, he had more important things to concentrate on.

"So, what did you want done again?" he asked Van, who was sitting in a nearby chair, flipping through a magazine.

"My wife's name, Katrina," he replied. "Over the two musical notes on the left side of my chest. I wanted some embellishment, but I'm not sure what. Some kind of Gothic design. Jerry said you were really good at freehand."

Talis nodded as he began to set up his makeshift station. "Go ahead and take off your shirt. I'm sure we can figure something out."

Kat came into the room, munching on a snack, and she smiled down at Van. "You sure you want to brand my name of you forever?" she teased, absently toying with his long, dark hair.

He looked up at her and, though his eyes were smiling, his face was serious. "Positive," he murmured. "Right over my heart, where you belong."

Talis put on a pair of latex gloves. He pulled a clean needle out of the package and attached it to his tattoo gun, trying not to look like he noticed the passionate kiss Kat delivered to her husband. He turned to Van and smiled. "You ready?"

Van nodded and returned Talis' smile. "Again, I appreciate you doing this here."

Talis waved it away. "Not a problem." As he began the business of shaving the area he was going to tattoo and drawing out a rough design, he mused on the fact that he was actually tattooing one of the most famous men in music.

He didn't care what anybody said. He loved his life.

Chapter Two

Cadence sighed in bliss as she sat on her friend Tawny's front porch, basking in the Arizona sun and enjoying the feeling of freedom. It had been too long since she had experienced this.

She let her gaze travel over the Pinal Mountains, which Tawny's house was nestled against the base of, and she closed her eyes. Globe, Arizona. Hopefully, Lance wouldn't be smart enough to think of looking for her here. He would think she had gone somewhere in Phoenix. He would never think she had sought refuge in a small mining town made up of Native American culture and Mexican restaurants. She wasn't even sure if he knew about Tawny. Probably not. He only ever paid attention to the things that were bad in her life. He never took the time to listen to what was good.

"Cade!" Tawny exclaimed as she bounded out of the house and flung her arms around Cadence in her usual, exuberant manner. "I'm so happy you're here! It's been great to wake up the past two days and have someone to talk to other than the scorpions."

Cadence made a face at the mention of the bugs, but returned her friend's embrace. "It's nice to be here. After sleeping on a bus for six months with a bunch of scroady, smelly guys and a few scary women who can belch the alphabet, being in the middle of nowhere is nice."

Tawny giggled. "How did you survive the whole tour without having to beat the guys off of you?"

"Are you kidding me? With Lance dogging every step I took, it was next to impossible for any guy to even look my direction." She rolled her eyes and wondered why the image of that man who had caught her at the concert suddenly flashed through her mind. He had been very attractive with beautiful, black hair that fell nicely around his face and the nape of his neck, and his eyes had been light blue and mysterious. Both his ears had been pierced in several places and his face had looked to her like it had been carved in stone and then covered by something soft. His features had been sharp, defined, but not harsh, and his lips were the most sinful things she had ever laid eyes on. Remembering his arms holding her so securely made her feel funny in the pit of her stomach. Her first instinct was to stop the feeling as soon as possible.

"I think he was afraid I'd start a brawl or something," she said, pushing thoughts of the handsome man out of her mind and finishing her sentence.

Tawny frowned. "Are you serious?"

"Yeah. You deck one security guard and you're branded for the rest of your life," she said with a snort. "Plus, the head of security taught me some self defense moves and I think Lance thought that made me even more dangerous."

Tawny's brown eyes lit up. "Really? I have always wanted to learn self defense. What did she teach you?"

Cadence thought for a moment. "Well, if you hit somebody in the nose with the base of your palm, you could break it. Just do like an uppercut motion." She demonstrated and laughed when Tawny followed her example. "Then, of course, there's the good ol' crotch kick, or," she laughed, "if someone's trying to sexually assault you, get a hold of their balls and twist."

Tawny winced. "Ow... Yeah, I see where that could come in handy." She sat down in the other deck chair across from Cadence. "So, I was thinking, we've eluded Lance for two days now and he's probably hunting down Danny as we speak to make sure you're not with him. Is it safe to go out in public now?"

Cadence laughed at the whine in Tawny's voice. She lived on a two acre patch of land on the very outskirts of town, and they'd only had her two horses for company for the past forty-eight hours. "Yeah, I don't see why not."

Tawny clapped her hands in jubilation. "Great! We should go to the river! It's sweltering and I want to go swimming! Sound like fun?"

"Sounds like a plan."

Tawny squealed and jumped up. "Yay! Come on, let's get ready! I absolutely cannot stand this heat any longer. I wanna get wet!"

Cadence followed her friend back inside, happy to finally be on her own again, making her own decisions without somebody constantly questioning her. It had been a bad idea to turn to Lance anyway. He would never see her as anything more than a delinquent child. She was better off on her own. It was how she worked best. On her own with no one to answer to, unless she was with Danny, but that man was more of a sick habit than anything else. She would be best off if she stayed away from him as well.

Talis laughed as his friend Ashton reeled in somebody's old, waterlogged sock. The joyous victory dance he had been doing on the shore over catching something immediately ceased; he stared down at the sock in dejection.

"Now that's definitely the catch of the day," his other friend, Tempyst, commented.

Ashton gave Tempyst a dismal expression and unhooked the sock from his line. He made his way back over to where Talis and Tempyst sat lounging in camp chairs, and dangled the sock in Talis' face. "Here, I caught you dinner."

Talis swatted it away as Ash plopped down into his chair with a pout. "Okay, this whole thing seriously sucks," Ash muttered. "The Arizona Renaissance Festival sucked, and now my fishing trip sucks. I don't even want to think about what the rest of the season is going to be like for me."

Tempyst rolled his eyes. "Ash, stop being such a baby. You were the one who wanted to go fishing in the first place."

"Yeah. Fishing. Not bobbing for socks." He flung the waterlogged piece of cloth off into a nearby bush with a scowl.

Tempyst frowned in disapproval. "Great, Ash. Jack up the ecosystem even more than it already is." He went over to where Ash had thrown the sock, fished it out of the bush, and shoved it into the trash bag.

Talis chuckled and turned back to Ash. "And what sucked so badly about the Arizona Renaissance Festival?"

Ash snorted. "Come on, Tal! The entire situation sucked, that's what! You got to be Sir Talis, the Courageous and Noble Hearted and I got stuck with Sir Ashton, the Heartless Mercenary."

"Gimme a break, Ash. That was not your title," Talis said at his friend's exaggerated, dramatic plight.

"So what?" Tempyst put in. "So you got stuck being the bad guy this year. Most guys would take the dark knight over the paladin any day."

Ash rolled his soft, blue-gray eyes. "Talis gets to be the paladin every year." He sounded like a little kid who wasn't getting his way.

"That's because Talis *is* a paladin," Tempyst said.

"Dude! So am I! I'm so chivalrous I make myself sick!"

Talis grinned. "Stop being butt-hurt, Ash. It's over now anyway."

Ash scowled. "Easy for you to say, Mr. Courageous and Noble Hearted. Why don't we just clothe you in rose petals and bask in your heavenly glow while we're at it?"

Talis laughed. "Come on, dude! Your dark knight self kicked my paladin butt in joust this year."

Ash continued to grumble as he situated his chair so that it was in more of the shade of the tree they were seeking refuge under.

Talis sighed as he sat back in his chair. Tempyst and Ash were only two of the five best friends he was going camping with. Next to his brothers, Tempyst, Ash, Raven, Draco and Devlyn were the best men he'd ever known.

Ash lived with him in Sedona and had been his roommate for years. He was blond and buff and the most genuinely good person Talis had ever met. There was nothing fake about him. He had a heart made out of solid gold, and he was the best jouster Talis had ever seen.

Raven was the best at everything, and he knew it. He'd won so many armored combat competitions that his opponents prayed before they fought him. If sword fighting was an Olympic sport, Raven would have too many gold medals to count. He was cocky, arrogant, and a bit of a womanizer, but he was fiercely loyal to everyone he cared about. Once Raven let someone in, they had a friend for life.

Tempyst was an enigma. No one actually knew his real name. He had been going by Tempyst for as long as Talis had known him. Ash had known him two years longer and he didn't know his real name either. For the most part, Tempyst was always quiet and calm. He was level-headed, a diplomat, and a magnificent blacksmith. He made a living out of crafting authentic medieval weapons and armor in the way they had been crafted centuries before. He was patient, and had an intellect that would put most professors to shame, and if he was provoked to the point of anger, everybody had better stay out of his way. Tempyst called himself Tempyst for a reason.

Draco was probably the most like Talis out of the five. He was a fine mix of modern and medieval. Tattooed, pierced and leather-clad. Leatherworking was his craft and his job at renaissance faires, but during the off-season Draco could usually be found with an electric guitar in hand jamming with his metal band. He was a rocker all the way. A hardcore musician with tons of talent and passion.

Devlyn was the most normal of them all. He was the one who was setting up camp at their designated spot in the Pinals as they spoke. He was the responsible one, the designated driver, and the one who always got his projects done on time. He was the one everybody looked to for guidance and comfort. He was everybody's brother and everybody's friend.

Talis loved all of his friends like brothers. They had been traveling to faires together for the past six years and they had stories they could tell for days. Adventure was what they lived on. Six souls displaced in time, pretending to live in an era long past. They were freaks and outcasts to the modern masses, looked upon like the nerdy kids who thrived off of role playing games, but when they were all together, they were a breed of men that no longer existed. They were warriors of old, the stuff of legend and myth, and Talis loved every single minute of it.

"I'm seriously going to burn," Tawny said as she slathered sunscreen across her shoulders.

"This was your idea," Cadence said with a giggle.

"Yeah, I know. I just think I'm stupid sometimes. 'Sure,

let's go down to the river in the middle of the day when it's a million degrees outside.'"

Cadence wrinkled her nose as her friend made fun of herself. "Come on, we're having fun. If we burn, we burn. At least it's cool in the water."

"Yeah, no kidding. Hey, I have to pee. Come over to the bathrooms with me."

Cadence had never understood that whole go to the bathroom in pairs thing, but she stood, followed her friend over to the restrooms, and waited outside. It really was about a million degrees. Especially considering it was only late April. It was going to be a horrid summer.

She sighed and leaned up against the wall, watching the group of guys down by the shore. She'd been watching them discreetly for most of the day, but that was greatly due to the fact that one of them had long hair down past his shoulders and another one of them was shirtless and had more tattoos than she could count. He had two full sleeves of ink on his muscled arms and many more across his shoulders and chest. It was too bad she and Tawny were swimming so far away. She wouldn't mind getting a closer look...except she couldn't see the tattooed man now. He must have gone somewhere else.

She tore her gaze away from the men and it trailed over to the highway where a familiar-looking white Hummer was making its way toward the recreation area they were all at. Her eyes widened in horror. Lance! Holy crap, the man knew no shame! He was actually searching for her like she was a fugitive. It was insane! She refused to go back to being his prisoner. One of these days he was going to have to learn that what she did with her life was up to her and no amount of holding her hostage was going to change that.

She turned to seek refuge in the women's room, but Lance would probably just send Rochelle in to look for her. She was pretty sure that the only reason Lance was searching for her in this area anyway was because Rochelle hadn't been able to keep the secret from him. She didn't blame her. Rochelle was Lance's wife. Her first loyalty was to him.

As the Hummer neared and she ran out of options, she flung open the door to the men's room and ran for the nearest stall, which happened to be the large, handicapped one. It wouldn't be as easy to find her in there. She didn't think

Lance was bold enough to go peeking under stalls.

She yanked the stall door open and closed it quickly behind her, peering out of the crack to watch the door.

"May I help you?" a deep voice drawled.

Cadence screamed. She spun and found herself staring straight at the tattooed chest of that man she had been watching all day. She blinked in bewilderment. Not only was he tattooed, but he was...well, ripped was a good word. She forced her eyes away from his six pack and all of his ink and looked up at his face. "Silly medieval tattoo artist?" she questioned, recognizing him from the Bleeding Passion concert.

The man winced and rubbed at his ear as if her shrill scream had pierced his brain. "Well, well, well, if it isn't the rude roadie," he grumbled. "What a pleasant surprise." His blue-eyed gaze raked over her body for a second before returning to her face.

Cadence crossed her arms over the green top of her two-piece swimsuit and scowled. "What are you doing here?"

"Well, I was going to the bathroom," he replied. "That's generally what one tends to do when they're in a stall. Guess I'm just lucky to get the stall with the busted lock." He folded his arms, mirroring her posture, and gave her a questioning look. "So, do you make it a practice to just chill in the men's room, or—"

She rolled her eyes and turned back to peer out the crack in the door. "Don't be stupid. I'm not chilling. I'm hiding."

"Oh, so you make it a practice to hide in the men's room?" He snickered. "At least I was fortunate enough to have zipped my pants up before you came barreling in."

"Would you shut up?" she spat over her shoulder. "I'm trying to pay attention."

"Who are we hiding from?" he whispered against her ear.

"My brother." She tried to ignore the involuntary shiver that went through her as his breath tickled her neck.

"Ah...okay. And why are we hiding from your brother?"

"Because he's looking for me and I don't want him to know where I am. That good enough for you?" She shot him an irritated scowl. "And how dare you call me rude. I wasn't rude to you."

He snorted. "So, laughing in my face doesn't count as being rude?"

"When did I laugh in your face?"

He turned away from her to lean nonchalantly back against the wall of the stall. "Well, you asked me about renaissance faires, and when I told you about what I did in them, you laughed at me. Not to mention you just called me the 'silly medieval tattoo artist.'"

She waved it away. "Oh, come on. It's not every day I meet someone who says they pretend to be a knight for a living. It was funny."

"Yeah, well, I think it would be pretty funny if I hauled you out of this stall right now and threw you outside." He stood up straight and grasped her arm.

She gasped. "No, don't!" She looked up into his eyes. "Please! I'm sorry I laughed at you, okay?"

He studied her for a second with a frown. "Why are you so afraid of your brother?" he questioned.

"I'm not afraid of him. I just don't want him to find me. He treats me like I'm a little kid and tries to run my life."

"Why?"

She sighed in exasperation. "Because I was arrested last year."

"For what?"

"I beat up a security guard."

His eyes widened in surprise. "You what?"

"It was self defense! He was sexually harassing me. I was let off, but Lance freaked out. Of course it was him who I called to bail me out of jail. I don't know why. He's been attached like a barnacle to me ever since."

He looked as if he was considering something for a moment. "Wait, what? Lance? Who's Lance?"

"Lance Lawson. My brother."

"Lance Lawson!" His eyes bulged. "Lance Lawson is your brother?"

"Yes, and the fact that he's a mega star doesn't change the fact that he's an overprotective pain so just be quiet and let me hide, okay?"

Talis looked down at her and contemplated his choices. She was rude, had mocked him, and didn't seem necessarily sorry about it. It would be what she deserved to have him turn her over to her brother. On the other hand, it wasn't his place to interfere. He didn't know the situation and it would be wrong of him to just stick his nose in and act like he knew what was best. Or... He grinned devilishly and let his eyes study the beautiful tattoo across her shoulders while she continued to peer through the stall door like a spy.

It was a dragon. An amazing green and yellow dragon breathing fire. So, she must have some appreciation for medieval mythology. "Why should I hide you?" he asked her. "You were rude to me. Give me one good reason why I shouldn't squeal on you."

She turned and looked at him again, as if she couldn't believe he was actually thinking about giving her away. She rolled her eyes. "Man, I am never going to laugh at anyone ever again," she grumbled. She heaved a defeated sigh. "Look, I'm sorry, okay? It wasn't right for me to laugh at you. I'm an idiot sometimes. I don't think before I speak."

His lips quirked at the corners in amusement. She seemed sincere, but he was going to milk this for all it was worth. "Apology accepted, but not good enough."

She gave him a genuinely pained expression. "What is your name?"

"Talis."

"Please, Talis, you don't even understand. He's driving me crazy. I can't do anything without him asking me about it. He keeps tabs on me all the time like I'm his kid. I can't keep living my life like this. I'll go insane."

An idea was whirling around inside of Talis' mind. An absolutely absurd and reckless idea. He grinned. "I'll make a deal with you. I'll keep you hidden, but you have to be my squire for the rest of the summer."

She frowned. "Your squire? Isn't that like a servant?"

"Assistant. At the renaissance faires."

She raised both of her eyebrows and laughed. "Oh, that's funny."

He shrugged. "You would travel with me, go to the faires as my squire. I'd pay your way, your food, your lodging. Think about it. Your brother would never think to look for you there."

She met his eyes, which he knew twinkled with devilish mirth. "You're out of your mind if you think I'm going to just go off with a stranger and play warrior like some kind of—" She paled as she heard the door open, and she whirled to look out the crack of the stall again.

"Cadence!" Lance's voice shouted. "Are you in here?"

"Lance!" Rochelle chastised from behind him. "What is

wrong with you? You think she's hiding in the men's room? Come on! Leave her alone! She's a grown woman!"

"You're the one who said you recognized the car in the parking lot," he retorted. "Honestly, Rochelle, I can't believe you plotted against me."

There was a distinct feminine sigh. "I just thought maybe she could use a break," she said. "You dog her all the time!"

"And with good reason! She was arrested, Rochelle! Not to mention she's been in and out of trouble since she was fourteen years old! If I don't watch out for her, no one will. She's proven that she's definitely not capable of watching out for herself." He took a step inside the bathroom. "Cadence?"

Cadence climbed up on the toilet seat so that Lance couldn't see two pairs of feet. Her heart felt heavy in her chest as her brother's words echoed through her mind. She hated that he thought she was such a screw up. She hated that he never gave her credit for anything. She hated that he only saw bad in her, never good. She met Talis' eyes in desperation. "Please?" she mouthed.

He arched an eyebrow and shrugged.

She swore under her breath and hung her head in defeat. She couldn't let Lance find her. She would either lose her mind or end up hating him forever and she didn't want either one of those things to happen. Maybe being a squire wouldn't be so bad. Talis had a point. No one would look for her amongst a traveling bunch of medieval reenactors. She had done worse things on spur of the moment. "Fine," she breathed.

"Deal?" he murmured.

She looked at him and nodded.

His flippant smirk morphed into a roguish grin.

"Cadence?" Lance called again.

"Dude!" Talis shouted. "I'm trying to take a crap, man! Either take one yourself or get outta here!"

Cadence put her hand over her mouth to stifle her laughter.

"Sorry, my bad," Lance called as he quickly made his exit.

Talis turned to Cadence and held his hand out to help her down from the toilet.

She put her hand in his, climbed down, and tried not to pay attention to the gentlemanly gesture. She looked up at him, feeling kind of sick as she realized that she had just bound herself to this man for the rest of the summer.

She thought she had gotten over doing stupid things like that. Maybe what Lance always said about her being too wild was true. She never thought before she acted. It had always been her downfall. She just did what she thought sounded good to her at the time. People got in trouble that way. She would know.

"Planning on running from me now?" Talis assumed. "Reneging on our deal?"

"No, I keep my word. You have yourself a squire, warrior boy." She plastered a smile on her lips. She was good at smiling. She was good at hiding.

He grinned, elated in a way that was disturbing. He didn't know what it was about this girl, something in her eyes... He couldn't put his finger on it, but he wanted to get to know her, wanted to know what it was that intrigued him so much. He knew that there was more to her than her glib exterior. There had to be. He saw it. He felt it. And he wanted to know what it was. If he had to trick her just to get to know her, so be it. He only had one life and he was determined to live it with as few regrets as possible. The fact that he had run into this girl twice in two days was enough to make up his mind.

"Do I have to come with you right away?"

He nodded, deciding a few days of camping wouldn't hurt her. He didn't want to lose track of her and have her disappear.

"All right, I have to tell my friend."

He opened the stall door and motioned for her to go out first, pleased with himself. He knew she was far from happy about this, but he felt strangely at peace with the entire situation. He didn't know why. Especially since, generally, it was kind of a skuzzy thing to do, tricking a girl into being with him. Oh well. He had spent his entire life trusting his instincts, and they had never steered him wrong. Everything in his gut was screaming that this was the right thing to do, so he listened. Sooner or later, he would figure it out.

Chapter Three

Cadence was seriously pondering whether or not she had lost her sanity as she walked out of the bathroom stall and headed toward the door with Talis. She had just agreed to tag along with this complete stranger for the entire summer. Not only that, but she was going to be traveling to renaissance faires. How ridiculous was that? Who did that for a job anyway? It was a bunch of people playing dress up. People who had no lives. She heaved a sigh. *Nice going, Cadence,* she said to herself. *You've really gotten yourself screwed this time.* Her summer was going to suck.

She stepped outside just as a blond man was coming in, and he rammed right into her.

"Oh geez!" he shouted. "I'm sorry!" He stepped back and shook his head in obvious bewilderment. "Wait a sec, why are you coming out of the men's room?"

Talis chuckled as he emerged from behind her. "Long story, Ash. Meet Cadence. She's going to be traveling with us this summer."

Ash looked down at Cadence and blinked as if trying to figure out this new development. "Oh...okay. Nice to meet you. I'm Ash." He extended his hand to shake hers and he frowned at Talis. "When did this happen?"

"Let go of her, you sick freak!" a voice shouted.

Talis and Cadence looked up just in time to see a frantic woman barreling toward them. She launched at Ash and swung her arm upward, belting him in the nose with the heel of her palm. Ash immediately let go of Cadence's hand and grasped at his nose right as the woman kicked him in the crotch. He let out a whimpering wheeze and sunk down to the ground. He rolled over onto his back, pulling his knees to his chest.

Cadence's eyes widened. Great. Of course it had to be Tawny. Most of the time, her friend was very level-headed. Other times, like now, not so much.

Tawny turned furious eyes to Talis next and he stumbled back, holding his hands up.

"Tawny!" Cadence cried in horror. "Stop it! What are you doing?"

Tawny turned to Cadence and flung her arms around her. "Oh my gosh! I was so scared! Did these men hurt you?"

Cadence frowned and pulled away from her. "No, they didn't hurt me at all. What's the matter with you?"

"You disappeared!" Tawny cried. "I came out of the bathroom and you were gone! Next thing I know I see you coming out of the men's room with two strange guys and one of them was holding onto you. What was I supposed to think?"

"That I had a perfectly good reason for being in there, and that men who are assaulting someone usually don't stand placidly around the person they're assaulting." She knelt down next to Ash and put her hand on his shoulder. He groaned and she tried to help him into a sitting position. He was bleeding rather profusely from his nose and she sighed. Great, great and double great. Things just kept getting better and better. "Well, obviously you broke his nose," she said, looking up at Tawny. "Can you fix him?"

Tawny chewed on her bottom lip, looking sheepish. "Well, yeah, but I have to take him to the hospital."

"Help me get him up and to a car," Cadence said to Talis. "Tawny is a nurse."

He raised an eyebrow. "Are you sure she's not a hit man?"

Tawny shook her head and blushed. "Oh, I am so sorry. I panicked."

Talis waved it away and bent to help his friend. "No, it's all right. It was a misunderstanding. It was valiant to try and help your friend." He gave her a warm smile.

Tawny looked down and smiled shyly.

"Yeah, says you," Ash groaned.

"Cadence, could you do me a favor?" Talis asked. "Our other friend is over under that far tree where we were fishing. Could you please tell him to go on up to the camp site with Devlyn and we'll be there later?"

She nodded and hurried to obey, wanting to get that man to a hospital as soon as possible. He was bleeding so much, and he looked very pale. This couldn't possibly get any worse.

Why did disasters follow her wherever she went? It had been that way since she was a teenager. No matter what she did or where she went, chaos followed. She just wanted some kind of a normal life. She didn't want to be labeled "wild," "irresponsible," or "reckless" anymore. She wasn't any of those things. She was just a free spirit who had a little bit of a problem thinking things through all the way. It wasn't like she sought out trouble. It just seemed to follow her, and she was very, very tired of it.

Tawny was pissed. Cadence had actually never seen her so pissed. They had taken Ash to the hospital, patched him up and had driven back to the river to return to their own car. Somewhere in all of that, Cadence had managed to explain to Tawny about Lance and her deal with Talis. Tawny had promptly gone off on a tangent about how that was the dumbest thing she had ever heard, and she was not going to allow Cadence to do such a foolish and irresponsible thing. Hearing her friend use the same words that Lance liked to use when speaking to her, Cadence had become even more determined to go with Talis. One of these days maybe she would show everyone in her life that not every decision she made was a bad one.

They were now at Tawny's house because Cadence had needed to grab her things before she went up to the mountains with Talis, but her friend had other ideas.

"Cadence, you are completely out of your mind!" she was shouting. "You absolutely can not just run off with a strange man! You do not have to honor some stupid deal you made in a bathroom stall, for crying out loud! It's not like you signed a contract. Things aren't settled on a handshake in this century."

Cadence sighed, but it came out more like a growl. "Tawny, don't be like Lance, all right? I think I'm old enough to figure out what to do with myself."

"Don't be stupid, Cadence! He could be some psycho murderer rapist!"

"Who gets his kicks out of being a chivalrous knight?"

She could see Talis smirking as he listened to the argument. He was standing in the doorway, trying to be invisible. Poor Ash was sitting in the car waiting for his pain killers to kick in. Cadence shot Talis a glance, but said nothing. He probably thought the entire situation was hilarious.

"I don't care how chivalrous he pretends to be. You don't know him and you definitely don't know his five friends that he's camping with. They're all men, Cade! Hello! One woman and six guys! That's a bad situation just waiting to happen! Use your brain for once in your life!"

Cadence blinked and, as she processed the words, her brows drew together in an irritated frown. "Excuse me? Please tell me you did not just say that to me because I know you know me better than that and would never start treating me the way my brother does."

Tawny averted her eyes and sighed. "Cadence, you know I love you," she said quietly, "and I know that you aren't a troublemaker by nature, but..." She shrugged and looked up at her again. "You do have a knack for being irresponsible."

Cadence stared at Tawny for a long, silent moment and her throat constricted with rage and pain. She said nothing more, but pushed past Tawny and went into her bedroom.

"Cade!" Tawny called with a sigh. "Wait a sec!"

"Shut up!" Cadence spat. "I have nothing more to say to you."

"Cade, listen to me—"

Cadence whirled. "No, you listen to me! I am sick to death of having people tell me what I am and what I'm not. You, of all people, know how much I hate that and yet you label me anyway." Angry tears burned behind her eyes. "How in the world am I supposed to prove to anyone that I'm not a screw up if nobody ever gives me any room to breathe? I can't even think with all of the restrictions people try to place on me! I am not seventeen years old! I am a grown woman! I can make my own decisions, and if I mess up my life, it's my business! So lay off!" She shoved random things into her duffle bag with vehemence.

Tawny heaved an exasperated sigh. "Why can't you just find somewhere to breathe around here? Why do you have to go gallivanting off across the country with a stranger?"

"What am I supposed to do, Tawny? You work every single day. I don't have a job until the band goes on tour again. At least this would kind of be like a job! Or would you rather me just wander around Wal-Mart for eight hours every day while you're at the hospital? How many quarter pounders at McDonald's do you think I can eat in a day? Or maybe you think I should take up knitting, or needlepoint, or something equally as dull and boring. Maybe then you will all get off my back!" She crammed one more thing into the duffle and zipped it up, then shoved past Tawny and strode angrily back into the living room.

Talis' eyes followed Cadence as she re-entered the room. She opened up the storage closet and yanked out a sleeping bag.

"Oh, no way!" Tawny cried, flying back into the room as well. "You are not taking my sleeping bag!"

Cadence glowered, flung the sleeping bag back into the closet and slammed the door. She flopped her stuff down by Talis' feet and pulled on a sweatshirt. It was going to be dark soon and she knew that, even though the days had been hot, the desert nights were still chilly. It would be even worse in the mountains.

Talis glanced between the two women. Tawny was standing with her arms folded and she looked extremely irate. He shot Cadence a small smile and went over to her. "Tawny, I can understand your apprehension and your skepticism," he said. "You're right, I am a stranger. You do, however, know my name and the name of my friend. Do you think I would have given you any information about me at all if I was planning on hurting Cadence?" He spotted a small pad of paper and pen on the kitchen counter and he went over to it. "Here is my cell number," he said. "As well as the numbers of all of my friends. Most of us usually get a signal up there. We're camping on this side of the Pinals, so, if you need to find us, just keep driving on up your road until you find our campground." He looked up at her. "Would you like my social security number too so you can track me?"

She rolled her eyes and snorted, obviously trying to ignore his small, teasing smile. His grin was too sexy for words. "Don't be stupid."

"Look, I promise you Cadence will be safe. My friends are nothing but honorable." He handed the list of phone numbers to her.

Tawny looked down at the list and frowned. "Tempyst? Draco? Raven? What, are all of your friends from a fantasy novel or something?"

"Ash, Raven and I are very skilled with blades of any kind. Raven is the champion in armored combat, Ash is the best jouster known to man, and I took first in knife and axe throwing this year. Devlyn is a champion archer, as well."

Tawny stared at him for a moment before she folded her arms and fixed him with an expression that would have withered any less of a man. "Well at least I know that if my friend gets attacked by a bunch of angry, medieval Celts, she'll be protected," she said, her voice saturated in sarcasm.

Talis sighed. "Look, if it makes any difference, Traevyn Whitelaw is my brother."

"Traevyn Whitelaw? The famous artist?"

Cadence's eyes widened at this new information.

He nodded. "The one and only."

Tawny gave a thoughtful frown. "Oh..."

"I'm ready!" Cadence called, not wanting to have to stand around any longer. She was irritated by Tawny's lack of faith in her and just wanted to be away from everyone. Talis was a stranger. He couldn't make assumptions about her. Neither could any of his friends. She was starting to think that maybe the best place for her to be *was* with all of them. At least they couldn't condemn her right away. Maybe Talis had done her a favor.

Talis nodded and turned back to her. He picked up her duffle and went to open the door for her, but she didn't wait. She flung her hand up in a halfhearted wave at Tawny and blew out the door. The sound of his car door slamming seemed to resonate.

Talis glanced back over to Tawny and saw her expel a sad sigh. He gave her an understanding smile. "I promise she'll be safe."

She looked up at him, shooting daggers with her eyes. "Why are you doing this? Is this some kind of game for you? You think Cadence is a nice catch? Wanted to have yourself a little fun?"

He shook his head and held his free hand up. "No, that was never my intention."

"Then why are you doing this? She's messed up! She doesn't deserve to be jerked around by you and get more messed up than she already is!" She huffed and let her arms drop to her sides. "You don't understand. Most people have some kind of path in life, something that drives them. They know where they're going, where they want to get and what roads to take to get them there. Cadence has no path. She just wanders from situation to situation with no forethought and she usually ends up getting herself into something she can't get out of. She doesn't need any more drama, okay? She needs some stability."

Talis chose his next words carefully. He knew what Tawny was saying and he knew she was concerned, but he also knew what it was like to need to feel free. He had been a wanderer and a free spirit his entire life. There was nothing wrong with it so long as you gave your decisions proper thought. He got the feeling, just from what he had heard, that Cadence had spent her life being stifled, and that sometimes led to bad judgment.

He'd had a friend like that once. The desire to be free had been so strong that it had impaired his decision making process. He'd barrel into things before thinking them out. Cadence just needed to be shown that she could be free and still make good choices.

"I know that there's not a lot I can say that will convince you I'm a decent person," he said. "But I swear to you, I won't bring drama to her life. She's not a game to me. She's..." What could he say? That he was intrigued by her in the strongest way possible? That, for some unknown reason, he wanted to get to know every facet of her personality so that he could know why he was so intrigued by her? He sighed. "Well, I'm not sure what she is exactly."

She huffed. "That's comforting."

"Just know I have no bad intentions. I promise you that."

She still didn't look pleased, but she stopped arguing, so he stepped out of the door and made his way to the car. Cadence was sitting in the back seat, scowling at everything, and Ash was slumped in the passenger seat with his head resting against the window, his nose stuffed with so much cotton it looked twice its normal size.

Talis sighed, wondered what in the world he'd managed to get himself into, and got in the driver's seat. He glanced at Cadence in the rearview mirror as he started up the road and hated how sad she looked. She looked lost and lonely, and it made his heart ache in the worst possible way.

Chapter Four

Cadence was silent for the entire ride to the campground. She felt awkward and didn't know what to say. She hoped that Talis' friends didn't get irritated at the fact that she was there. She didn't want to feel like an intruder. She just wanted to feel like she was in charge of her life for once.

As they pulled into a barely visible campground, her stomach fluttered nervously. Talis parked next to a campsite dotted with colored tents and illuminated by a large, blazing fire. Three other men sat around it. Cadence took a deep breath. She really hoped this didn't end up being another stupid, hasty decision. She jumped as someone pounded on the driver's side window.

"Talis!" he shouted. "Get outta the car, man!" He pulled his ears out and pressed his lips up against the glass, blowing his cheeks out to look like a monkey.

Talis chuckled, opened the door and got out, followed by Ash. "You're a nut job, Draco," he muttered.

"You were gone forever," Draco commented. He made a face when he caught sight of Ash. "Dang... Nice nose, bro."

As Cadence got out and shut the door, Draco glanced over at her. He gave Talis a questioning frown.

"Draco, meet Cadence," Talis introduced as she came to stand next to him. "She's going to join us for the weekend. She's my squire for the summer."

Cadence looked up and met the eyes of the man in front of her. Shoot, he was just as hot as the rest of them. He was dressed entirely in black and his hair was black and spiky. He had several ear piercings, like Talis, as well as an eyebrow and lip ring. He was tall and broad-shouldered, and had the prettiest aquamarine eyes she had ever seen.

"Oh, okay," he said, smiling down at her. "It's good to meet you, Cadence. I'm Draco."

She shook his hand and smiled.

Draco turned to Ash and put his arm around his shoulders as they walked up to the camp. "You look terrible," he commented.

Ash gave him a withered expression.

"Well, at least you have a good war story now," he commented with a shrug.

"What is noble about getting belted in the nose because some woman thought I was attacking her friend? That's not much of a war story. Not to mention I think she kicked my balls up into my throat and they may never come back down."

Cadence smirked. "Just be happy she didn't get a chance to do the other thing I taught her to do."

Ash raised an eyebrow at her. "Do I even want to ask?"

She shook her head and looked up at the other two men who sat by the fire. One of them had blond hair about the same length as Talis' that fell carelessly around his sculpted face. His jaw was square and his cheekbones were high. He was beautiful, like a Greek statue, or those carvings of Alexander the Great.

The other man Cadence recognized as the one who had been at the river. Tempyst, or whatever his name was. He had long brown hair that fell well past his shoulders with a few braids interspersed throughout it. On the left side of his face was a tribal design tattoo that ran from his temple down to his jaw. His eyes were dark and looked like they held a thousand secrets.

Hey, this whole traveling with these guys for the summer thing might not be so bad. She hadn't seen so many attractive men in one place since she'd seen *The Thunder from Down Under.*

"Guys, this is Cadence," Talis introduced. "Cade, this is Devlyn and Tempyst."

Devlyn gave a warm smile and Tempyst stood. He took Cadence's hand in his and bowed over it slightly. "A pleasure," he said in a voice like satin.

Cadence raised an eyebrow and her face burned. "Um...thanks."

Talis grinned. "Raven will be here tomorrow."

"Raven?" she queried.

"Our other friend."

She nodded, set her things down and took a seat in the camp chair Ash offered her. She sighed and looked around at everyone, feeling very uncomfortable.

"Cadence thinks renaissance faires are silly," Talis said with a wicked grin as he sat down across from her.

As all attention focused on her, she tried to retreat into her chair. She shot Talis a dangerous look, but he just chuckled. "I just think it's kind of amusing is all," she said quietly. "A bunch of grown men playing with swords..."

Draco burst into laugher and a few other light chuckles followed.

Cadence cleared her throat and attempted to look dignified. "I was mainly just making fun of Talis when I said it. It sounded an awful lot like he was trying to impress me at the time."

Talis raised his eyebrows as the laughter and jeering turned his direction. He gave a helpless shrug. "Okay...so maybe I was trying to impress her a little. Most women would die to have a 'knight in shining armor.' The last thing I expected was to be laughed at." He gave her a halfhearted scowl.

"So, if you think renfaires are silly," Devlyn said, "why did you decide to be Talis' squire?"

Her eyes narrowed and she gave Talis a pointed look. "I owed him." She sighed and decided that, if she was going to have to be stuck with these people for the rest of the summer, she may as well get to know them. "What is it that all of you guys do anyway?"

"Well," Draco jumped in, "Tal and Ash do most of the combat stuff. I do leatherwork, Tempyst is a blacksmith, and Devlyn is an archer."

"And what about that Raven guy? What does he do?"

"Leeches off society mostly," Ash grumbled, "and tries to mack on all the girls."

A collective laugh went around the fire and Talis smiled. "Raven is the best and youngest warrior in the SCA," he explained.

She frowned. "SCA?" She felt like she had entered a completely different world. She was still having trouble wrapping her mind around the fact that all of these attractive men played medieval times for a living. She had been ex-pecting pimple faced teenagers and geeks with glasses who hadn't bathed in days. She had not been expecting six virile, beautiful men.

"Society for Creative Anachronism," Talis supplied. "The granddaddy of all historical re-enactment societies."

She nodded like she understood, but she still really had no idea what they were talking about. There were actual or-ganizations set up for people who liked to play like they were in a different century? Man, guess there was a whole culture she knew absolutely nothing about. She'd always thought renaissance faires were employed by desperate actors or something. She never would have guessed there were peo-ple who really did it for a living.

"Guess where Cadence works," Talis said with a grin. "She's a roadie for Bleeding Passion."

Draco practically fell right out of his chair. He stared at her, his jaw almost on the ground. "Shut up!"

Cadence couldn't help but giggle. "I'm actually Lance Lawson's sister."

"Uh oh," Devlyn said, "you shouldn't have told him that. You'll have a stalker now."

As if on cue, Draco stood and knelt at Cadence's feet. He took one of her hands and kissed it delicately, bowing low over it. "My lady, I am your humble servant."

She rolled her eyes. "Oh please," she grumbled, but she couldn't keep the amusement out of her voice, especially since Ash was making gagging noises.

Talis grinned. "Hey, does anybody happen to have a spare sleeping bag or something? Cadence doesn't have one."

"I have two," Devlyn said. "I usually unzip them all the way and use one as a blanket and the other to sleep on, but that's all right. Go ahead and grab one."

"The yellow tent, right?" Talis asked as he stood.

Devlyn nodded.

Talis grabbed a lantern off of the picnic table that was strewn with food, gear, and odds and ends, and he motioned Cadence to follow him with a smile.

She obeyed and trudged after him, shivering as she walked further away from the fire. She had never understood how the desert could be so bloody hot during the day and so friggin' cold at night. Her breath clouded out in white puffs, and she stuffed her hands into her pockets as she came up to where Talis had set the lantern. He unzipped the yellow two-man tent and crawled inside. Moments later, he handed her a sleeping bag.

She took it and watched him as he zipped the tent back up, noticing how the muscles in his broad shoulders moved beneath his shirt. It had been awfully nice of him to ask for a bag for her. She'd figured she would just have to sleep in the car or something. She cleared her throat, wondering where exactly she *was* supposed to sleep. "Talis? I don't have a tent."

He smiled as he turned to face her. "Neither do I."

"Where do you sleep?"

"Under the stars."

She arched an eyebrow. "Are you joking?"

He grinned, his features illuminated only by the moon and the lantern's glow. "No. Why would I want to stare up at an artificial ceiling when I could look up at that?" He inclined his head up to the sky.

Cadence followed his gaze and drew her breath in at the sight that met her. It looked as if the entire sky had been sprayed with diamonds. She had never seen the stars without the interference of city lights and, if she'd ever had the opportunity, she hadn't taken the time to pay attention. It was incredible and, for some reason, it made her want to cry. She didn't know why and she felt stupid for it. It just...

"Now *that* is freedom," Talis whispered.

Cadence snapped her attention to him and a tremor went through her. How had he known that's exactly what she had been thinking?

He met her eyes and his smile faded. "What's wrong?"

She shook her head, dispelling the strangeness of the situation. "Nothing, I just...uh..." She cleared her throat. "I've never actually been able to look at the stars like that before." She gave him a small smile.

"Never?"

She shrugged. "I grew up in L.A. There are no stars anywhere near there." She gave a soft laugh. "At least not the kind you find in the sky."

He grinned, and for some reason, her heart did something funny at his smile. She didn't like it.

She cleared her throat, which had gotten extremely dry all of a sudden, and looked down. "Talis, why did you make this stupid deal with me anyway?" she murmured.

"Why?"

"Yeah." She looked up at him bravely. "I mean, what's the point? What are you trying to prove? Why me?"

Talis sighed and ran a hand through his hair. "I don't know," he stated with a shrug.

She blinked. She'd kind of expected more of an answer than that. "You don't know? What, you just decided on a whim?"

His smile was disarming. "Kind of. I don't know, Cadence, there's just something about you..."

She folded her arms, waiting for his lame pick up line to come next. "Something about me that what?"

He looked her straight in the eyes. "Something that seems so lost."

"You mean I look like one of those poor runaway kids you see at the homeless shelter?" she grumbled. She dug the toe of her shoe into the dirt and focused on that for awhile so she didn't have to look at him. "Sounds about right. Reckless. Irresponsible..."

"No," he said, lifting her chin with his finger. "You just look like you need to get away from the life you know and live something different. Something that has nothing to do with anything or anyone in your past. Something that's all your own. That's why I made the deal with you."

If it was possible, her dry throat felt got even dryer. There was a drought going on inside her body.

His voice...

It was the most beautiful thing she had ever heard. It was so soft. Soft and husky like warm velvet. It was dangerous. Dangerous because it carried more power than Danny's and Danny had been able to make her do anything just by whispering in her ear. Talis' voice was much more compelling, and the fact that he was speaking her own thoughts made it that much worse.

She took a step away from him, trying to gather her composure and seem tougher than she felt. "You know you took a risk by just allowing me to come along with you. You don't know me at all. I could rob you, or steal your car."

He smiled a slow, sexy grin. "You could, but I'm willing to

risk it." He stepped closer to her to make up for the step she had taken in retreat. "You get to know people by taking chances."

She pushed a wayward strand of hair out of her face and tried not to notice how her heart raced at his nearness and at the way that grin of his looked highlighted by the lantern light. The shadows playing on his face made him look evil in the best kind of way, and that was not a good thing. She could never resist the bad boys. She'd never been able to... And Talis was gorgeous. And ripped. And tattooed. She suppressed a groan. This was just getting worse.

"Tal!" Draco's voice shouted from the campfire. "What are you guys doing over there, man?"

"Yeah, if you're doing stuff in my tent I'm gonna make you clean it!" Devlyn added.

Cadence laughed, grateful for the distraction.

Talis rolled his eyes and sighed, but he smiled when he heard her laugh. "Forgive them; they're vile," he stated.

"It's fine. Makes me feel like I'm back on the road. And even though my brother's a pain, I really like being on the road."

"That's because you're not tied down. Am I right?"

She met his eyes and gave a slow nod, swallowing hard. How did he keep doing that? It was like he was reading her mind.

He picked up the lantern and winked at her. "See, that's what it is."

She cocked her head to one side and frowned quizzically.

"That's what I see in you. Your soul is the same as mine." He grinned enigmatically. "I'm a wanderer too."

He started back to the campsite and Cadence couldn't help but shiver as she followed him, although it had nothing to do with the cold. She shivered because something about what he had said and the way he had said it struck a chord so deep within her that it made her heart tremble. It was not something she was used to, and she knew it should alarm her, but strangely, it didn't. It intrigued her. *He* intrigued her, and that was much, much worse.

Chapter Five

She couldn't take her eyes off of the sky. She just kept staring, drinking in the beauty and basking in it. She couldn't help it. It was so mesmerizing. Talis was right. It did feel like freedom. It was the first moment of real peace she had felt in too long and she wanted to soak it right into her soul.

She and Talis were alone now. Ash had been the first to retire, but that wasn't really surprising considering the poor guy was miserable. Draco had followed him soon after, claiming he had been up for twenty-four straight hours working on a project for a customer. Tempyst and Devlyn had stayed awake a little longer, talking with Talis about something that had happened to Devlyn earlier that week. Finally, however, they had turned in as well.

She had spread her sleeping bag out beside the fire, next to where Talis had spread his. She still didn't like this whole idea of sleeping out in the open with no kind of protection whatsoever, but she was trying not to be a baby about it. She heard the distant footsteps and cry of an animal she couldn't distinguish and it made her jump. Okay, there went that plan about not being a baby. She swallowed and glanced over at Talis, who was tending the fire quietly. "Talis?"

He glanced up at her. "Yeah?"

"It's a little scary out here," she admitted. Outside the glow of the fire, everything was pitch black. She couldn't even see where the others' tents were. Anything could be out there, watching them, waiting. She shivered. "Do you have a weapon or something?"

He reached down by his chair and held up a sheathed sword.

She stared at it for a second, her brain trying to process

the fact that he was serious. "Okay, that really doesn't make me feel any better. I mean do you have any kind of weapon that shoots bullets?"

He frowned and glanced at his blade. "Hey, Tempyst made this sword. Besides, I took second in armored combat this year."

She stared at him in disbelief. "Yeah, but the thing trying to kill you would have to get close enough to maim you by the time you could use a sword."

"That's what Devlyn is for."

She opened her mouth to retort, but found that she couldn't. How was she supposed to respond to a half-crazy man who thought that fighting with a sword was adequate protection?

Talis chuckled at the dumbfounded look she knew was on her face. He went and sat down next to her, leaning toward her with a playful grin. "Have I let anything kill you so far?" he teased.

She raised an eyebrow and pulled her knees to her chest. "Not yet."

"I saved you from falling on your head at the concert. I hid you from your brother. Do you really think I'm going to let something eat you?"

She smiled in spite of herself. She liked how the firelight shone in his eyes. The flames reflected in his pupils and made the light blue seem darker and more intense. A soft sigh escaped her lips.

"All of the food is locked in the cars. Nothing is going to hurt you, Cadence. Nature is beautiful. Enjoy it."

She snorted. "I enjoy it just fine in daylight away from mountain lions and bears."

"Just think of this as a trip back in time. It's like a fairy tale. We're the wandering band of roguish warriors and you're the damsel in distress."

She scrunched up her face. "Ugh, no way."

He couldn't mask his surprise. "You don't want to be the damsel in distress? I thought every woman wanted to be rescued."

She shook her head. "If some 'dark knight' was trying to do something bad to me, I'd kick his sorry butt into next week."

"Is that before or after you'd hide from him in a bathroom stall?"

She huffed and scowled at him. "That was low."

He laughed and prodded at the fire. "Come on, you have to admit it. I rescued you. You can't deny it. You were a damsel in distress. I *am* a knight and I *do* drive a white Mustang...." He shrugged. "All the pieces fit."

She rolled her eyes. "You're ridiculous."

"So you keep telling me." He flashed her a wicked grin.

She tried to maintain her air of indifference, but that was almost impossible to do when he smiled like that. She cleared her throat. "How did you get involved in all this renaissance stuff anyway?"

"My tattoo partner, Jerry, and I went one year and I was like, 'hey this is cool.' So I joined."

"Just like that?" she asked in surprise.

"Sure, it fit my lifestyle. My brothers always teased me about being born in the wrong century." He met her eyes. "Always wanted to be a warrior on a horse instead of a businessman on a subway. The middle ages have fascinated me my whole life. When I found out I could make money off of playing like I'd traveled through time, I went for it."

"Do you make good money?" she questioned skeptically.

He chuckled. "Not at all. That's why I do tattooing. Renfaires are my passion. Tattooing is my bread."

A different animal made a noise that sounded much closer to their camp and she let out a startled shriek before she could stop herself.

"Shhh," Talis commanded, not unkindly. "Don't start screaming. You'll scare my friends to death. Then Devlyn will come out with his re-curve bow and start shooting arrows into the night like Legolas. And Ash and Tempyst will come out wielding swords. Not to mention Draco sleeps naked and no one really needs to see *that* springing into the night."

Cadence laughed at the picture he created. She shook her head and sighed, gingerly easing herself into the sleeping bag.

Talis glanced at her and the way that she clenched the sleeping bag in her fists. "Cadence," he murmured, remnants of his magnificent smile still playing around his lips.

She glanced up at him.

"I won't let anything happen to you," he swore. "Trust me."

She hoped he was right and decided to just try and go to sleep while he was still awake. It would make her feel better to know the fire was going and there was someone alert and watching in case something should happen to wander their way. She closed her eyes and listened to the crackling and popping of the fire. She must have been more tired than she thought because she fell asleep almost instantly.

Cadence awoke slowly, her ears filling with the sound of birds chattering high in the treetops and the stillness that only came with being away from civilization. She shivered and opened her eyes. A thin layer of fog rolled across the ground and she figured it had to be somewhere close to seven in the morning. She rubbed at her eyes and sat up. Talis was stoking the fire, trying to get it to go again, but no one else was up. She yawned and tried to blink the sleep out of her eyes.

Talis glanced up at her and smiled. "Good morning."

She ran her fingers through her hair, which was a tangled mess, and she frowned. "Did you ever go to sleep?"

"Yeah, I just woke up a few minutes ago. Did you sleep all right?"

She nodded and took the liberty of studying him in the hazy morning light. He was wearing a black thermal shirt that hugged his body and a regular pair of blue jeans. She couldn't even remember what he had been wearing the day before, and she couldn't remember when he had changed. All she remembered was how delicious he had looked without his shirt on. She spotted the edge of his tattoos peeking out from under his sleeve. "Did you do your own tattoos?"

He looked up at her and smiled as he threw a larger log onto the fire. "The ones I could do without messing them up by moving around. Jerry did the rest."

She chewed on her bottom lip, knowing she should just leave it at that, but curiosity nagged and that was always a bad thing when it came to her. "Can I see?"

He made sure the log was stationary and the fire was going strong before he put the stick he had been using as a poker down and went over to her. "Sure." He pulled his shirt off in one fluid movement and stood in front of her, open to her inspection.

Cadence tried not to stare, or drool, but that was a difficult thing to master. She had described him as ripped the day before, but she realized that didn't even do him justice. He was gorgeous. Like the cover of books gorgeous. Like model gorgeous, only less manufactured-looking. He looked like... She couldn't believe she actually thought it, but he really did look like a warrior. Like a real, live warrior of old who swung a sword and wore armor. She had seen her fair share of muscle men and vain model wannabes growing up in L.A. Talis did not look like he pumped iron at the gym every other day with his personal trainer, and then drank his liquid protein dinner. His physique looked natural and beautiful.

"So, where do you want to start?" he asked, breaking her from her thoughts.

She blinked and shook her head as sense returned to her. "I'm sorry?"

He grinned. "Front or back?"

She hated that she felt a blush creep into her cheeks. She didn't blush. What the heck was the matter with her? "Oh, um..." She stood. "Back, I guess." He turned obligingly and she looked her fill, enjoying every minute of it. He had some kind of tribal design up both sides of his lower back and a gigantic Phoenix across his shoulders. "That's beautiful," she commented.

"Thank you."

She studied his muscled arms, which were mostly an intricate collage of images of Norse mythology, Celtic patterns, medieval weaponry and ancient myth and lore. As he turned, she saw that he had identical dragons on both sides of his chest. She gasped. "Oh wow!" She loved dragons. She had one of her own.

"Dragons and Phoenixes are my two favorite mythical creatures," he said. "I know you share a love of dragons as well."

She looked up at him with a quizzical frown.

"I saw your tattoo yesterday when we were in the bathroom. It's lovely."

She smiled and nodded. "Dragons are extraordinary." She turned her attention back to his tattoos, studying the rich, vivid color. "They're so strong and invincible. No one messes with a dragon." Before she even knew what she was doing, she traced her finger along the outline of one of the dragons, fascinated by its intricate detail. Reality came slamming back almost instantly and she jerked her hand away, her cheeks burning. "I'm sorry," she murmured.

He shrugged one shoulder lazily and smiled. "A beautiful woman touching me..." He reached for her hand and placed it back on his torso. "It's not like I minded."

Cadence's breath caught. His skin felt very hot, even though it was cold outside.

Talis smirked and moved her hand slowly up his body and across his chest, forcing her to feel all the lines of muscle.

Her throat went dry again, and her heart made a funny flip-flopping in her chest. This was not good. He felt so strong, so masculine. She had a weakness for strong and masculine. Crap, what was she thinking? She just had a weakness for masculine. Talis being drop dead gorgeous did not help matters. *Stop it, Cadence,* she told herself. *Just be strong. Use your head.*

She braved a look up at him and he gave her one of those cheesy seductive looks with the raised eyebrow. A roguish smile was quickly on his sensual lips. She scowled and gave him a light shove. "You're evil," she stated.

He laughed. "Maybe a little." He wrinkled his nose in a playful manner and she looked back up at him coyly from under her lashes. A smile tugged at her lips and she giggled, shaking her head. He grinned and she felt some of her brash bravado slip for a moment. "Come on now, I made you laugh," he said, touching her cheek briefly.

Her heart continued to do that flip-flopping thing and she had trouble meeting his eyes. She'd never had that reaction to a man. Not even to Danny. Danny was... Geez, she didn't even know what Danny was. A mistake? A disease?

"Eight in the morning and Talis is already getting naked."

Cadence looked over to see Draco stepping out of his tent, fully clothed, thank goodness.

He stretched and yawned as he approached. "Save some of it for later," he teased.

Talis rolled his eyes.

Draco came up to Talis and patted his stomach, looking

at Cadence. "Just look at that hot bod," he said dramatically. "Don't you just wanna lick it?" He grasped Talis around the shoulders and ran his tongue up his neck, then tried to do some kind of serpent thing in his ear.

Cadence raised her eyebrows and laughed.

Talis shoved Draco off of him and gave him a pained look. "Dude," he said, "that's nasty. I have to go sterilize myself now, thanks."

Draco laughed and headed over to the picnic table.

Talis shook his head and pulled his shirt back on. "It is way too early in the morning for you," he muttered.

"You think I enjoy looking at your ugly mug this early in the morning? Aw, why you covering up, stud?"

Talis gave him a sidelong glance. "Because I feel violated."

Draco's grin was contagious. "Hey, what do you want for breakfast? I'll cook for everybody."

Talis shrugged. "I don't know. Surprise me."

Draco pulled his keys out of his pocket and headed toward his car. When he returned, he proceeded to make everyone French toast and scrambled eggs. Almost as soon as he started cooking, people began to meander out of their tents and join them at the fire.

Cadence could get a good look at the campsite now that the sun was up; it really was rather lovely. It was nestled right against a hill and pine trees surrounded them in every direction. It was peaceful in a way that she hadn't experienced before. Then again, she hadn't experienced a whole lot of "peaceful," period.

"Hey, Ash," Talis greeted as Ash came stumbling out of his tent sporting two black eyes. He winced. "How are you feeling today, man?"

"Like I had my nose broken," he muttered. "What's for breakfast?"

"French toast!" Draco exclaimed. "Come and get it before Devlyn eats it all."

Devlyn looked up from his plate and frowned.

"Hey, Tal, did you bring your throwing knives and axes?" Tempyst asked as he sat down with his plate.

"Of course I did. Brought two rattan swords, as well."

"You up for a duel after we eat?"

Talis chuckled. "Sure, I'm always up for a good duel."

Not only did Cadence not understand half of what these people were saying, but she couldn't believe they were actually calmly discussing dueling after breakfast. She could swear she had somehow managed to fall into some kind of alternate universe. These people weren't normal.

Suddenly, a car turned into the campground and made its way over to their site. Cadence watched as a tall, muscular young man got out. He was dressed in a bright red shirt and his black hair was pulled back into a short ponytail. He was wearing a stylish pair of black shades and he waved and grinned at everyone. His smile was mischievous, playful, and Cadence could have sworn that he'd definitely taken a double look at her before he started to unload his gear. She couldn't blame him for it, really. He had been expecting to meet his friends for a weekend of male bonding. She imagined he hadn't been expecting to see one lone, out of place girl in the midst of them.

"Never fear, the party is here!" he called as he shut his trunk and made his way over to the others.

Everyone chuckled.

"Hey, Rave!" Draco exclaimed. "Right on time! Breakfast is served!"

He nodded and set his stuff down. "Of course. I always know when to show up." He grinned and gave Draco a brief embrace before turning and doing the same to Talis. "Hey, Tal." His gaze slid over to Cadence and he smirked. "Who's our guest?"

"This is Cadence," Talis said. "She's going to be traveling with me for the summer. Cade, this is Raven."

Cadence raised an eyebrow as he gently took her fingers and went to do that medieval kiss on the back of the hand thing all these guys seemed so fond of. She sniggered. "So, you're the guy who leeches off society and macks on all the girls?"

Devlyn spit out some of his coffee and started to laugh hysterically.

Raven arched an eyebrow. "Hmm, I see my brothers have been singing my praises again." He sneered playfully at everyone. "So nice of you." His eyes focused on Ash for a moment and he frowned. "Crap, Ash, what happened to you?"

Ash looked up dismally from his breakfast and glanced at

Cadence. "She has a very protective friend."

"Overprotective is more like it," Cadence muttered.

"We were talking about sparring a little after breakfast," Talis said. He nodded his head in Cadence's direction and grinned. "Show Cadence what we're all about. She thinks we're silly anyway."

Raven fixed her with a shocked expression and she sighed. She shot Talis a scowl. "Do you have to keep bringing that up?" He shrugged and gave her that devilish smile she couldn't look at without her heart doing funny things.

Raven put his hands on his hips and stood with an arrogant posture, like he owned the world. "Why wait? Devlyn is finished eating already. Let's start now."

Devlyn frowned. "What the crap? I'm an archer, remember? Besides, do the competitions have to start immediately upon your arrival? Can I maybe let my eggs digest first?"

"I'll play," Talis volunteered. "It was my idea anyway. Besides, I still have to get you back for that nasty trick you pulled on me last year."

Raven gave him a cocky grin. "Bring it on."

Chapter Six

After Talis had retrieved two large, wooden swords out of his trunk that looked like they were made out of really thick bamboo, he came back to the campsite and tossed one to Raven.

"Beat the crap out of him, Tal," Tempyst said.

Raven snorted and swung the sword nonchalantly. "Not likely."

Cadence frowned and shook her head in the disbelief that just kept on coming. "Big men playing with wooden swords," she muttered.

"They're rattan," Talis explained with his ever-present, easygoing smile. "We aren't allowed to compete with actual weapons so we use these instead, wrap the would-be blade in duct tape and paint the hilt how we want."

"Well, that's dumb," she stated. "How come you can't use real swords?"

"Because people like Raven would end up getting life in prison for murdering too many people," Draco commented.

Raven laughed and turned to face Talis, who had adopted a warrior's stance, and the two squared off.

"They're idiots for fighting without armor," Ash remarked. "Those things hurt like heck when you get hit."

Cadence tried not to act like she was interested, but she couldn't help herself. She had to watch. She wanted to say it was ridiculous, but there was something so old world about the entire scene. They both looked so powerful and skilled as they struck and evaded one another. She had assumed it would be like two big kids playing with sticks, but she was wrong. This wasn't a game. It may have only been a friendly competition, but it was serious to them. Their moves were planned out. They really were sparring, the way soldiers of long ago must have.

Talis was defending mostly. Raven attacked with a kind of fervor that made her head spin, and Talis matched him. The sound of their swords clapping together echoed through the trees. She couldn't help but smile. It looked almost like some kind of barbaric dance.

Without warning, Raven's sword came in contact with Talis' elbow and made a sickening thud. Cadence winced.

Talis grabbed at his elbow and let out a frustrated, pain-laden growl. "Sonofa..." He rubbed it and scowled at Raven.

Raven chuckled and gave a flippant shrug.

With a sigh, Talis put his injured arm behind his back and switched to swinging the sword with his left arm.

"Isn't that just like Raven?" Ash mumbled. "Hack off limbs till you're dead."

"Wait, so Talis can't use that arm anymore?" Cadence asked.

Ash shook his head. "No, if you're hit in the arm or leg, you can't use it. A blow to the stomach, chest, or head is a killing one."

Her eyes widened. "Couldn't that really injure someone?" She had already seen Ash get his nose busted. She really didn't want to see Talis get his head bashed open or have his lung collapse or something.

"They won't hurt each other," Tempyst assured. "They're friends and they're only playing around. They won't hit hard while they're unarmored."

Cadence wanted to say that it looked like Talis had gotten his elbow whacked pretty hard, but she bit her tongue. She continued to watch with morbid fascination, but within minutes, Raven out maneuvered Talis and stabbed the point of his sword right into Talis' stomach. A collective chuckle went through the other men.

Talis shook his head and laughed as Raven patted him on the back.

"I told you not to go up against the master," Raven said arrogantly.

Cadence snorted with derision and folded her arms across her chest.

Raven cocked an eyebrow and looked at her. "Ah, Lady Cadence does not approve of the victory."

She met his gaze pointedly. "I don't approve of the attitude," she spat. "You show up here acting like we've all just been waiting to bask in your glory. It's disgusting."

Talis raised his eyebrows and laughed. "Man, Rave, she's got your number," he teased.

"She's an outspoken one, isn't she?" Raven asked, giving Cadence a playful smile.

"Oh, yeah. I'm silly and you're disgusting." Talis made a face at his friend. "Suddenly, silly doesn't sound so bad."

Raven gave a halfhearted scowl.

Talis grinned and held the sword out to Cadence. "Wanna try?"

Was he actually asking her if she wanted to swing around a wooden sword? "Are you serious?"

Raven flashed her a grin that was probably the most arrogant she'd seen so far. "Yeah, come on. I'll teach you."

Her eyes narrowed and, before she even knew what she was doing, she had yanked the sword out of Talis' hand and was turning to face Raven. "What am I supposed to do with this thing?" she grumbled to Talis.

"Try and hit him," he replied, "before he hits you."

She gave him a bland expression and turned back to Raven. "If you hurt me, so help me, I'll kick you where it counts."

His grin was wolfish. "Whatever stings, I'll make better." He winked.

Talis let out a groan.

"Raven is not making the situation any better," Ash commented. "He doesn't know when to quit."

"Cadence is going to get obliterated if she holds her sword like that," Devlyn muttered.

She held her sword like a baseball bat, only it looked more like a girl who didn't know how to play baseball attempting to hold a baseball bat. She knew that's what it looked like because that's what she felt like, but she had way too much stubborn pride to ask for help.

Talis frowned and shook his head. "Cadence, wait." He strode over to her. "You look like a girl."

She spun, letting her sword drop in irritation. "I am a girl, Sherlock!"

"Well, Raven will kill you if you hold your sword like that," he chuckled. He stood behind her and adjusted her hands.

"Don't hold it like you're about to hit a home run."

Cadence laughed in spite of herself. She couldn't help it. She was trying to seem all tough and kick-butt in front of Raven because he was irritating her, but Talis was right. She had no idea how to hold the thing. She tried to pay attention as he coached her, but she was really paying more attention to the way his hands felt on hers than she was to his words.

He had magnificent hands. Strong and warm, rough and gentle all in one. For some reason, feeling his touch made her heart shiver. She didn't know which was worse, having it flip-flop at his smile, or having it shiver at his touch.

"Okay, try now," Talis instructed.

She faced Raven again and he flashed her that cocky grin.

"I'll try to go easy on you, but no promises," he bragged.

Her eyes narrowed. She did not want anyone to go easy on her. She was far from a porcelain doll. "Bring it on, hotshot," she grumbled. Laughter came from the others, and she smirked.

Almost immediately, he went for a killing blow, but she dodged it.

"Don't let him win, Cadence!" Draco shouted.

Raven snorted. "Right." He expertly blocked a few vehement strikes from her. "If Talis can't beat me, I doubt a little girl can, however pretty she may be."

Cadence glowered in irritation and her fingers tightened around the hilt of the weapon. She swung the sword again and it connected with his. They sparred some more, but she got the distinct feeling that he was just toying with her and that annoyed her on the highest level.

"You know what's fun about you?" Raven said playfully.

She wiped her hair off of her sweating forehead. "What?"

"You don't think anything out before you do it. You don't pay attention. Your moves are all spontaneous and reckless." His grin was taunting.

Cadence felt something inside of her snap and she let out a mighty yell. She looked at Raven and saw her brother and Tawny both telling her the same thing. *You're too reckless, Cadence. You never think anything out before you do it. You're so irresponsible.* Well, here was something she'd thought through first. She was going to pulverize this punk.

She launched an attack at Raven, hitting her sword

against his harder than she probably should have. It was enough to make him back up a bit with a surprised look on his face. She continued to attack, her arms burning from exertion. She hated that no one ever gave her credit for having a brain. Why did no one think she could do anything right? Why did everyone assume she was just going to mess up? That she was reckless and irresponsible? Why couldn't anyone ever just *cut her some slack*?

A unanimous gasp went up around the camp fire as Cadence hit Raven's sword so hard it went flying. Raven's eyes widened as she pressed the tip of her weapon against his throat.

"Holy flying crap," Draco murmured.

"Talk about beginner's luck," Ash said.

Raven shook his head, his look of shock morphing into admiration. "That wasn't luck," he said. "That was passion." He turned toward Cadence and smiled. "A warrior with skill is no match for a warrior who has something to fight for. What are you fighting for, Cadence?"

She looked up at him, her emotions in turmoil. She wanted to cry. She wanted to scream with rage. She wanted to laugh because she had won. She was a mess. She sighed and shook her head. "Freedom," she whispered.

"Freedom is the most noble of all causes." He gently reached down to remove the sword from her grasp and took her hands in his. "You stick with Talis. He is the freest person I have ever known. You'll find your freedom with him. Until then" —he bowed at the waist— "I'd hate to piss you off."

She giggled and met his eyes. Her opinion of Raven quickly changed. He may be completely arrogant, but he was treating her with a great amount of respect. He didn't think that she losing her temper and lashing out was a bad thing. She had a horrible temper. Everyone had always chided her for it. She'd gotten into so many fights in school. She'd beat up a security guard, for crying out loud! But Raven didn't act like her aggression was awful. Neither did any of the others. They were actually staring at her in awe. Maybe this combat thing wasn't so bad after all.

Raven winked at her. "I need some breakfast. I'm done sparring for now. Cadence has wounded my pride enough for one day."

"You should register her in the hand-to-hand combat,

Tal!" Draco called.

Talis put his arm around Cadence's shoulders with a grin. "You all right?" he asked her as they walked back to the camp fire. "You looked a little crazed for a minute there."

She swallowed, forcing her emotions down. "I'm fine."

"No one's ever beaten Raven before," he said. "None of us." He laughed suddenly. "Raven's needed a good butt kicking for awhile now. It's even better that he was beat by an inexperienced woman."

"I can hear you," Raven grumbled, shooting Talis a half-hearted glare.

"Talis," Cadence said, frowning thoughtfully. "Can women enter this combat competition?"

He looked down at her. "Of course." His eyes traveled over her for a moment before his lips turned up in a soft grin. "If you want, I can teach you the rules and stuff later. You liked beating up on Raven, huh?"

She smiled as she felt her cheeks grow warm. "I've always had an awful temper. After I beat up that security guard, they sent me to anger management classes. I don't think they really worked, though. As much as I hate to admit it, I really liked how powerful wielding that thing made me feel."

"Ah ha," he said in a teasing tone. "Not so silly after all, eh?"

She glared up at him.

He chuckled, and they joined the others at the fire.

Chapter Seven

All was lively around the fire that night. The day had been spent rather lazily with some occasional combat. Talis had taught Cadence the basics of sword fighting, and she had enjoyed sparring with him for a couple hours. Tempyst had also set up a tree stump with a target on it and the guys had thrown axes and knives at it for half of the day. She'd attempted that as well, but after sending a throwing knife into a tree about ten feet farther than the target, and almost decapitating Ash with an axe she'd sent flying, she realized that she was definitely better with a sword than she was with missile weapons. Poor Ash had avoided her like the plague for the rest of the day. She didn't blame him, really. Every time he got near her, he ended up having something awful happen to him.

A fire blazed in the pit now and the alcohol was flowing right along with all the insane stories they were telling. Everyone was trying to talk at once or correct one another, and no one was somber. Cadence watched and listened, enjoying how everyone was so free to laugh.

"Hold on, do you remember that time Talis and Draco got tanked and ran through the renaissance camp completely naked?" Devlyn laughed.

"It doesn't take a lot to get Draco naked," Tempyst said with a chuckle.

Talis shook his head and frowned. "No one needs to remember that, Devlyn."

Draco scratched at the back of his head. "I *don't* remember that."

Cadence smiled and glanced at Talis. He was sitting on the ground, absently strumming his acoustic guitar. The firelight played upon his midnight hair and she gave a soft sigh. "Do you guys always camp at renaissance faires?"

"At a lot of events we do," Draco replied. "We all sit around in our garb, play music, dance. It's like disappearing into the middle ages for awhile."

"We'll be staying at my brother's house for the big renfaire," Talis supplied, looking up at her. "He lives in Big Sur and it's just easier to stay with him considering the renfaire runs for about two months."

"Your brother Traevyn?" she asked, arching a brow. At his nod, she continued. "You're really the brother of Traveyn Whitelaw?"

He grinned and met her eyes. "You're really the sister of Lance Lawson?"

She said nothing. Yeah, she guessed that put them both in about the same boat. Famous artist sibling, famous rock star sibling.

"It was funny how that piece of information was what diffused Tawny's anger," Talis remarked. "For some reason, everyone seems to think I'm an okay kind of guy when they find out who my brother is."

"So, tell us about being a roadie, Cadence," Tempyst interjected.

She looked up at him in surprise. So far, no one had really asked her anything about herself. She had assumed they just accepted she was there and left it at that. She hadn't thought anyone was really interested in her.

"Yeah, tell us about touring with the greatest metal band ever," Draco urged. "We all claim to be gypsies, but you're the real gypsy. You've been all over the world!" He shook his head. "Man, what I wouldn't give for that life."

Cadence smiled and began to talk about touring with the band. She had only planned on giving a brief summary of what she did, but one thing lead to another and, with every encouraging word and response from the others, she told more about her experiences until she was laughing and talking over everyone just like the rest of them.

They all continued to talk and share stories late into the night and, one by one, everyone started to file off to bed, leaving Talis and Cadence alone by the fire again.

Talis was still strumming softly on his guitar as Cadence rolled out her sleeping bag. She watched him for a minute, remembering how she used to hang out with Bleeding Passion in their hotel rooms. Van had always been constantly strumming on his acoustic.

She sat down and pulled her knees up, resting her chin on them. Talis looked so calm and serene while he played. She wondered if she had ever, in her entire life, felt as serene as he looked. Probably not. She was all chaos and destruction. She'd never been serene.

He must have felt her eyes on him because he looked up. He smiled softly and set his guitar aside. "Are you cold?"

She shrugged. "I'm okay."

"Do you want anything? I was going to make some coffee."

She gave a small smile. "Sure."

He set up a grill across the fire and set the percolator on it. He sat down next to her and sighed. "So, are you ever going to tell me anything about you?"

"What do you want to know?" She avoided his gaze by playing with some pine needles.

He shrugged. "Just, something. I feel weird toting you all over and not knowing anything other than that your brother is famous, you think I'm silly, you were arrested for beating the tar out of a security guard, and you wield a mean sword."

She giggled in spite of herself. "I didn't really beat the tar out of him, per se."

"Oh, you only gave him one black eye instead of two?" he teased. "At least you weren't throwing an axe at him."

She burst out laughing. "Poor Ash! I feel so bad for him. He needs to stay far, far away from me." She shook her head and sobered. "I guess that can be said for most people, though."

He frowned and folded his hands in his lap casually. "Why do you say that?"

She shrugged one shoulder. "I seem to mess up everything I come around. It's just a gift, I guess."

"Who told you that?"

She sighed and flung the pine needles she'd been messing with off into the darkness. "My mom, my brother, half the people I've known in my life. Take your pick." She was quiet for several seconds, debating on whether or not to tell him anything else. He remained silent, letting her work it out.

She didn't usually like to tell people about her past. She didn't like to remember most of it herself. "See, my mom and dad were divorced." It came out of her mouth before she registered that she'd made a conscious decision to tell him. She didn't know why. Maybe because he wasn't pushing, wasn't trying to pry. He was just patiently waiting out of curiosity.

"My dad had custody of us, but I wanted to stay with my mom. That was a stupid idea, but I was too little to know that at the time. She was drunk ninety-five percent of the time. I ran away from home when I was fourteen and that's when it started. Cadence's path of destruction. I got suspended from school three times from fighting and was sent to juvenile hall because some stupid girl got me into drugs for awhile. My mom didn't really care. All she did was tell me that I always messed everything up. Her favorite thing to say was that I had messed up her life just by being born. You can imagine how fantastic that makes a little girl feel."

Talis kept his face carefully devoid of expression. She appreciated that. She hated when people felt sorry for her or looked at her with concerned, puppy eyes. "Where were your dad and brother during all of this?"

"I really didn't see a lot of my dad. My fault, not his. I was ashamed and didn't want to face him. I felt like I had chosen to live with my mother so it was only fitting that I take the punishment for it. Lance had no idea what was going on. He was off with his band at that point. That's why he's so protective of me. He feels guilty that he wasn't there for me. When I turned eighteen, I dropped out of school and moved out. I finally started to have a semblance of a relationship with my dad. I told him some of the things that had gone on and he told them to Lance. Lance and I actually got pretty close for awhile, but then I met Danny and blew that too."

"Danny?"

"My ex-boyfriend. My bad habit. Lance hates him, thinks he's the worst thing that could happen to me. After I was arrested last year and he bailed me out, he took it upon himself to be my permanent lord and master."

"You don't need a lord and master, Cadence," he said softly.

"You don't think so? You're the first."

He shook his head. "You just need some kind of guidance, some kind of path. You're not a walking disaster.

You've just had some bad luck."

She heaved a sigh and dismissed the thoughts of her past. Seriously, what was she even telling him any of this for? "So, tell me about your brother," she said, changing the subject. "What is he like?"

"Well, I have two, actually."

She appreciated how he didn't continue to prod her and she was grateful for the change of topic.

"Julian is a veterinarian. He's very gentle, probably the most kind-hearted person I have ever known. He's not shy really, but he's quiet, more reserved. He's a great listener. Traevyn is..." He smiled to himself. "How do I define Traevyn? He's a genius. That's really the only way I can say it. He's a complete creative genius. He's read more books than I even know the names of."

"Is he a free spirit like you?"

He chuckled softly. "Traevyn is...Traevyn. He's probably the most complicated person I have ever known. With creativity comes intensity. Traevyn is very intense, very dark. He's stoic and brooding and doesn't show his emotions except to those he trusts and loves." He paused for so long she looked over at him to see if he was all right. "We all thought we were going to lose him a few years back."

"Lose him? What do you mean?"

"His first wife cheated on him with his best friend, then divorced him after their daughter was killed in an accident. He recluse himself for three years, barely even talked to Julian and me. Our parents couldn't even reach him. I've never seen him so black, so hopeless. We were all terrified he would try to do himself in one day."

"What happened?"

Talis met her eyes and smiled. "Evie happened. My sister-in-law, Traevyn's wife. She worked miracles." He shook his head with a kind of reverent wonder. "There's no one like Evie. He worships her. They have a four-year-old daughter named Julia and they are expecting their son in a few months."

Cadence smiled, relieved that the story he'd been telling had a nice ending. "That's wonderful! Is Evie an artist too?"

He nodded. "Evelina Whitelaw. She makes a pretty decent living. She's not as famous as Traevyn yet, but she's only been at it for five years."

She studied him quietly. "It sounds like you admire her a lot."

"I do. She gave life and love back to my brother again. Evie and Julia are his life. I don't even want to think about what would happen to him if he lost them. They are everything that keeps him sane, grounded and alive."

"I wish I could meet her." Evie sounded like the people Cadence always wanted to be like. She'd always wanted to be someone's light and savior. That's why she constantly went for the bad boys and why she constantly went back to Danny, but she had come to realize long ago that she would never be one of those people. She couldn't even take care of her own life, let alone fix someone else's.

"You'll get to meet her," Talis said. "We're staying with them, remember? You'll get to meet both my brothers. We're going to Julian's right after this trip. There's a renfaire up in South Lake Tahoe, California, and Julian lives there. We're staying with him for about two weeks." He got up and checked the percolator, then made both of them a cup of coffee. "As far as being a walking disaster, Cadence, that's crap."

She blinked in surprise as his statement seemed to come out of nowhere. "Oh, yeah?"

He looked at her. "Yeah."

He left it at that without bothering to elaborate and she just stared at him. Well...okay then. She let her eyes roam across his profile, his defined jaw and beautiful lips, all of the piercings in his left ear. Man, those lips... His mouth was just wicked. And it didn't help that such a perfect mouth spoke words that touched her directly in her heart.

Her eyes continued their appreciative journey and settled on his hands. He had several Celtic rings adorning his long fingers and, before she could think about it, she grabbed his left hand and began to look them over.

Talis seemed slightly surprised by her sudden action, but he smiled as he watched her look at his rings. "Did you dance at one point, Cadence?"

She met his eyes in bewilderment. "Yeah, I did ballet for years. How did you know that?"

"Just the way you hold yourself. I work around dancers and your posture is the same as theirs, elegant and graceful." He shrugged. "Just a hunch."

She raised an eyebrow. "Either I am really transparent or

you are a creepy psychic."

He chuckled and let her continue her study of his jewelry as he continued his study of her.

"Did you get all of these at renaissance faires?" she asked, trying to keep the conversation going. His silent inspection was unnerving.

"Most of them."

"Let me see the other hand." She pulled his right hand over to her, causing him to have to move closer to accommodate the position. She loved his hands almost as much as she loved his lips. She took an extra long time studying his rings just so she could keep touching them. Something about them was so masculine, yet so tender.

"How come you don't dance anymore?" he queried.

"No time."

"Did you enjoy it?"

She swallowed hard. Enjoy it? She had loved it. It had been her only real happiness growing up. "Yeah, it was fun." She said it in a way that greatly undermined how much it had really meant to her. It had been the only thing that had made her restless spirit feel at peace. When she had gone into that dance studio, for two hours, she had been free. Free of worry and pain. It had been her one and only release.

One of the black strands of Cadence's hair had escaped her ponytail and was hanging in her face. Talis reached out gently and tucked it back. Her heart lurched at his innocent touch. In all her life, no one had ever done something so infinitely tender. For no reason at all. She looked up into his eyes and was torn between wanting to stare into those light blue depths for all time and wanting to run as far away from him as possible.

Talis was dangerous. He was dangerous to the thin barrier of protection she had put around herself. He was everything she had sworn to stay away from: sensual, alluring, dark, sexy, and so free. He lived the kind of life she had always wanted. He did what he wanted when he wanted and answered to no one but himself. How did he do it? How did he wander like a medieval warrior and be so poised and assured? She couldn't even venture to a different state without something awful happening to her. She wanted to know his secret. She wanted to know how he could live the life she dreamed of while she only screwed hers up. She also wanted to know what it was about him that made her heart behave so strangely.

An unknown creature sounded its call suddenly, making her jump. Talis' hand came up to her shoulder to soothe her and her heart shivered. His touch... Holy cow, what was it about his touch?

"Why are you jumping?" he teased her softly. "You didn't get eaten last night."

She gave him a bland expression. "Yeah, well, maybe the chupacabras were hibernating last night." His laugh was a deep rumble and it set her blood on fire. She braved another look up at him and the words flew right out of her mouth of their own volition, much like everything else she usually said. "Talis, you are the most beautiful man I have ever seen."

He arched his eyebrows in surprise at her sudden declaration.

Cadence's eyes widened and she snapped her mouth shut. What was wrong with her? Was she a complete lunatic? Her cheeks burned and she looked down, feeling betrayed by her own mouth. "Sorry," she murmured.

His smile was soft, and he lifted her chin with his finger. "Cadence," he said, forcing her to meet his eyes. "You don't have to censor yourself with me... Ever."

She averted her gaze. "That's a brave statement."

"I mean it."

She chewed on her lip and stole a glance into his eyes again. She wanted to tremble at the way he was looking at her. No one had ever looked at her with such acceptance. This stranger gave her more acceptance than her own brother did, more than her own best friend. Slowly, he tipped her head back so that she was gazing up at the sky. She grinned as peace stole into her as she studied the stars.

Talis watched her quietly for several moments before he trailed his fingers slowly down her throat. Cadence closed her eyes at the touch. She swore he had to have some kind of magical powers. He made her feel like her blood was boiling when he touched her, like she was going to incinerate. That was strange, even for her. She didn't react that way to strangers. It was dangerous and reckless to feel such desire for a man she barely knew.

She pressed closer to him on instinct, her heart hammering as she felt his arms go around her shoulders. She pulled her gaze from the stars and looked back at him. His eyes met hers and the shadows that played on his dark face from the flames turned her molten. He was gorgeous. Gorgeous and free and everything she should not be attracted to, but Talis didn't seem irresponsible. He didn't seem like the kind of guy that would get her into more trouble. He somehow managed to live his life completely free while still being in control.

What is his secret? She wanted to know. She wanted to know *him*. She wanted to feel more of his divine touch, even though it was against her better judgment. She wanted to be close to him because, for some bizarre reason, she had the feeling that his arms would feel more like paradise than anything she had ever experienced. Maybe, if she was in his embrace, she would finally know what peace was. Maybe she could finally rest. She wanted to see if those sinful lips of his felt as divine as they looked.

She jumped as the blaring ring of her cell phone tore through the night. She scrambled to pull it out of her duffle bag before it woke up the entire camp and she really did get to see Devlyn shooting arrows and Draco bounding out of his tent naked.

She scowled at the phone as she flipped it open, irritated that it had dared interrupt her moment with Talis. It was her brother. Well, that just figured. He'd probably felt a disturbance in the force and somehow knew she had wanted to kiss a guy. What was her phone even doing on? She swore she had turned it off to avoid this kind of thing.

Talis pulled back, trying to return his mind to the present. He sighed, trying not to think of what might have been. Her barrier had slipped for a moment; she had almost let him in. She had almost *kissed him*. He could kill whoever was on the other end of that phone.

"Hello?" Cadence spat. She heaved a sigh and rolled her eyes. "I was abducted by aliens," she grumbled. "...No, I'm not in trouble. Contrary to popular belief, I can cross the street without someone holding my hand and be pretty okay. What are you doing, Lance? It's the middle of the night... You are absolutely *not* coming to get me!"

Talis raised an eyebrow since she was all but shouting, and cast a glance back to where everyone else was sleeping.

"You really have some kind of nerve," she went on. "I am not your child, or your wayward pet, or your slave for that matter. I can do what I want, when I want, with who I want!" She huffed in agitation. "I'm with a man."

"*What?*" Lance screeched.

Talis blinked. He'd actually heard that. This wasn't going to be good.

"Yeah, a really sexy one, actually," she continued. "And I'm not coming home, and you're not coming after me, so you can just deal with it." She stabbed her finger down on the off button and flung her phone back into her bag. "Jerk," she spat.

Talis smirked. He took a sip of his coffee and stayed his distance, figuring their momentary closeness had just been a fleeting thing. He knew she would be pissed after talking to Lance and he didn't want her to feel like he was intruding on her space. He was happy that she had told him so much about her past. He knew she hadn't told him everything, but that was okay. She was used to keeping to herself. He understood that. He was surprised she had told him as much as she had.

It pained him to know that she felt like she damaged everything she touched. He wanted to show her that she could attain the freedom she desired. That she could live the life she wanted to and not be seen as a perpetual screw up.

He sighed, resigning himself to just sit there quietly and try not to think about how delectable her lips had looked and how he ached for a taste of them. His eyes widened as he felt her rest her head against his shoulder. He glanced down at her and frowned in concern. "You okay?"

"I'm fine. I just..." She swallowed visibly. "Do you mind?"

He shook his head and moved his arm so he could place it around her. "No, I don't mind at all."

She sighed and closed her eyes as his arm encompassed her. She snuggled against him and seemed to struggle with her emotions for a bit before her body relaxed against his.

She said nothing. She just sipped her drink and stared into the fire. He didn't break the silence either. There was nothing that needed to be said. She had let him in a small bit, had chosen to let him close and show a smidgen of vulnerability. He didn't need any explanations, and he definitely wasn't going to ask any questions. He was holding her, and that was enough for him at the moment.

Chapter Eight

"It's your turn," Cadence said with a grin as she stuffed another onion ring into her mouth.

Talis thought for several minutes. They had been traveling for five hours and were about two hours outside of Las Vegas. They had just fueled up and gotten some food. Cadence had spent the first several hours sleeping, but now they were taking turns asking one another questions to pass the time. "What kind of movies are your favorites?"

"Action and suspense movies, I think. I love when things blow up."

He laughed. Cadence was definitely not the typical girl. No romantic chick flicks for her. No way. Destruction and mayhem all the way.

"Okay, so I know about how you got involved in renaissance faires, but how did you get involved in tattooing?" she asked.

"I was always good at drawing," he replied, "but I didn't really want to go into the art field like Traevyn. I didn't have enough discipline. I had a friend who was five years older than me when I was in high school. He started a tattoo shop in Sedona, Arizona and invited me to come out and be his apprentice when I graduated. It sounded cool, so I did it."

She shook her head in what looked like admiration. "I can't understand how you are able to live your life like that, so free and unattached. Whatever sounds good to you, you do. And you somehow managed to make a success out of it. Whenever I do something on a whim, I mess it all up and wind up getting really screwed."

He chuckled. "All right, who's your favorite band?" he asked. "Besides Bleeding Passion."

"The Cure."

"Good choice."

"Who's yours?"

"AFI. I love the lyrics. They're so poetic." He chewed on his bottom lip as he thought of his next question. "All right, tell me about this Danny guy," he blurted. "What's wrong with him?"

Cadence's smile faded for a minute and she looked down at the food in her lap. "Well, nothing's really *wrong* with him..." She sighed. "He's just kind of a bum. You know, can't keep a job, wears wife beaters while he drinks beer in his trailer. You get the idea."

Talis smiled.

"He claims to be a 'musician,' but he's really just lazy."

"Understood."

"How come you don't have a girlfriend?" she retaliated.

He smirked and shrugged. "I don't know. A relationship is not something I actively pursue. I'm content with my life the way it is."

Her frown was thoughtful. "But wouldn't you like to have someone to live your life with? A partner in crime?"

"Well, of course. The need for love is in all people. I'm no exception. I just don't look for it. I've had a few relationships, but none were serious."

She smiled playfully. "What about one of those belly dancers you say that you play music for?"

He rolled his eyes. "Please. One of them used to date Raven and is still totally stuck on him, even though she won't admit it. Another one is the biggest airhead I have ever known and the other is about two shots shy of being a complete alcoholic."

Cadence laughed. "Okay, I can see the problem there."

"Besides," he continued with a chuckle, "I've always felt like when I meet the girl I'm supposed to get close to, I'll know."

"How?"

"Intuition," he replied simply. "Instinct." He met her eyes for a second and smiled. "Kind of how I felt when I first looked at you."

Her mouth opened in surprise. She felt her cheeks burn and she looked away nervously, not knowing how to respond to that statement. Part of her was screaming that she should leap out of the car and make her way back to Tawny, but deep down inside, she knew that it had been the same with her. When she'd looked up at him after he'd saved her from falling at the concert, she'd felt a strong connection. It had unnerved her and she had looked away, but she couldn't pretend it didn't exist. She felt it every time she met his gaze or got near him. It scared the absolute crap out of her.

Talis grinned. "Anyway, that was like five questions. Tell me how that's fair."

She forced a smile, even though her heart was still racing at his previous statement. "Sorry, go ahead. Your turn."

He seemed to toss around a few questions before deciding which one to ask. "So, what do you think of me?"

She blinked in bewilderment. "That's kind of a broad question. Do you mean what do I think of your looks? 'Cause I already blurted that out like an idiot last night."

He chuckled. "No, what do you think of me as a whole?"

She let her eyes take in his beauty for a minute before she looked back down at her lap. "I'm here, aren't I? I came with you. Shouldn't that speak for itself?"

He gave her a playful look. "I bribed you."

She snorted. "No, you forced me."

"Then your reasoning isn't valid."

She growled in irritation. "I'm pleading the fifth on this question."

He let out a surprised noise. "You can't do that! It's against the rules!"

"I can and I will," she stated haughtily. "I don't know you well enough to answer that question."

"Cadence, you've spent the last three days around me. I think you should have formed some sort of opinion by now."

"Yeah, I think you're a silly, medieval tattoo artist. Now shut up. It's my turn." She couldn't look at him for fear he would see how red her face was. She wanted far, far away from that question. She was not going to tell him that she thought he was gorgeous and fascinating and that she was attracted to him in the worst possible way.

Talis sighed. "You are exasperating on the highest level."

She gave him a withered expression. "Thanks... Okay, so where were you on New Year's?"

"At home on my sofa in Sedona watching the ball drop with Ash. You?"

"I was on a tour bus." She looked over at him with a grin. "You know, a friend of mine told me that wherever you are on New Year's is what you'll be doing all year. What do you think that means?"

He smiled. "It means you'll be free, Cadence. All year." He glanced over at her, then chuckled. "And I'll be sitting on my couch with Ash, like I am every year."

She laughed, but hoped he was right about her being free. That was all she wanted. A life like his. No attachments, nothing holding her down.

"We're going to be spending two nights in Vegas," he stated.

She frowned. "Huh? I thought we were going to your brother's."

"We are, but I have a friend who performs in the Tournament of Kings dinner show at the Excalibur and I told her I'd say hello. You don't mind, do you?"

She shook her head. Mind? Vegas? She loved Vegas. There was so much to do. A twenty-four hour party. She smiled and lapsed into thought as she watched the barren desert landscape go by out the window. Talis put a CD on and she sighed. She decided she would call Tawny once they got into Las Vegas. Even though she had pissed her off royally, Cadence didn't want her to worry. She was still her best friend, after all. Lance could just deal. She didn't care if he worried. He deserved it.

Talis' earlier comment about knowing he was supposed to be close to her when he first saw her surfaced in her mind. She felt her face flush just thinking about it. She stole a sidelong glance at him and her heart betrayed her by skipping a beat. What would it be like to be with someone like Talis? Someone so free and easy going? Danny claimed to be free and easy going, but he was really just a lazy leech. He hid behind the "free spirit" front to avoid having to get a job and be responsible. Talis was far from lazy. He had everything in his life in order. She frowned in thought and swallowed. "One more question?"

He smiled. "Ask away."

"How would you treat a woman you were in love with?" She needed to know. She needed to know if he would be as wonderful as she imagined.

"A woman should be treasured and adored," he replied.

"If I loved someone, I would do everything in my power to make that person happy and give them anything they want. When I give my heart to someone, I want to give them all of me. I want to experience everything with that person. I can't say I've ever been in love, but when I do fall, I have a feeling it'll be the end of me. I'm not so different from my brother, Traevyn, in that sense."

"Is that why you're reluctant to get into a relationship?"

He frowned. "I'm not reluctant at all." He slid his gaze over to her. "I just need to find the right girl."

Cadence looked down, her cheeks turning hot. "Why do I get the feeling that you're hitting on me?"

He shrugged casually. "Maybe I am. You're beautiful. Besides, you only live once, right?" He flashed her a playful smile.

Cadence giggled, flattered by his words. She lapsed into silence for the next several hours, just listening to the music that was on and staring out the window.

She smiled when they reached Las Vegas, remembering the last time she had been there. It had been on the tour. Bleeding Passion had played at the House of Blues in the Mandalay Bay casino. She and Lance had actually managed to have a really good time. It was one of his off days when he wasn't hounding her and he had gotten tickets for her, Kat and Rochelle to go see *The Thunder from Down Under*. Kat had been mortified, but Cadence and Rochelle had a blast. The entire time they had been in Vegas Lance had been fun and playful. Cadence wished he could be like that all the time. That was the brother she remembered, the one he'd been before she'd gotten with Danny. She wished he could return to that. She missed him. She needed him as a friend, not a guardian.

Talis checked them into their room at The Excalibur and almost immediately hit the shower. He was dirty, scruffy and stinky from camping, and he really didn't want to go meet his friend looking like a mountain man. After he was finished, Cadence took her turn and he laid down on the bed to watch TV and relax while he waited for nine-thirty to roll around.

They had gotten into the city around six-thirty and the second performance of Tournament of Kings was at eight-thirty. He would meet his friend at the stage door afterward.

"So, what are we going to do tonight?" Cadence asked as she came out of the bathroom.

Talis glanced over at her and his heart stopped for a minute. He hadn't seen her with her hair down since he'd met her. It was always been up in a ponytail. She had it down now and it fell around her face and shoulders in straight, jagged chunks. She was wearing a tight, black tank top and a black skirt that stopped a few inches above her knees. He forced himself not to drool and he shrugged. "I have to go meet my friend. I figured we'd just get a bite to eat or something."

She wrinkled her nose. "Well, that's boring," she stated. "We're in Las Vegas and all you want to do is get something to eat?"

He smirked. "I'm a little tired, Cadence. I drove for seven hours."

She smiled. "Well, do you mind if I go over to the Coyote Ugly bar in the New York, New York casino? They play decent music there and I want to dance."

"Go ahead. I'm not your keeper. Just be careful, okay?"

She winked at him. "Of course." She grabbed her purse and one of the key cards and headed for the door. "You should come and join me later," she said, throwing a flirty look at him over her shoulder. "No girl likes to dance alone."

He smiled. "I don't know... Are you gonna dance on the bar?"

"Only if you're really nice to me," she said with a giggle.

He chuckled. "Have fun. I'll see you later." He watched her go and sighed. He really, really wanted to take her up on her invitation, but he had to meet his friend and was actually very tired. Maybe he would revive later and go find her. If not, there was always the next night.

Chapter Nine

Talis couldn't find Cadence, and it was really starting to bother him. He'd met up with his friend, Leila, after the show, and they'd gone to the coffee shop to get some food. They'd talked for awhile and he told her that he would go and see the show the next night and hang out. When he'd returned to his room, Cadence had still been gone and, as he remembered her in that sexy outfit, he thought he'd go track her down. What was the use of going to bed when all he would do was think about how what he really wanted to be doing was watching her gorgeous body move to the music as she danced?

He'd gone to Coyote Ugly, but hadn't been able to find her there. That had bothered him a little bit. Now, he was halfway up the Strip and had been to every club in every casino along the way and still couldn't find her.

He wasn't trying to be overprotective or controlling. He would never do that to someone, but he was concerned. Cadence was in his care. She was his responsibility and, given her history, he wasn't feeling very good about her disappearance.

Loud music caught his attention as he walked past an outdoor club where a lot of people were dancing. He skimmed the crowd and the people at the bar and his eyes widened as he spotted Cadence bumping and grinding on the dance floor with some guy who had his hands all over her backside. Talis watched as she stumbled and almost fell, then laughed, took a drink of something she was holding in her hand, and flopped one of her arms around the man's neck. Talis heaved a sigh. Great.

He turned to the entrance, paid his admission, and

headed straight for the dance floor. Much to his dismay and great irritation, the man Cadence was dancing with whispered something in her ear as Talis approached and took her hand, leading her off of the dance floor and away from the club. Talis shoved his way past the people who were bottlenecked at the bar and ran after Cadence, grasping her arm and pulling her away from her companion.

She wheeled around and stumbled again as she faced Talis. She grinned. "Hey, sexy," she purred, "decided to join me after all?"

The man she was with scowled at Talis and grabbed Cadence's other arm. "Hey buddy, find your own girl," he snapped.

Talis turned a black glower to the man and shoved him hard with one well placed hand on his chest. "Back off," he snarled.

Cadence giggled and grasped onto Talis' arm. "Now, now boys, play nice," she slurred. "There's plenty of me to go around."

Talis couldn't mask his disgust at her skanky behavior and he shook her off of him. "Shut up and sit down," he ordered, "before you make even more of a fool out of yourself." He turned back to the man and glowered. "Seriously, dude, you do not want to take me on right now." He was, by nature, a very calm person, but he had gone from calm to concerned about two blocks ago and now he was just annoyed. Annoyed that Cadence hadn't even respected him enough to let him know where she was.

Something in Talis' demeanor must have set off a warning in the other guy because he held his hands up and went back to the dance floor to scope out other prey.

Talis turned back to Cadence, who immediately latched onto him again. "Why don't you buy me a drink?" she suggested.

He let out a frustrated sigh and shook her off of him again. "I think you've had enough."

She stuck her lip out playfully. "Are you my knight coming to rescue me?"

He stared at her for a moment and knew that, if anyone who knew his family had walked by at that moment, they would have thought he was Traevyn. The Whitelaw men tended to get this steely, cold, clenched-jaw look to them when they were angry. Traevyn was the master of it. Talis could feel his face morph into his brother's. He folded his arms as he faced Cadence, repulsed by what he was looking at. Not only had she completely disrespected him, but she was continuing to mock him when she was so drunk that she could barely stand. *She* was mocking *him*. "No," he stated. "I rescue ladies. Besides, I coddle babies, not selfish little girls."

She frowned. "Whatever." She tried to push past him, but he blocked her path.

"Sit down, Cadence," he said, pushing her toward the table and chairs behind her.

"You're not my mother," she snorted.

"Sit down!"

His voice snapped like a whip and she quickly obeyed. She stared up at him as the message sunk in that she was in big trouble.

Talis ran his fingers through his hair in frustration and let out an aggravated growl. "I cannot believe that you were just going to leave with that guy!" he shouted.

"What's the matter? You jealous?" she sneered.

He met her eyes, but knew his were cold. "Hardly. Who you screw is none of my business."

She flinched at his icy, venomous tone.

"I am, however, greatly upset by the fact that someone who I am *paying for* to come on a trip across three states with me would not have enough respect to tell me where she is going. I am responsible for you, Cadence! *I* am! And if something awful happens to you, I don't really feel like being taken to court by Lance friggin' Lawson because he thinks I kidnapped you and did horrid things to you! I searched the Las Vegas Strip for you, Cadence! You own a cell phone. One I happened to program my phone number in to. You couldn't call me and let me know what you were doing? Send me a text message?

"I went into every club from the Excalibur all the way to here and, when I finally do track you down, you're falling down drunk and leaving with some sleaze who just wants to get lucky! You expect me not to be just a little ticked off? Who goes out drinking in Vegas by themselves? Do you have a death wish? That's a recipe for trouble right there! I thought you were going to Coyote Ugly to dance! I didn't think you were going to wander halfway down the Strip to get plowed!"

She blinked up at him and sniffed. "I told you I was a screw up," she muttered. "You shouldn't really be surprised."

He rolled his eyes at her flip tone and excuses. "Oh, bull. You grew up with your mother telling you were a screw up so, of course, you think that's what you are. You make stupid choices because you think it's expected of you. You know why else? So that you can hide behind the idea of being a 'fated screw up' and not have to take responsibility for your actions." He shook his head, so far beyond angry that he could actually hear his pulse pounding in his ears. "Well, you know what? That's fine. Just keep living up to people's expectations of you. Keep being a child for all I care, but I'm not ready for children in my life yet. Grow up, Cadence. And when you do, gimme a call. That is, if you remember you actually have a damn phone." He turned and started to walk away from her.

"Talis, wait!" she cried. "Where are you going? You're just going to leave me here? What am I supposed to do?"

He shrugged and kept on walking. "Figure it out."

"Talis!" She stood and her voice reflected the fear she suddenly must have felt at the thought of him abandoning her on the Las Vegas Strip. "Talis, wait!" She stumbled after him, but tripped and fell. She put her head in her hands and groaned.

Talis stopped and battled with himself for a moment. He couldn't bring himself to take another step and, at the same time, he couldn't bring himself to turn around. *Leave her.* She probably deserved it. It was what his brother would do, but then again, with anyone who was not his family, Traevyn tended to have a curious absence of conscience.

He sighed in defeat. He couldn't leave her. She'd made him angrier than he'd been in who knew how long, but it went against everything he stood for to just walk off and let her fend for herself. She could get seriously hurt in the state she was in and he couldn't live with that. He could hear her muffled sobs.

He drew in a deep breath to calm himself and let it out in a long, slow exhale, then he turned and went back to where Cadence was crumpled on the ground. He hefted her into his arms and carried her out of the club. She said nothing. She just wrapped her arms around his neck and rested her head on his shoulder as he carried her. He caught a bus back to the hotel because, strong as he was, he was *not* Hercules and didn't feel like breaking his back carrying her back down the Strip.

She remained quiet all the way up to the room and, when he set her down on the bed, he turned toward the window, unable to look at her. He was still angry. He felt disrespected, taken advantage of and hurt. Hurt that she would treat him like he was just her chauffer, or her employer, or something. He thought he would at least fall into the friend category by this point. He had been worried about her, genuinely concerned, and she hadn't even cared. She'd laughed at him, and he was quickly growing very tired of being laughed at.

"Talis?"

He sighed and looked over at her. She was slumped on the bed, her eye makeup was smudged under her eyes, and she looked completely helpless. He hated that his heart ached at the sight. He hated that he felt anything at all when all he wanted to do was strangle her.

"You know, all that stuff you said back there... It was pretty harsh, but you were right..." She looked up at him. "Something about the way you said what everyone else has been trying to tell me really hit hard. Guess I've been needing to get a clue for awhile now." Did she really get herself into stupid situations on purpose? When she thought about it, she realized she did. Because it was easier. It was easier than changing. She shrugged. "I've just been this way for so long... I don't know how to be different."

He crossed to her bed and stood in front of her. "You have to want to be different. Cadence, you're not a stupid girl. You just don't think before you act. I know you hate hearing that, but it's the truth. You need to realize that the choices you make have consequences."

She sniffled as more tears came. "I just want to be free like you."

He arched an eyebrow.

She looked up at him. "You're such a free spirit, such a nomad. I mean, you wander around the country pretending you're in the middle ages. Talis, that's the kind of life I've always wanted."

"Well, I may be free, but you don't see me getting com-

pletely wasted and leaving clubs with perfect strangers. Cadence, the difference between you and me is that I realize
that freedom and recklessness are not one in the same. You
can live a free spirited life and still be smart. You can even
get wasted and still be smart about it! Just don't go out
drinking alone. That's just asking for something bad to happen. I had a friend once who went out drinking alone and got
so hammered she ended up breaking out her own front
tooth. You want something like that to happen to you? Or
worse?"

She studied his handsome face and, even though she
was still drunk enough to have her vision tinged with bright
colors, she was coherent enough to follow the conversation
and know she would remember it the next day. "I don't know
how to express myself," she blurted as more tears gushed
out of her eyes.

"I beg your pardon?"

"My emotions. I don't know how to express them. I never
have. That's why I'm always doing stupid crap. When I'm
angry, I explode. I beat people up. Security guards, for in-
stance. When I'm happy, or having a good time, I do stupid
things like I did tonight because I just want more of it. I've
never known how to channel my emotions properly. Everything's always so over the top. It's like I have no healthy outlet..." She frowned and shook her head. "I don't think I'm
making sense."

He smirked and sat down on the end of the bed next to
her. "Yes you are." He sighed and reached up to brush back
her messed up hair. "You just have to find something that
gets all your emotions out so that they don't get pent up and
come out at the wrong time."

She stared down into her lap. The only thing that had
ever done that for her was dancing. Everything she'd been
feeling—angst, anger, sadness—she had always been able to
dance it out and feel complete afterward. She hadn't had
that feeling since she'd had to stop. "I'm sorry I disrespected
you, Talis," she murmured. "You didn't deserve to be treated
that way."

He knelt down in front of her to remove her shoes. "Well,
you're going to pay for it tomorrow. I told my friend Leila I
would watch her show tomorrow night. You're coming with
me."

She frowned. "What? Why?"

He looked up at her and gave a wry smile. "Because you need to learn that your actions have consequences. I no longer feel comfortable leaving you by yourself."

"I'm not a child, you know," she said with a scowl.

"Stop acting like one and I won't treat you like one." He pulled back the covers and motioned for her to get under them. "Come on, you need to rest."

She was completely bewildered by the fact that he was obviously very upset with her and, yet, he was still being considerate. She gave a quizzical frown as she looked up into his gorgeous blue eyes. "Who are you?"

His lips quirked. "I'm your knight coming to rescue you," he replied quietly. "Now go to sleep." He waited for her to crawl under the covers, then pulled them over her, switched off the light and resumed his place by the window.

"Talis?"

He looked down and a muscle twitched in his jaw, showing his annoyance. "Yeah?"

Cadence was drunk. There was no sense in even trying to pretend otherwise, but she knew the difference between thinking someone was attractive for real and seeing through beer goggles. That guy at the club—beer goggles all the way, but Talis standing in front of the window, his powerful body silhouetted against the bright, blinking neon lights... She had never seen anything more beautiful in her life. He took her breath away and it frightened her, but it also made her realize that she didn't want to do anything to jeopardize what she'd found in him. Talis had been nicer to her in the past few days than a lot of people had ever been. She would be a complete idiot if she wrecked that. "I'm really sorry for upsetting you," she murmured. "I was immature and careless. Please don't be mad at me."

All of the anger that had been etched into the lines of his body seemed to dissolve and he heaved a sigh. He tangled his fingers in his hair, then walked back over to her bed and sat on the side of it, gazing down at her. "I'm not mad at you, Cadence."

She smirked, then giggled. "Yes, you are."

A spectacular grin split his lips and he shook his head. "Okay, yeah, I was pretty pissed, and I'm not going to tell you it's okay because it's not, but..." He sighed and reached out to touch her face. "I'm willing to give you another chance."

She chewed on her bottom lip for a moment and shivers worked up her spine at his touch. "You're the only person who's even remotely tried to understand me," she whispered. "Half the time I don't even understand myself."

He rubbed a strand of her hair between his fingers. "Someone's got to be in your corner, Cadence. Everyone needs a champion." He met her eyes. "Just don't abuse the privilege, and don't take my kindness for granted."

She shook her head. "I won't. I'm sorry."

He gave her a soft smile, located her hand, and kissed her fingers gently. "Go to sleep, beautiful."

She smiled and felt warm all over at his term of endearment. She watched him go back to the window and she stared at him for a long time until her booze-induced brain couldn't take it anymore and finally shut down.

Talis knew when Cadence fell asleep, and only then did he allow himself to look over at her and marvel at her beauty. He briefly wondered if he had finally just lost his mind. He should be running far, far away from Cadence right now. He didn't go for women like her. They were dangerous. They sucked you dry and dragged you down with them. But there was something so vulnerable about her that he couldn't disregard, no matter how hard he tried. It was like she was lost inside a trap she'd built for herself. She self-destructed because she didn't know any other way to be.

He decided that, if she really did want to change the way she lived her life, he would be her champion. Lord knew she needed one. It was apparent that no one else in her life was going to try and understand. Paladin. That's what Tempyst and Ash had called him. He just hoped his chivalry didn't end up getting him screwed over, or worse, hurt because he let himself care when he shouldn't have.

Chapter Ten

Cadence woke up with a massive hangover, which really wasn't all that surprising. She sat up with a groan and rubbed at her pounding temples as the night before came flooding back to her. Good lord, what was the matter with her? She was in serious line for the stupid award. She glanced over at Talis, who was still asleep, and her heart made a funny flip in her chest.

Guilt washed over her and she sighed. She couldn't believe how she'd treated him. All she ever did was complain about how no one took her seriously, or trusted her to make her own decisions. She griped constantly about how everyone called her reckless and irresponsible. Talis had never said those things about her. Not before last night. He had trusted her to do her own thing and hadn't tried to control her at all. She was the one who had royally botched it. She'd treated him the way she treated everyone else in her life who'd ever judged her. Like he didn't matter.

She groaned again and put her head in her hands. Talis had never judged her. Not once. And, even after she'd disrespected and laughed right at him for his concern, he'd still taken care of her. Sometimes she disgusted herself. She didn't even deserve to be in the same room with a man like him.

She rolled out of bed, her stomach churning in protest, and she ran her fingers through her disheveled hair. She glanced at Talis again and wondered when he'd actually gone to sleep. He looked beautiful lying there, his black hair in stark contrast to the white of the pillow. He was shirtless and she let her eyes roam over his magnificently tattooed arms. She smiled. Someone who saw Talis on the street would think he was a bad boy, the worst kind of rebel who probably had a wealth of emotional problems. Why else would he have two full sleeves of tattoos and have both of his ears pierced in several places? It would be a surprise for them to know that he was probably more balanced than half the people who looked "acceptable" to the world's standards.

Talis was the walking picture of everything Cadence had never thought possible. She'd always thought that, in order to be an individual in any way, you had to be a rebel. In order to be a rebel, you had to do the typical rebellious things. Drink, party, not give a crap who you hurt along the way. Every man for himself. Always look out for Number One. She had learned that this was not the best course of action to take, but by the time she'd realized that, she hadn't known how to break herself of the pattern.

Apparently, she was still having problems with that.

Talis boldly strode the path of individuality. He wore his uniqueness with pride, but he didn't try to force his views on anyone, didn't feel the need to make a spectacle of himself just so that everyone on the planet would know he was an individual. He just...was. He lived his life the way he wanted to live it and did it with ease and confidence. He was who he was. He did what he wanted, but he did it in a way that was so responsible and smart. He still thought about others when he made his decisions. That had been made more than clear to her when he'd turned back and picked her up at the club, even though he'd been so angry at her.

She admired him more than she'd ever admired another living soul. Then why did she keep making fun of him? Because it was her defense mechanism? Because she didn't quite understand his occupation? Because she was a shallow, evil witch? Yeah, she definitely decided it was number three.

Well, screw that! She was sick of being stupid.

Setting her mouth into a determined line, Cadence stood, pulled some clothes out of her duffle bag, and headed for the shower.

Talis was more than pissed. He'd thought maybe, just maybe, he'd gotten through to Cadence the night before, but no. As soon as he'd woken up, she was gone again. And he was not going looking for her this time. If she had such little respect for him, she could fend for herself. He didn't like being walked on and taken for granted. He was a good-natured, easy-going guy, but he had his limits. He wouldn't be anyone's doormat, no matter how beautiful she was.

He pulled his pants on and left the bathroom, his hair still wet from the shower he'd just taken. He could not believe his luck. What was the matter with his intuition? Was it having an off day? Decided to take a vacation?

A knock sounded on the door, followed by an announcement of, "Room service!"

Talis frowned. Room service? He hadn't ordered room service. He opened the door to tell the person that there had been a mistake, but to his surprise, there was nobody there. There actually wasn't even a cart with food on it. There was, however, a clear plastic container with four snail pastries and some sort of gigantic coffee something next to it. He blinked in bewilderment and stuck his head out into the hall.

He looked both ways, but saw nobody. "O...kay," he muttered. He picked up the pastries and the coffee and set them on the dresser, where he proceeded to stare at them and try to figure out what he should do with them. He didn't know where they'd come from. He would be stupid if he actually ate them... They did look really good, though.

Another knock. "Housekeeping!"

Talis frowned. What the crap? He had the privacy please sign on the door. Couldn't the maid read? With an irritated snarl, he went back to the door and yanked it open only to stop short, the heated words he was prepared to speak dying on his tongue.

Cadence was leaned in a flirty fashion against the doorframe, twirling some kind of pink fabric rose in her fingers. She was in a simple pair of jeans and a black Bleeding Passion shirt, but her hair was down again, falling around her face in all its multi-colored glory. His heart beat sluggishly for a moment before he got a hold of himself and frowned. "What are you doing?" he all but growled. "I wake up and you're gone again! I thought I—"

Cadence forced her way into the room and held the rose out to him. "For you, grumpy tattoo man," she said sarcastically.

He blinked in stunned silence and took the rose she offered. He studied it and frowned.

"Yeah, I couldn't find any actual flower shops anywhere near here," she said. "So that was the best I could do. I found it at some sleazy convenience store. It's made out of women's panties." She shrugged.

Talis raised both eyebrows and couldn't help but chuckle. "It's fitting for Vegas, I guess."

She grinned. "The breakfast is from me, too."

He eyeballed her, not knowing her motivation and not knowing whether or not he should completely trust her. "Why?"

"Because I was a jerk and you weren't," she stated matter-of-factly. "Here, I got you something else. Close your eyes."

He frowned, but obeyed. He felt her slip something around his neck and clasp it. When she pulled away, he looked down at it and couldn't have masked his surprise if he'd tried. It was a silver dragon with green stones for its eyes. He reached up and touched it. "Where on earth did you find this?"

"I had to search very hard so you'd better like it."

He looked up and met her gaze. "Like it? Cadence, it's fantastic. Why did you get me this?"

"Because..." She swallowed and looked at her feet. For a moment, she seemed vulnerable and shy. She must have hated it. "Dragons are powerful and strong. They're also free. They do what they please and no one messes with them..." She chewed on her bottom lip. "I guess it just reminded me of you."

He watched her quietly for a moment, smiling at how unsure of herself she looked. His heart all but melted at her thoughtfulness. And to think, he had been ready to kick her to the curb earlier. Maybe his intuition hadn't taken a vacation after all. "Thank you, Cadence," he said softly. "I love it."

She looked up at him, her face lighting up with jubilation. "Really?"

He grinned and moved to encircle her waist with his arm. He pulled her close against him and pressed an unhurried, tender kiss to the place where her jaw met her neck. "Really," he whispered.

Cadence drew her breath in sharply as electricity coursed through her body at his soft touch. Those lips... Oh lord, they were so perfect. They felt so perfect. She wanted so badly to know what they felt like against her own.

"Thank you." He breathed it against her ear and she had to hold onto him in order not to fall over. Both of her hands reached up to grip his arms, but this only brought her in contact with his bare skin and sculpted muscles. As a result, she just felt dizzier than before. What kind of magic was this man made of? No one had ever made her react that way to a simple touch or a hushed voice. She had dated some serious hotties, but none of them had caused her to lose control. Not like Talis did.

She cleared her throat and stepped back a bit to put some distance between them. "So...what exactly is this show you're dragging me to tonight?" she asked, pushing her hair behind her ears self-consciously.

"It's a medieval show and dinner. We all get to eat with our fingers while we watch actors joust and fight."

She gave a quizzical frown. "And you have a friend who does this?"

"I met Leila at a renfaire several years ago. She was a belly dancer at the time. Now she lives here and dances in the show."

Cadence's attention snapped to him. "She dances?"

He nodded, smiling at the way she reacted to that information. He cocked his head to one side and his eyes narrowed. "Would you like to go dancing tonight, Cadence?" he asked. "After the show?"

She raised her eyebrows and met his curious gaze.

He smiled. "We can all go out together. Leila apparently has some new boyfriend she wants me to meet. We can go back to that club you were at last night."

She smirked. "That depends. Are you going to yell at me again?"

"Only if you disappear on me again."

"You were mean," she stated.

He shook his head. "I don't like to be mean."

His voice was a whispering caress and it made her stomach clench in a delicious kind of way. "Then don't be."

"Don't give me a reason to be."

She was very aware of how close he was to her, his body

hovering so near, his lips only inches away from hers. She could almost feel the electricity between them. He was so sexy it was wrong.

"So, what do you say?" he prodded. "You want to dance with me tonight?"

She bit her bottom lip and gave him a coy smile. "I don't know. Are you just trying to get lucky?"

He made a purring noise and put his lips to her ear. "In the worst possible way," he whispered.

She shivered.

He chuckled and walked past her to retrieve a shirt and pull it on.

She stood there for a minute until she wasn't dizzy anymore, then turned and wagged her finger at him halfheartedly. "You—" she stammered, her senses still reeling. "You're just wrong." She shivered again as she recalled the feeling of his breath on her skin.

He flashed her that devilish smile of his. "Oh come on, Cadence," he teased. "You pride yourself on being such a tough, hardened chick. Don't tell me you can't handle a little flirting." He winked at her.

Cadence sighed. A *little* flirting? A *little* flirting she could handle. Heck, she could even handle a *lot* of flirting. She could handle crude remarks and lewd gestures, but what she couldn't handle was Talis. He was a weakness she couldn't explain. All she knew was that he made her blood burn and she never wanted to go another day without seeing that taunting, evil grin of his. She loved it. It was perfect.

Chapter Eleven

Las Vegas would never be the same for Cadence. Las Vegas would never be the same just like the stars would never be the same. Every time she looked up at the night sky, she would think of Talis, and every time she thought of Vegas, she would remember how dancing with him had been the most erotic few hours of her life.

The dinner show had been surprisingly entertaining. They sat in a large arena and were served a three course meal while jousting and combat competitions went on, ladies danced, and gymnasts performed acrobatics. The audience was encouraged to scream and yell like barbarians and, at first, Cadence had felt very out of place. With Talis urging her on, however, she had managed to shout out a couple of "huzzahs" and found herself enjoying the spectacle.

Leila had met them at the stage door after the performance with her boyfriend, James. They were both friendly and fun and they'd grabbed a bite to eat before heading down to the club where Cadence had been the previous night. She'd felt awkward and unsure of how to behave, afraid she was going to do something stupid and make Talis angry at her again, but he hadn't given her much time to fret about it. He'd taken her out onto the dance floor and proceeded to show her just exactly what poetry in motion meant. He was completely beautiful, his body moving in the most sensual, beguiling way. She'd danced with her share of men, but Talis left them all behind to eat his dust.

The man was pure sex appeal at its most elegant. It drove her crazy. Men with muscles like Talis shouldn't be elegant. It was always usually ripped and masculine, or elegant and slightly effeminate. She had never seen a ripped, masculine, elegant man before. Talis defied all categories.

It took a good nine or so hours to get from Las Vegas to South Lake Tahoe, California and it was dark when they finally arrived. Cadence could tell they were high in the mountains due to the thick forest lining both sides of the highway. Homes appeared here and there before they hit the main strip of town, which consisted of many tourist-friendly shops and several casinos all stuck together. She could see the glassy sheen of water off to the side, but it looked like obsidian in the darkness.

She watched the scenery go by and sighed. *Talis...* Always, it was about Talis. Heaven help her, but the man invaded every thought she had. Against her better judgment, he had managed to just stride on into her life, and she liked it that way. Something about him was so refreshing. He was sexy, but real; nothing fake about Talis. He didn't put on fronts to hide behind. He didn't wear plastic smiles and tell people what they wanted to hear. He lived and breathed complete freedom. He was eccentric, but so comfortable in his own skin that no one would ever think to label him as a freak or an outcast. He was one of those extremely rare individuals that transcended all stereotypes. He was not her type at all, but she couldn't help but be drawn to him. She was helpless to resist his devilish charm and his extremely balanced way of living. He was the most intriguing human being she had ever met.

Talis guided his car into the driveway of a beautiful two-story home with a deck that wrapped around the top floor. She couldn't see much because of the dark, but the lights were on and it seemed warm to her, like it was inviting her in. She smiled. She didn't think she'd ever felt like a home was welcoming her in. She'd hated the house she grew up in, and she never really felt comfortable in Lance's home, but that was greatly due to the fact that she felt like he always watched every move she made, expecting her to destroy something.

"Well, here we are," Talis stated. "Finally." He turned off the engine and stretched his back, obviously more than sick of driving. He blinked a few times, yawned, then opened his door and went around to get the trunk.

Cadence got out also and was blasted by icy air that instantly made her shiver. The smell of pine was heavy in the air and everything was so silent it was eerie. "Holy crap," she muttered as she rubbed her arms and shoved her hands into her pockets. Talk about a temperature change. She pulled her duffle bag out of the car and slung it over her shoulder, then walked over to Talis, shivering in place. "Okay, it is frigid up here."

He smiled. "There's still snow on top of the mountain. It snows here all the way through May sometimes."

She folded her arms across her chest. She was used to warm places. She'd lived in Arizona for the past several years. The coldest she'd ever been was when Bleeding Passion had played in Finland, but they had only been there for two days.

She followed Talis up to the front door and waited as he rang the bell. Moments later, the door opened and a beautiful blond man greeted them with a grin that should have illuminated the darkness. She blinked in bewildered surprise. This was Talis' brother? She took the liberty of giving him a once-over as they made their way inside.

He was taller than Talis and had hair that looked like spun gold that fell just past his shoulders. His facial features resembled Talis', but the angles of his face were sharper and more defined. His eyes were a startling blue-turquoise color and his lips were full and sensual...sinful like Talis'. She briefly wondered if all of the Whitelaw men were so gorgeous. If they were, she could hardly wait until she saw Traevyn.

"You made it!" the blonde Adonis exclaimed, holding his arms out.

Talis set his bags down and embraced his brother. "Hey, Julian."

Two large dogs came barreling into the foyer, panting excitedly. One was a black lab and the other was a Husky. Talis grinned and knelt to rub them. They licked his face and he laughed.

Julian turned to Cadence and offered a warm smile. "Hi, I'm Julian." He extended his hand.

Cadence smiled and shook it. "I'm Cadence."

"You a friend of Talis'?"

"Yeah, sorta. He conned me into being his squire for the summer. I hope me being here isn't a problem."

He shook his head. "No, not at all. I have plenty of room.

Make yourself at home."

She grinned, liking how warm and friendly he seemed.

"Come on, let's get you settled." Julian grabbed one of Talis' suitcases and led them up a carpeted staircase.

The entire house was built to look like a log cabin and the whole bottom level had hardwood floors of a warm, mahogany color. The front room had a high, vaulted ceiling and a large fireplace where a brown leather sofa and chair sat before it on a red oriental rug.

The top floor was carpeted with the same marbled tan and beige as the staircase, and Cadence walked through what must have been a den as she followed Julian and Talis. All of the furniture was lovely and everything seemed in its place, but it wasn't cold and sterile. Everything seemed warm. The color scheme, the lighting, the fact that she had already seen two cats wandering through the rooms and a gigantic fish tank in the den, not to mention the two dogs at their heels.

"Tal, your room is the same as always. Cadence, do you mind sleeping in the room next to him?"

"It's fine, thank you." She went in to set her things down, enjoying that everything in her room seemed to have a maroon theme. She grinned when she saw a fat calico cat curled on her bed.

"Oh, you aren't allergic, are you?" Julian asked in alarm.

She shook her head and reached out to stroke the feline. "I love cats."

Julian smiled. "Well, I have plenty of them. That's Josie. Just push her off if she annoys you. She likes this room best."

Josie began to purr contentedly as Cadence rubbed under her chin, and she smiled.

"The bathroom is at the end of the hall," Julian continued. "I know you probably both want to freshen up after your long trip, so I'm going to go do some paperwork in my office downstairs. Come on down when you're ready. Maybe we can go get some food. I haven't eaten dinner yet."

"Thanks, bro," Talis called from his room next door.

Cadence smiled and nodded her thanks to Julian as well. She sat down on the bed and sighed, rubbing absently at a sore spot in her shoulder.

"Did you want to shower, Cade?" Talis asked, poking his

head in the door.

She looked up at him. "Uh...sure."

"Are you okay?"

She nodded. "I just have a tension headache." She shrugged and gave a small smile.

He leaned against the doorframe and folded his arms. "You stressed?"

She tried to keep her eyes from boldly assessing his body, but it was a difficult impulse to master as he stood there, the picture of everything manly and sexy. "I guess..." She shrugged again. "I don't know, Talis. Even though being with you has been a nice change of pace, I just keep thinking about my brother and what kind of lecture he's going to give me when he sees me next."

Talis gave her a soft smile. "Cadence, don't worry about your brother right now. Go take a hot shower. Later tonight, I'll give you a back rub, okay?"

She met his eyes and he grinned and winked at her. She smiled. "Okay."

"Besides," he said as he made his way out of the room, "no one's lecture could be worse than mine a few nights ago." He gave her a teasing smile before going back into his room. He opened his suitcase and rummaged through it until he found some clean clothes. He heard the bathroom door click shut and smiled to himself before grabbing his clothes and heading downstairs. "Jules!" he called.

"Don't call me that," Julian grumbled from his office. He turned in his chair just as Talis came into the room. He frowned. "That's what everyone calls Julia and, the last time I checked, I wasn't a girl."

Talis grinned, knowing his brother hated the shortened name. "Hey, Traevyn named her after you. You should be flattered. They'd better name this new one some variation of Talis or I'm going to be offended."

Julian chuckled.

"I'm going to use your shower, okay? It'll save time."

"Oh sure," Julian said. "Go ahead."

Talis went down to Julian's bedroom and quickly stripped his clothes off as he entered the bathroom. He needed a hot shower as bad as Cadence did. His back was killing him.

"So, you really don't know this girl at all?" Julian asked as he leaned up against the kitchen counter.

"I know, it's crazy. I don't even know what I'm doing. This isn't really like me."

Julian looked completely unconvinced. "What are you talking about, Tal? This is totally like you. It's insane, out of the ordinary and completely impulsive. How is that *not* like you?"

"That's not what I meant. I mean, it's not like me to really be attracted so strongly to a woman."

"You'd rather be attracted to a guy?"

Talis heaved an exasperated sigh. "Could you maybe be serious for, like, two seconds?"

Julian chuckled. "All right, I'm sorry. Go ahead."

"Julian, I'm telling you, it's weird with this girl. I've been attracted to girls before, but when I first saw Cadence, my heart nearly stopped. I don't know what it is. She's abrasive, reckless, irresponsible..." He sighed and shrugged. "And no matter how many times I try to tell myself this is a bad idea, something inside of me just keeps telling me that I can't get rid of her. I feel like she needs me or something even though she pretends she doesn't need anyone."

Julian's smirk was so big-brother like. "You're acting just like Traevyn when he first met Amy."

Talis stared at his brother for a second before he rolled his eyes and made a disgusted noise. "Gee thanks, Julian. That's real comforting. I remind you of Traevyn when he met his heinous ex-wife who cheated on him and ripped out his heart!"

Julian laughed. "That's not what I meant. I just mean that I've never seen you this hung up on someone before."

Talis held his arms out helplessly. "Julian, this has disaster written all over it."

"Look, you said the girl had a horrible past, right?"

"Yeah."

"And she claims she wants to change her reckless ways, right?"

"Yeah."

"Then maybe you are just what she needs. Tal, you're

the most honorable, goodhearted person I have ever known. You see something good in her or she wouldn't be here with you right now. You always had the best judgment out of all of us. Trust that."

"I know..." He shook his head to banish his convoluted thoughts. "Man, I can't think when I'm this tired. I'm going to turn in."

Julian nodded. "I work tomorrow so you have the run of the house. When's the renaissance faire?"

"This weekend. Thanks for listening to me ramble, Jules. I'll see you tomorrow."

Julian scowled. "Would you quit it with that?"

Talis grinned and yawned as he mounted the staircase and made his way toward his room. He stopped in Cadence's doorway and chuckled at the sight. She was lying on the bed watching TV with both dogs across her legs and Josie up by her head. It was endearing and showed a softer side of her that he hadn't seen.

He leaned against the doorframe. "Apparently, they like you."

Cadence looked over at Talis and giggled. "I guess. Did you have a good talk with your brother?"

"We were talking about you, actually."

She didn't look pleased at that information. "Me?" She sounded suspicious.

He nodded as he made his way into the room. She looked so fresh from showering earlier, and she hadn't reapplied her makeup. She was beautiful even without it, one of those rare natural beauties. Her skin looked soft and clean, like satin. He wanted to touch it. "I was telling Julian about how insane I think I am for dragging Cadence the walking disaster along with me for the summer." He flashed her a teasing grin.

She scowled. "Nice," she grumbled.

He chuckled and scooted Harry, the black lab, and Lucy, the Husky, out of the way so he could sit on the end of the bed. "Did you call Tawny?"

She nodded and rolled her eyes as she pushed herself up into a sitting position. "She still thinks I've lost it. I guess somewhere in all the midst of this Lance remembered I had a best friend and has been calling her non-stop. I think she's about ready to kill me... So is Lance."

He smiled gently, couldn't really blame her brother and friend for being worried, but couldn't really blame Cadence for being annoyed either. He motioned for her to turn around. "Come on, let me give you that back rub I promised."

She grinned and obeyed, turning so he had access to her back and shoulders.

"Go ahead and lay on your stomach," he commanded. "Hope you don't mind if I straddle you. I can't do it right if I don't."

She tried to ignore the lewd joke that came to mind at his words, *"I can't do it right if I don't."*

"It's fine. Just don't crush me." She'd had back rubs before. Having him straddle her shouldn't have been a big deal, but as she felt him settle himself across her hips, her heart leapt into her throat and started to pound. Having him there seemed so much more intimate than it should have. She swallowed and buried her face in the pillow so he wouldn't see her blush. She closed her eyes as she felt his hands run up her back briefly before resting on her shoulders. He applied gentle pressure and began to work the knots from her muscles.

She'd put on a sweatshirt due to the cold and she noticed that it was difficult for him to give a proper massage with the bulky material bunching up under his fingers. He let out a frustrated growl and tried to tug her shirt down.

Cadence giggled. "Talis, this is stupid," she said, tugging at the collar. "You're choking me. Here, just let me take it off."

He moved to let her sit up and Talis blinked in bewilderment as she wiggled her way out of her sweatshirt and discarded it on the floor. A faint blush colored his cheeks as his eyes raked over her bare skin and he shook his head. He glanced toward the open door and cleared his throat. "I'm gonna close the door," he said. "The last thing we need is Julian wandering by and thinking who knows what."

She laughed. "Oh, come on. It's only my bra. It's not like I'm naked or anything." She laid back down on her stomach.

He cleared his throat again. "Yes, well..."

She turned her face to look at him as he closed the door and made his way back to the bed. She grinned. "Do I make you nervous, Talis?" she teased.

He raised an eyebrow. "Quiet, vixen," he scolded. He resumed his place across her hips and placed his fingers on her skin, hesitating a moment before running both of his hands up her back slowly, as if wanting to feel the texture. Cadence's stomach somersaulted at the touch of his hands. They were warm and gentle and they ignited a fiery path as they traveled up her back and shoulders. The breath left her body as he ran just his fingertips down the bumps of her spine and across her sides. She shivered. Okay, maybe taking off the shirt hadn't been such a good idea. She had not been prepared for the way her body reacted to his touch.

Talis shook his head and tried to regain some kind of sense. What was he doing? What kind of a back rub was that supposed to be? This wasn't doing anything productive at all. He shifted uncomfortably and frowned, wondering if sitting across her hips had been such a good idea. *Hey Talis, is that a banana in your pocket, or—* He shook his head again. Okay, either he was way too tired, or this woman really was an evil temptress.

He forced himself and his thoughts to behave and put his hands back on her shoulders where they belonged. He kneaded her muscles gently as he studied her beautiful tattoo. He frowned as he realized there was a name written underneath the dragon in small, cursive letters. "Katydid," he read. "What does that mean?"

"A nickname Lance gave me a long time ago. That's what everyone on the crew calls me."

He arched an eyebrow and smirked. "You mean your evil, horrid brother gave you a cute nickname?"

"A long time ago before he was evil and horrid."

He frowned thoughtfully. "You know, Cadence, we all have issues with our siblings from time to time. I mean, I'm close with both of my brothers, but there are still times when I want to kill them. Traevyn can try the patience of a saint and Julian, as nice as he is, still put my boxer shorts in the freezer when I was sixteen to get back at me for embarrassing him in front of a girl."

Cadence laughed.

Talis smiled. "My point is, all siblings can get on our nerves, but they're family. Your brother may be overprotective, but it's just because he loves you and he worries about you. Maybe he goes overboard, but at least he cares. That's more than can be said for some families."

She fell silent and seemed to mull on his words for a moment before she gave a soft sigh.

Talis finished his massage reluctantly and trailed his fingers down her spine one more time just to savor the feel of her skin. His hands came to rest on her sides and he grinned. "Cadence, I have a question for you."

"Hm?"

"Are you ticklish?" He ran his fingers across her ribs playfully.

She squealed and wiggled beneath him in an attempt to get away.

"Ah ha, I see someone *is* ticklish." He tickled her sides again, and she kicked her legs, bending one at the knee and causing her heel to connect with his lower back. He grunted in pain and rubbed at it. "Gee thanks," he grumbled.

She laughed. "I'm sorry!"

He arched an eyebrow. "Not as sorry as you're gonna be." He moved off of her hips and grabbed one of her feet, tickling it relentlessly. She screamed and flailed her legs. Talis laughed until her foot made contact with his jaw in a way that sent him somersaulting backward off the bed. He landed on his back and stared up at the ceiling in stunned silence.

"Talis!" Cadence gasped. She jumped up and ran to where he was lying. "Oh my gosh, Talis! Are you all right?"

He cracked his jaw and met her eyes. "Dang, Cade," he muttered. "You don't fool around, do you?"

She shook her head in horror. "I am so sorry."

His lips quirked. "Well, if you want to play rough like the boys..." He stood and grabbed her by the waist, hauling her up over his shoulder.

She screamed and tried to clutch his shirt. "Talis, put me down!" she cried. "I don't like to be upside down!"

"I grew up with two older brothers, little girl," he snarled. "You think I can't take you on?"

"Talis!" she half-laughed, half-screamed. "Put me down!"

He hefted her back over his shoulder and flung her onto the bed, flopping down on top of her in a body slam. She squealed with laughter right as a rending crack ripped through the room and the end of the bed collapsed. Talis' eyes widened and he heard Cadence gasp. He raised his head enough to see that the entire end of the mattress was sloping toward the ground. "Oh, crap," he murmured.

Cadence put her hand over her mouth and stared up at him. "Did we break it?"

He looked down at her and nodded, then frowned. "Man, you must weigh a ton."

She slapped her palm against his chest playfully.

"Is everything all right in here?" Julian burst into the room and stopped dead in his tracks as his gaze fell on Talis on top of a shirtless Cadence. His eyes widened. "Oh man, I am so sorry," he mumbled, averting his eyes. "I just heard a lot of noise and I thought—" He closed his eyes and waved his hands. "I'll just leave now."

Talis laughed as his brother turned to go. "Julian, wait! It's not what you think." He shook his head. "Trust me, I don't like it *that* rough." Cadence's laughter was music to his ears. "We were just playing," Talis explained as he pushed himself off of her and stood.

"You were playing half naked?" Julian questioned skeptically.

Talis rolled his eyes. "Do I look half naked to you? I was giving her a back rub."

Julian turned toward his defeated bed and winced. "I liked that bed frame," he whined.

"I'll replace it. Go back to bed, Julian. We can do something about this tomorrow."

Cadence frowned and sat up. "Where am I supposed to sleep?"

"Talis' room, I guess," Julian muttered. He glanced at Talis and eyeballed him. "I'm sure he's not gonna mind."

Talis shooed his brother out of the room, then turned to Cadence, who was pulling her shirt back on. He met her eyes and grinned.

"Poor Julian. I think we gave him a heart attack," she giggled.

"He'll live. Come on, let's move you into my room. I can sleep on the couch in the den."

She frowned. "Don't be stupid, Talis. I'm not going to chase you out of your room. I'll sleep on the couch."

"Cadence, please. I am not going to make you sleep on the couch. It won't kill me to sleep on it one night. Some time tomorrow, I'll dismantle the bed frame and put the mattresses on the ground."

She rolled her eyes and huffed. "Okay, this is ridiculous. We're both adults and it's just for a night so let's just share the bed in your room, okay? You don't need to be a gentleman *all* the time."

His heart skipped a beat and he met her eyes. He knew he should keep his mouth shut, but he couldn't. He had a devil living inside him...and it liked to come out around Cadence. "What if I want to sleep naked?" he teased.

She gave him a flat expression, refusing to show him that his taunts affected her. "Well, unless Talis Jr. takes up more than his fair share of the bed, I don't see a problem."

Talis arched an eyebrow and chuckled. She never failed to surprise him. She got flustered when he was close to her, but she didn't need help in the retort department.

Cadence grabbed her pillow and duffle bag and followed Talis into the bedroom. She was quick to crawl under the covers, but that was mainly due to the fact that her heart was beating much too fast at the thought of being so close to him. She tried desperately to put on a false bravado, but she reacted to Talis in a way she'd never reacted to another living soul.

Talis switched off the light and slid into bed beside her. Her heart beat erratically for several minutes, but when she heard him sigh and felt his reassuring weight next to her, she eased unexpectedly.

"Goodnight, Cadence," he murmured. "I hope you sleep well."

She smiled and flipped over on her side so she could see him. "You too, Talis."

He turned his head to glance at her in the darkness and gave a soft smile. "Are you cold?"

She wasn't really, but she shrugged. There was a definite chill in the air, but she was comfortable under the covers.

He searched her face and bit his bottom lip slyly. "You can always share my body heat," he suggested. "Since you gave me permission not to be a gentleman and all."

She grinned. His teasing was merciless. He was a fine balance of mystery and humor. His playfulness made her feel at ease when his divine beauty would unnerve her otherwise. Deciding to be a bit devilish herself, she scooted close to him and rested her head on his bare, tattooed shoulder. She knew it was the thing he least expected. "Sounds like a plan," she stated simply.

Talis tensed for a moment, giving away his surprise, but he was quick to mask it by bringing one hand up and delving his fingers into her hair. "Good night, Cadence," he whispered.

She smiled and snuggled a little closer, liking the husky note in his voice. "Good night, Talis." And for the first time in longer than she could remember, she felt peaceful as she lay next to him.

Chapter Twelve

Cadence had lived in hot places her entire life. She'd grown up in L.A and had lived in Phoenix for the past several years. She was accustomed to a little rain now and then, but she was not prepared for the silent chill of a morning in South Lake Tahoe.

She knew that the heater was on, but she imagined that Julian wouldn't have it cranked up to ninety degrees. He was used to living there. She, however, was not.

She didn't know where Talis was. He'd been gone since she woke up and she couldn't bring herself to get out of bed. She was comfortable and warm under the covers, and the chilly air that kept brushing across her exposed face was a constant reminder of how badly she did not want the rest of her body to have to endure it.

Summoning all her strength, she flung the covers off and swung her legs out of bed, shivering as the cold air attacked her. She grabbed her duffle bag and searched through it until she found some decently warm clothes, then headed for the bathroom where she planned on taking the hottest shower of her life.

When she had finished, she headed down the hall and out into the den where she stopped at the sight that met her through the sliding glass door. Talis was standing on the deck and, behind him, stretched a lake of the most gorgeous shade of blue she had ever seen. The lake was surrounded by pine trees that spanned out as far as she could see, and Talis was leaning nonchalantly against the rail in a black sweatshirt and a relaxed fit pair of blue jeans. She smiled as she realized that she would be very content waking up to that sight every morning of her life. That strange feeling of peace came over her again, and she closed her eyes for a moment, relishing in it. What was it about him?

Talis had shown her more in the past few days than she had ever seen. She considered herself very knowledgeable about the world. She had lived in two major cities and had traveled all over the planet with a famous rock band. She had seen Europe and Japan and Australia, places people dreamed their whole lives of seeing, but she realized that she'd never really appreciated any of it. Being a roadie was a constant job of tear downs and set ups. She always saw more of the inside of the arena the band played at than she did of the place they were in. Even when she did get to go out, she usually took off with some of the other guys on the crew and hit the nearest bar. She'd never taken the time to look around at the beauty of the world, but that might have been because she'd never really seen any beauty in the world. Not until now. Not until she'd stopped for a second to slow down and look at life through Talis' eyes.

She headed toward the door with a smile and slid it open.

Talis turned to look at her over his shoulder and offered her a warm grin. "Well, good morning. I thought you might sleep all day."

She wrinkled her nose at him as she joined him at the rail. "Whatever, Talis. It's only ten o'clock."

"I've been up since six."

"Good for you. Ask me if I care."

He chuckled and extended his arm out to indicate the beautiful expanse of blue in the distance. "Welcome to Lake Tahoe."

"It's so amazing." She took a deep breath of the crisp, pine-scented air and sighed.

"I got rid of the bed frame in your room and put the mattresses down on the floor," he said. "So you can sleep on your own bed tonight."

She glanced up at him. "You don't waste any time. Do I snore that bad?"

He smirked down at her and gave her an expression that said more than any words could have. It actually succeeded in causing her cheeks to flush warm.

He turned his attention back to the lake, not wanting to embellish on the fact that he had loved sleeping next to her. She'd been soft and warm and, her presence had done something funny to his heart. She was vulnerable in her sleep, childlike almost in the innocence on her face. It contrasted so greatly with the harsh demeanor she presented to the world.

He'd never been a needy guy. He was self sufficient, independent, and he liked it that way. He'd never been lonely. He loved his life and everything in it, but at one point in the night, Cadence had been pressed up completely against him. He'd been able to smell her, feel her steady heartbeat, and luxuriate in what it was like to be so close to someone. He'd never thought he needed that in his life, but now that he'd experienced it with someone like her, he didn't think he'd ever be able to go without it. Something about her called to him so strongly. He wasn't content just being her traveling companion and friend. Not at all.

"Talis!" Julian's voice came.

Talis looked over and frowned as he saw his brother coming out onto the deck. "What are you doing? I thought you went to work."

Julian rolled his eyes. "You know all that paperwork I was doing last night? I forgot it. Had to come back. Look, I've got to get out of here. I have two appointments that are late now because of this. Your entourage is here."

Talis arched an eyebrow. "My what?"

"Your entourage. You know, Draco, Raven, Dopey, Sleepy, Sneezy. Whoever they are. They're downstairs."

Cadence laughed as Julian ran back out. "I didn't know the guys were going to be here," she said.

"Draco, Raven and Tempyst are. Ash will be here next week and Devlyn is going to catch up with us in Big Sur." He started toward the door. "We have to go register today. All the fighters have to register for the competitions beforehand."

"You're competing?"

He nodded. "Armored combat. Draco and Tempyst aren't fighting, but they have to set up their vendor stations."

"Is Ash fighting?"

"No, this renfaire runs for two weekends and he can't come up until next week, so he misses out. He's just going to hang out with us."

"Do you want me to go with you today?" She followed him back into the house and downstairs.

"You don't have to. It'll be pretty boring. Just take my car and wander around town, go to the beach, relax. We'll be back by evening."

She nodded and followed him down to where Raven, Draco and Tempyst were sitting in the front room. All three of them immediately stood up like the men in old movies did whenever a lady entered the room. "Hey guys," she greeted.

Raven stepped forward, took her hand and bowed over it, then looked up at her with an impish grin.

Cadence rolled her eyes, but didn't fight the smile that came to her lips.

"How are you?" Draco questioned. "Talis drive you crazy yet?"

Talis scowled at his friend and Cadence giggled. "No, he's too busy trying to keep me in line. I'm going to get some breakfast before I starve. You boys have fun today." She flashed a playful grin and swaggered on into the kitchen.

Talis stared after her, watching the way her hips swayed tantalizingly as she walked.

Raven chuckled. "Well, when Talis picks his jaw up off the floor, we can head out and get started."

Talis glanced at Raven and smirked. "All right, let's go. We have a lot of stuff to get done today. Cade!"

"Yeah!" she shouted from the kitchen.

He smiled and went in, where she was surveying the contents of the refrigerator. "Have a good day today, all right?"

She shut the door and returned his smile. "Don't worry, Tal. I promise to not go get plastered somewhere."

"I wasn't trying to be snide" he said as he approached her. "I was just being nice." He leaned forward and kissed her on the cheek. "I'll see you later." He winked and disappeared out the door with his friends.

Cadence sighed as deafening silence filled the large house. Silence bothered her. It was too...silent. She didn't know what to do with it. It made her restless. Being restless was a dangerous thing for her.

Maybe she would go into town later. She needed to get some warmer clothing anyway. That would take up some time.

Cadence was bored. It was nearing four o'clock and Talis still wasn't home. How long did it take to register and set up a couple vendor stands anyway?

She had gone to town, managed to get herself some more suitable clothing and was feeling much warmer because of it. She'd wandered along the beach for awhile, enjoying the peace and serenity of nature, but she could only do that for so long before the restlessness ate at her.

She had gone back to Julian's, thinking that the guys would be back, but they weren't. She was still all by her lonesome and getting more bored by the second. Maybe there was some kind of club in one of those casinos she could go to. There had to be. It was happy hour, too.

She shook her head. *No, no, no!* What was the matter with her? Was she a glutton for punishment? Two seconds away from being a complete alcoholic? A boredom drunk? Talis would throw a tantrum if he came home and found out she had gone to a club by herself again. She couldn't risk blowing it and having him dump her off at the nearest bus station and ship her back home. She needed to use her brain for once and do something productive. Just because she was bored didn't mean she needed to go off and get herself into trouble. She really needed to stop acting like an eighteen-year-old girl who didn't know any better.

She ran through her options as she wandered aimlessly around the living room. She could watch TV, but she wasn't much of a TV fan. There was never anything interesting on. She was kind of hungry. She could always try her hand at cooking dinner for everyone. She was used to take-out and restaurants so that would at least take up some time, if she didn't manage to burn the kitchen down.

That was definitely something Talis wouldn't expect. It was productive, would keep her busy, and it was also something nice to do. Julian had worked all day and he was nice enough to let her stay in his home when he didn't know her at all. She was sure he would appreciate coming home to a meal for once, and Talis and the guys had been working all day. They were bound to be hungry.

Making up her mind and feeling good about her decision for once, she went purposefully into the kitchen and started to look through the cupboards to see what she could create.

"Holy cow," Draco murmured as he and the others trooped into the house. "What smells so good in here?"

Talis frowned as he caught a whiff of the heavenly aroma as well. Julian hadn't gotten home yet, so it had to be Cadence.

"Hey, guys!" she called excitedly as she came in from the kitchen. "You're just in time. I just finished dinner!"

Talis couldn't have hid his surprise if he tried. "You made us dinner?"

"I made it for everybody. We just have to wait for Julian, but you can all go sit down." She motioned everyone toward the dining room as she disappeared back into the kitchen.

Raven arched an eyebrow and gave Talis a wicked grin. "Have you claimed her yet because if you haven't..."

Talis rolled his eyes. "Come on, Raven. Claimed her? What are we, a vampire clan?"

He shrugged. "Hey, they would have done that in the middle ages."

"Yes, well, contrary to what we do for fun in our lives, we aren't in the middle ages. Now we have things like women's rights and sexual harassment. I can't just club her over the head and drag her back to my cave." He wandered over to the dining room and sat down at the head of the table.

Raven chuckled as he and the others followed. "Maybe you can't drag her back to your cave, but I somehow don't think she'd mind if you dragged her back to your bed." He raised his eyebrows playfully.

Talis sighed. "Raven, you're hopeless." But he couldn't stop the way his body reacted to that suggestion. Just the thought of being intimate with Cadence made his blood catch on fire.

"I just call it as I see it," Raven said. "And you'd better stay sitting or else everybody else is gonna see it too."

Lucky for Raven, Cadence strode into the room. Talis didn't have a chance to find some sort of object to throw at him.

She was carrying plates of pasta with some sort of

strange, brown sauce covering it. She set one down in front of Talis and one down in front of Raven, then went back into the kitchen to retrieve two more for Draco and Tempyst.

Raven frowned down at the pasta. "Dude, what is this?" he whispered.

Cadence came in and delivered the other two plates, then set a basket of rolls on the table. "There you go! You can go ahead and start eating if you want. I'll get Julian's when he gets here."

"Hey, Cadence," Talis called, clearing his throat discreetly. "What is this, exactly?"

"It's pesto, silly," she said as she returned to the kitchen.

Draco frowned. "Isn't pesto supposed to be green?" he whispered.

"Shut up," Talis scolded in a hushed voice. "She didn't have to do any of this for us. I'm sure it's not that bad, so just eat it."

Draco stared down at it in dismay for a minute before he bravely took up a fork and twirled some of the pasta onto it. He stuffed it in his mouth while the others watched, monitoring his response. He dropped his fork down on the plate with a clang and covered his mouth as if he was going to retch. He squeezed his eyes shut and forced it down, then shook his head and gave Talis a pained look. "That tastes like motor oil," he croaked.

Talis sighed. "Come on guys, she tried."

Draco stuck his tongue out as if he was having trouble getting rid of the taste. "She failed."

Tempyst decided he would be safe and go for the bread. He grabbed a roll and tried to cut it in half with his knife, but it was so hard that the knife didn't even want to go through. He sighed and stabbed the point of his knife into it, trying to saw through the bricklike monstrosity.

"Dude, gimme that," Draco said, grabbing the knife and roll from Tempyst. He tried to retract the knife from it, which was next to impossible, and he scowled. He turned it upside down and tried to shake the roll loose, but all he succeeded in doing was flinging it off and backwards as Julian walked through the doorway. The bread bounced off of his forehead and rolled to the ground.

Julian frowned and rubbed his forehead. "What the?"

Draco raised his eyebrows. "Sorry," he muttered.

Cadence came back in with a plate for Julian and one for herself. She sat down next to Raven and smiled at everyone. "How is it?" she asked.

Draco forced a smile and nodded. "Mmmm," he said.

She grinned and dug into the pasta. She took a big bite and stopped chewing midway. She scrunched up her face and shook her head, then spit it unceremoniously back onto her plate. "Ew!" she cried. "Oh my gosh, that tastes like raw sewage!"

Draco wrinkled his nose. "I was thinking more like petroleum... Although, it does *look* like raw sewage. "

She stood and grabbed her plate. "This is disgusting! Why didn't you say anything? Is the bread at least decent?"

Tempyst cleared his throat. "Ask Julian. It hit him in the head when Draco was trying to dislodge my knife from it."

She gave him a horrified expression and headed back into the kitchen. "Well, forget this!" she cried.

Talis winced and rubbed the bridge of his nose. "Now she's going to be upset," he said, shooting an irritated scowl at his friends.

Draco frowned. "What were we supposed to do? Force it down and die a horrible death?"

"She tried to do something nice and it all went to crap." He could imagine what she would be thinking. That she'd messed up again, that she screwed up everything she touched. She would be heartbroken. He sighed again and stood, starting to clear the rest of the plates.

"That sucks," Raven muttered. "It smelled really good, too."

"Well, that does it!" Cadence declared as she came back into the room. "Pizza is on its way!"

Talis stopped and looked up at her. He frowned because she was still grinning.

"I figure pepperoni and sausage is a much better alternative to gasoline and concrete, don't you?"

Everyone chuckled and unanimously started to help clear the table as the tension left the room.

Talis set down the plate he was carrying and followed Cadence into the kitchen where she started to scrape off plates and load the dishwasher. "Cadence."

She looked over her shoulder and smiled at him.

He placed his hand consolingly on the small of her back.

"You're not upset about dinner?"

She shrugged. "No, why should I be? I've never cooked anything besides TV dinners and macaroni and cheese. I didn't know what I was doing. I'm just glad it was only pasta and not steak or something." She laughed. "Can you imagine if I'd tried a prime rib? It probably would have been mooing and trying to walk off the plate." She shook her head and flung some silverware into the dishwasher.

He smiled, still perplexed over the fact that she was so nonchalant about it. "Thank you for the gesture. It was very thoughtful of you."

She shrugged again, turning to face him with a warm smile. "No big deal. I was bored and figured that destroying dinner was at least productive." She met his eyes and giggled at the concern she must have seen mirrored in them. "Talis, stop looking so upset. I'm fine, I promise."

"I just don't want you to think that we didn't appreciate the thought."

"I know you did. It's fine. We'll all just hang out and eat pizza instead."

Talis hadn't expected her to be so accepting of her failure, but it was nice to see. Maybe she was starting to change her thought pattern. He frowned thoughtfully. "You seem like you're in a good mood." He ran his hand across his jaw.

She nodded. "Sure."

He moved his hand up his face to scratch at his temple. Here went nothing...

"Good... Now's a good time to tell you this then..." He cleared his throat. "I registered you in the armored combat competition."

Her eyes bulged and her mouth fell open. "You *what*?" She set the plate she had been holding down on the counter with a forceful clang.

"Yeah, but I registered you for next weekend only so that you can practice first and Tempyst can get you armored."

She stared as if her brain refused to comprehend what he had just told her. "Are you absolutely out of your mind?" she cried. "I don't know the first thing about armored combat!"

He frowned. "Oh, right. Need I remind you that you kicked the crap out of Raven? Come on, Cadence, it'll be fun, and I have a feeling you'll be really good at it."

She snorted and put her hands on her hips. "Why, because I have so much rage to channel?"

"Something like that," he said with a chuckle. "Don't worry, there are two separate competitions. One this weekend and one next weekend. You can watch this week and get a feel for the whole faire atmosphere. I'll work with you, and next week, you'll be ready to go."

She rolled her eyes. "Whatever my master commands," she grumbled. "You know, I thought I was supposed to be your squire. As in, I stand on the sidelines and bring you your armor."

"That was before I realized that I had such a warrior maiden in my company." He tucked a strand of her hair behind her ear.

Cadence's cheeks heated unexpectedly at his kind words and gentle touch. She looked down and swallowed as her heart picked up its pace. She couldn't even imagine putting on armor and going out to beat on some dude with a stick of rattan. It seemed so strange and foreign to her, but she had to admit, she'd liked dueling when she'd done it up in the mountains. And Talis believed in her. It was nice to have someone believe in her. She looked up at him and smiled. "Okay."

His grin was reward in itself. "This weekend we'll get you some proper clothes and Tempyst can fit you for armor. We'll get you all decked out and mean-looking."

She giggled and briefly wondered what in the world she'd gotten herself into.

Chapter Thirteen

Talis sighed and tapped his fingers against his arm in boredom as he waited in the clothing booth. "Cadence, are you ever coming out of there?"

"Shut up, Talis!" she shot back from the other side of the dressing curtain. "I don't see you wearing one of these things."

Talis smirked and exchanged a glance with Raven, who was dressed appropriately in his flamboyant red and black tunic and black breeches. A baldric was strapped securely around his chest, holding his magnificent broadsword in place across his shoulders. His black hair was pulled back and he was drinking water from a ceramic ale mug. Looking at Raven at a renfaire always made Talis chuckle. While they all enjoyed it, no one looked as at home at one as Raven did.

Suddenly, the dressing curtain was flung aside and Cadence flounced out in full serving wench attire. Talis blinked in bewilderment as his eyes were immediately drawn to her breasts, which were straining against the top of her brown leather corset.

"This is ridiculous!"

Talis raised an eyebrow, still not able to tear his gaze away from her cleavage. Holy cow. How come he had never noticed her perfect curves before? "You don't like it?"

She huffed. "I look like every other brazen, tavern wench hussy out there!" She put her hands on her hips and scowled. "I'm supposed to be some warrior woman and you make me dress like a common strumpet!"

Talis swallowed. His throat was dry. "I dunno... I kinda like it." He met her eyes and gave her an evil grin.

"Yeah, me too," Raven commented.

Cadence looked over at him to see his eyes glued to her bosom as well. She sighed in exasperation. "Well, as much as I love being on display for a bunch of lecherous guys, I hate this outfit."

Talis smiled and stepped forward. He caressed his hands down her arms and met her eyes. "You don't like it?"

She met his gaze and shook her head.

"Then find something you do like. Whatever you want."

"But half of these clothes cost a small fortune."

"Don't worry about it, Cadence. Just find something you like and I'll get it for you. Just...try to do it in a hurry. I have to compete in an hour."

She smiled, bit her bottom lip in an excited gesture and ran to the men's section.

Raven frowned. "She's...in the wrong section," he stated as he pointed after her in confusion.

Talis sighed and shrugged. "She's the one who has to wear the garb, Rave. She may as well be comfortable in it." He looked at his friend forlornly. "Too bad for us, though... I liked that last outfit."

Raven gave a knowing chuckle.

Several minutes later, Cadence emerged from the dressing room again sporting black breeches, a black peasant shirt and the brown corset minus the heaving bosom. Black, knee-high pirate boots added the extra spark to the outfit, and Talis grinned as he looked over her in appraisal. The entire outfit hugged her slender body in a delicious way, but she didn't look like all of the other women at the faire. She stood out. She was unique. She looked like the warrior he had registered her as.

"I don't think those boots go with the rest of the outfit," Raven commented. "The time periods don't match."

"Shut up, Raven. Who cares? What are you, the renfaire police? Not everything has to be SCA approved." Talis shook his head and let his eyes assess Cadence again. "It suits you."

She smiled. "It makes me feel strong."

"You should feel strong. You're a warrior, remember?"

She giggled. She'd never considered herself a warrior of anything. Having Talis call her one made her feel special somehow, even if it was only pretend. She stole a look up at him and couldn't believe that she actually thought he was sexy in battle armor. Since he was competing soon, he already had on his chain mail tunic and his leg pieces. He looked amazing. So strong and masculine.

She'd been reluctant to come to the faire that morning because she didn't know what to expect. All she had to go on was the dinner show at The Excalibur, but that was nothing compared to this.

A medieval style village had been erected for the event and it was nestled amongst the thick forest. Everyone was dressed up and performing constantly. Different acts of all sorts went on throughout the day, swordplay and acrobatics and comedy. There were archery competitions and knife throwing and vendors calling out to the people passing by.

It really did feel like she'd stepped back in time and, even though she had laughed at Talis when he'd first told her about all of this, something inside of her welcomed the eccentric lifestyle. It felt different there, among all of the actors. It felt real, like things were simpler and freer. Like chivalry and romance still existed.

"So, when I compete next weekend," she said suddenly, "do they announce me as me, or do I have some other name?"

"I registered you under a different name, but I tried to keep it as close to yours as I could," Talis replied with a smile. "You're Cadeyrn."

She frowned in question.

"It's Celtic. It means 'battle king.'"

"Did you know that's what it meant when you picked it?"

He tucked her hair back in a tender, delicate gesture. "Of course I did. That's why I chose it."

She met his eyes and her blood warmed as he smiled down at her. "Thanks, Talis," she said quietly.

He continued to let his fingers trail absently along her jaw line, or her neck, wherever he could get away with touching her. She didn't stop him. She didn't mind. "You've fought many battles in your life, Cadence. It's a fitting name for you."

She gave a shy smile and impulsively wrapped her arms around his waist, resting her head against his chest. The chain mail was rough against her skin, but she didn't care. What he had just said was the nicest thing anyone had ever told her. He'd validated every awful thing she'd endured in her life. He gave her credit for living through it instead of condemning her for it.

She closed her eyes and held on, her heart surging with overwhelming affection for him.

Talis caressed his hands through her hair. "Are you okay?"

She nodded.

His expression was curious, but she couldn't get out what she was feeling. She had a difficult time putting her chaotic emotions into words. She hoped her hug was adequate enough to express her gratitude for everything he had done for her. It was more than she deserved.

"Tal, we have to go," Raven interrupted.

Talis heaved a sigh and cast her a glance that was full of longing, and maybe even a little bit of annoyance at having his friend interrupt their private moment. The fire that smoldered in his eyes for that brief moment made her heart pick up speed. His gorgeous smile split his lips. "Are you going to come watch me?" he asked with hopefulness.

She grinned. "Of course I am! I need to study your moves."

"All right, come on then," he said with a chuckle. He paid for her outfit and the three of them headed over to where the combat competitions were being held. Tempyst's vendor stand was right across the way and Talis jaunted over to grab the rest of his armor. Cadence went inside the small, roped-off arena with Raven and waited, letting herself take in all the sights.

It still amazed her that she was having a fun time. She'd thought for sure that the entire affair would be ridiculous. The idea of a renaissance faire had always seemed so nerdy to her, but she saw now that it was more like a giant, inter-active play where she could become whoever she wanted to be...Cadeyrn, the battle king. She grinned. It wasn't silly like she'd said before. Something about the atmosphere seemed so much simpler. It was an escape, and she could definitely use one of those.

"Cadence, could you help me with this, please?"

She turned to see Talis trying to strap on his chest plate and having a difficult time doing it. She smiled and huffed playfully as she grabbed the straps and began to buckle them. "I'm supposed to be a warrior. How is it going to look if people see me strapping you in your armor like some common slave?"

Talis smirked. "No one knows you're a great warrior yet, Your Majesty. Right now you're still my squire, so do your job."

She giggled and continued to help him get suited up. She gave him a hard time, but she really didn't mind doing it. She found that being close to Talis was something she was growing to crave.

She finished strapping on his last shoulder plate and frowned thoughtfully when she caught sight of silver glinting from around his neck. She reached up and pulled a necklace free from beneath his tunic and chest plate. Her eyes widened in surprised recognition and she looked up at him.

He smiled down at her. "What? You didn't think I would go into battle without it, did you?" He tucked it safely back underneath his armor. "A warrior always wears his lady's token onto the battlefield."

She felt her cheeks turn pink and she averted her eyes. "Your lady, huh?" She tried to sound mocking, but she knew that her voice wavered. Why did the thought of him laying some kind of claim on her seem so appealing? She had never wanted to belong to someone else. Even when she'd dated Danny, she'd hated when he'd called her "his girl" while possessively putting his arm around her shoulders. She wasn't anyone's property. She didn't have a collar around her neck.

But it was different with Talis...everything was different with Talis. She wanted to belong to him in some way because, if she did, maybe she could sample some of that heavenly radiance he seemed to exude. That soft and mysterious light that made the world seem so much brighter and made life make so much more sense. He made her feel sane for the first time ever and she never wanted to relinquish that.

Cadence's breath caught in her throat as she felt Talis lift her chin so that she was looking up into his blue eyes. He smiled gently down at her and her stomach somersaulted.

He shrugged one shoulder in a lazy manner. "Well, you're the only lady around that's given me something to wear into battle," he replied. "That doesn't necessarily make you mine, but it does make you pretty special." He ran his finger in a slow line down her neck, then traced her collarbone.

She shivered involuntarily and looked down, shaking her head. "I'm not special," she murmured, trying desperately to hold onto her taunting humor. "I'm just your squire, remember?" She forced herself to look up at him again and smile.

He raised an eyebrow. "It wasn't a squire who gave me that necklace," he said, lowering his voice. "It was an evil temptress who made me give her a back rub while she was half naked, and then broke my brother's bed."

Cadence gasped and pointed an accusatory finger at him. "I didn't make you do anything, Talis Whitelaw, and if you recall, *you* broke Julian's bed after you *body slammed* me!"

She saw Talis' sinful lips morph into his evil grin too late and, before she could do or say anything more, he'd grabbed a hold of her wrist and was running his tongue along her still pointed finger. She froze and her heart pounded out an abnormal rhythm as he drew her finger into his mouth and sucked on it, his eyes flashing with devilish mirth as he watched her.

When he released her, she just stood there as if she'd been frozen in place. Shivers worked along her spine and she tried to force herself to breathe and remember how to speak. She frowned as sense slowly returned to her, and she met his eyes. "You're the Devil," she stated. His laughter made her scowl halfheartedly. "I am not the one who's a temptress," she hissed.

"Oh, I'm a temptress, am I?" he teased.

She frowned. "Well...a tempter...or whatever the masculine version of that word is." His chuckle was a low, sexy rumble and it didn't do anything to make the situation better for her. He was evil, in the worst possible way. He was evil, and she loved every minute of it. He was the first man she'd ever met who made her feel out of control. It had been strange at first because she was, by nature, a dominant person, but even when she tried to seem tough and unflappable around Talis, he did something to remind her that he could very easily get her to do anything he wanted. All he had to do was give her that roguish smile of his.

"Talis, is that you?"

The spell Talis had woven vanished as a petite, chestnut-haired woman in a teal belly dancing costume came running over to them, bells jangling the entire way.

Talis smiled at the approaching woman. "Heather! There

you are! I couldn't find you!"

"I have been trying to get a hold of you all week and I couldn't."

"I know, I'm sorry. I changed my cell phone number and I couldn't find where I put yours."

"We had to get Mike to play guitar for our first two shows," she grumbled. "And, even though he's a great musician, I get sick of him staring at all of our butts while we're trying to perform."

Talis laughed. "I'm so sorry. When's your next show? I'll change after I compete and come play for you."

"We perform every hour on the hour."

He nodded. "All right, I'll come find you right after Raven slaughters me."

"Okay, see you then!" She laughed and took off back in the direction she had come.

Cadence watched her go with a small sigh. She would love to do belly dancing. Dancing of any sort had always been so cathartic. She missed it more than anything. Back when she had been a dancer, she had done belly dancing for a semester just for fun. Her teacher had proclaimed she was a natural, but she had only stuck with it for that short amount of time.

"All right," Talis said, shoving his helmet on. "Time to get this show on the road."

Cadence forced her mind back to the present, grabbed his sword and shield and handed them to him. "Good luck!" she exclaimed.

He grinned even though he knew she couldn't see it. Having Cadence by his side seemed so right to him. Even though he loved to tease and taunt her, he genuinely loved her company. Just having her near made him feel warm all over and, the closer he got to her, the more he just wanted to lose himself in her arms and her kisses. He was coming to realize that it was her wildness he loved, her untamed spirit. It was the very thing he should be wary of, but he was drawn to it against his will. And the more he was around her, the worse it got.

As predicted, Talis did very well throughout the entire competition until he got to Raven, who promptly obliterated him. After a particularly nasty killing blow right to the side of his head, Talis made his way back to Cadence, his left ear still ringing. He'd won five rounds. He wasn't going to complain. He was used to Raven blowing him out of the water by now.

He pulled his helmet off and flung it down, his hair dripping with sweat. He rolled his eyes as he looked at Cadence, who was handing him a very unauthentic water bottle. "He could at least not make it so humiliating," he griped. "I mean, was it really necessary to blast me up alongside the head?"

Cadence smiled as she started to remove his armor. She'd loved watching Talis and Raven fight. Sword fighting was like a violent dance, and they were both so beautiful. She hoped that when she fought next weekend she wouldn't be taken out in the first round. She wanted the chance to kick the crap out of Raven again, as it seemed she was the only one who could. Even though she liked Raven, the man could seriously do with being knocked down a peg or two. He walked like he owned the battlefield, or the entire faire for that matter.

With an enormous, exhausted sigh, Talis shook out his arms and shoulders as Cadence removed his armor. "Don't worry about the leg pieces," he said as he gathered the discarded armor. "I can get those. Do you know what time it is?"

She arched an eyebrow. "No, Raven told me I had to take off my watch. He said it wasn't period. It's with my clothes over at Tempyst's."

Talis smiled. "All right, I'm heading over there anyway. I have to change and book it back over to Heather's dance show."

Cadence followed him back over to Tempyst's shop and she looked around at the display pieces he had out while she waited for Talis to get changed. Tempyst, himself, was busy doing a demonstration and she smiled because a lot of women were practically drooling over his nicely sculpted upper body. She could bet money that not half of them were actually listening to his lecture about blacksmithing. History looked to be about the furthest thing from their minds.

"You interested in blacksmithing?" a gravelly voice asked.

Cadence turned and frowned up at an enormous, sweaty man with a bushy brown beard that looked like it was swallowing the bottom half of his face. He was dressed in battle armor and carrying a helmet under one arm. "Uh...a little. I know the blacksmith. I was just watching."

He smirked. "You know Tempyst, eh? Figures. I wouldn't imagine a woman like you would be all that interested in combat."

Just what exactly was that supposed to mean? That he was lumping her in the same category as all of those ogling airheads over there? She put her hands on her hips. "As a matter of fact, I am very interested in combat. I'm competing in armored combat next weekend." He burst out laughing at her and she shrank back a little. Ouch. Was that how Talis had felt when she'd laughed at him?

"You? You're competing next weekend?" He laughed again. "You don't stand a chance, little girl. Go back to churning butter with the rest of the wenches."

Her eyes bulged. Was this guy for real? Anger simmered just below the surface. "I beg your pardon? Dude, I'm going to give you about two seconds to retract that statement before I yank your ratty beard up over your head."

His eyes narrowed even though he still chuckled. "You don't know what you're talking about, woman, and you don't know who you're talking to. Tread carefully."

"Stop flapping your jaws, Olaf," Raven's voice interrupted. He placed his hands firmly on Cadence's shoulders and maneuvered her away from the giant man.

Cadence was irritated that Raven was stepping in. She didn't need anyone to fight her battles for her. If he'd have stayed away just a second longer that stupid guy would have had about three less teeth. Then again, it was probably a good thing that Raven was intercepting. The last thing she needed was to get kicked out of the faire and blacken Talis' name.

Olaf glowered at Raven and he stood taller. "Put a leash on your woman, Raven," he snarled. "She needs to stay where she belongs and out of my way."

Any last shred of common sense Cadence had was knocked out of the way by the red tidal wave of rage she felt sweep through her. She lunged forward, but was stopped by Raven's arm. "I'm gonna knock you into Tuesday, you worthless sack of crap!" she shouted. "I'll show you where you belong! Your face under the tread of my boot seems about right!"

Raven still managed to stand very calm and give a nonchalant shrug while continuing to keep Cadence at bay. "I'd watch out, Olaf. She whooped the stuffing out of me and we all know that you can't even manage that. She'll pulverize you."

Olaf's face twisted into an evil, menacing sneer. "I'll see you next weekend, little girl," he growled at Cadence, "and after I finish you, I'll mop up your blood with this one." He pointed at Raven, then turned and swaggered away.

Raven rolled his eyes. "In your dreams, meat head," he grumbled. He turned to Cadence and grinned at her as he placed his hands on her shoulders. "I see you met Olaf."

"Who the hell does he think he is?" she spat.

"Cadence, you know how most of us perform and compete in renaissance faires because we think it's fun to pretend we've gone back in time?"

She forced herself to pay attention to Raven and not run off and jump on that giant's back.

"Well, Olaf thinks he really is in the middle ages. He's ridiculous and delusional. He used to be in the army, if you can imagine, but he couldn't cut it. He bailed like a weenie and decided to pretend to be a warrior from the Dark Ages instead. He thinks he's some amazing fighter, but he just fights dirty and mean. I beat the tar out of him every year."

"*I'm* gonna beat the tar out of him," she growled, still scowling at his retreating form.

Raven smiled and kissed her on the cheek. "I have every confidence that you will," he murmured. He winked at her just as Talis came back out. "Cadence just had her first encounter with our old friend Olaf," he said.

Talis raised an eyebrow. "Oh, that's marvelous. I'm surprised she didn't knock him out."

"Almost," he laughed.

Talis grinned and looked down at Cadence, who was still glowering. "All right, ready to go?"

She still felt her pulse pounding out an angry rhythm, but when she looked at Talis, it dissipated. A smile twisted her lips in spite of her annoyance. He had removed all pieces of armor and was now wearing a simple, white peasant shirt and brown draw-string pants with a maroon scarf tied around his head. He looked like a gypsy and it made her giggle, but not because she thought it was silly. She actually thought it was adorable...and strangely appealing, but she was quickly coming to realize that Talis was appealing in everything.

She sighed and went to him, wrapping her arms around his waist in much the same way she had done at the clothing shop.

Talis stiffened for a moment, but it was probably due to surprise. "Why do you keep doing that?" he asked, touching her hair in a gentle caress.

"I'm sorry I laughed at you."

"What?"

She looked up and met his eyes, still keeping her arms around his waist. "When I first met you. I'm sorry I laughed at you. It was a mean thing to do, especially when it was just because I didn't understand. I had no good reason to laugh."

"Why the apology now?" he asked as he clasped his hands behind her back and pulled her closer.

"Because I just realized how much it must have hurt."

He smiled softly and pressed a tender kiss to her cheek. "Thank you." He shook his head. "I can only imagine what Olaf said to you. That man is the worst kind of bully. Come on, I have to run before Heather's show starts and she kills me. This is my job while I'm here, Cade. I can't be late."

She grinned and took his hand. "We'd better run then."

He chuckled and they jaunted off toward the stage where the show would be held.

Cadence forgot about Olaf and her rage toward him as she ran. She forgot about it because it wasn't pertinent at the moment. All that really seemed to matter was that she was holding Talis' hand. He anchored her. He reigned in her erratic emotions. He made her stable and, at the same time, he set her free.

Chapter Fourteen

Talis yawned as he headed up the stairs and toward his bedroom, stretching as he did so. His shoulders were stiff and aching from competing and he just wanted to lie down and relax. He wondered if Cadence was still up. After the faire, they had spent the evening unwinding with Julian. She had decided to go take a hot bath about an hour ago, and she had never come back downstairs. Talis figured she must have gone to sleep. She'd had a long day.

He was pleasantly surprised with how well Cadence had taken to the renaissance faire. She'd seemed awkward at first, but once she'd put on her new outfit, it seemed like she'd gotten caught up in the atmosphere, and he had a feeling she'd enjoyed herself.

He sighed as he remembered the way she'd hugged him after she'd met Olaf. Sure, they'd been playing and teasing one another ever since they'd met, and he was always trying to make her squirm with his relentless taunting, but she had never shown him affection like that before. It had been so sweet and genuine, like the gesture had really come from her heart. It made him melt every time he thought about it and he had a feeling that was a bad sign. What in the world was this woman doing to him?

He passed by the sliding glass door and stopped in his tracks with a frown. He went back over to it and gazed out, surprised to see Cadence lying on the deck, staring up at the sky. His frown deepened as he slid open the door. "What are you doing out here?"

Cadence glanced over at him and grinned. "Freezing to death," she giggled. She shrugged. "I don't know. I was just looking at the stars. It's so peaceful out here... I'm just being stupid, I guess."

He shook his head. "No, you're not being stupid at all..." He let his gaze roam over her and he put his hand over his heart. She was so beautiful. Seeing her literally made his chest ache. "Do you mind if I join you?" He had to be close to her. It was a desperate need that he couldn't contain.

"No, I don't mind."

He smiled and disappeared back inside for a moment only to return a second later with the quilt off his bed. "Here," he said, "at least this way we won't freeze." She sat up and he knelt behind her. He wrapped the quilt around his shoulders, then pulled her close up against his chest so that he could share the blanket with her. He took the opportunity to slip his arms around her waist. "Better?"

She closed her eyes and let the warmth of his body wrap her in bliss. She nodded. "Much." She snuggled close to him, leaning her head back to rest against his shoulder.

"Did you have a good time today?" he asked.

She smiled and nodded as she thought about how fantastic he had looked fighting and how she'd stared more at him during the belly dancing show than at the actual dancers. "It was fun. I just want to show that Olaf dude what-for next weekend."

He chuckled. "Olaf adopted a Viking persona, and I think he's played it for too many years. Don't worry about him. He's just a sore loser. He hates Raven with a passion because he can never beat him."

"Do you really think I stand a chance in the armored combat competition?" The cold air made her face tingle, but Talis' warmth made her ache and burn. Her face was cold, but her blood was molten. She burrowed deeper into his embrace.

"If I work with you, I think you stand a very good chance. You have a natural killer instinct."

She giggled and he tightened his arms around her. She closed her eyes with a sigh. What was it about him that made her feel so completely serene and blissful? She'd never been serene, or calm at all. She'd always been explosive, a chaotic storm of turbulent emotions. Talis made all of it go away. He calmed the storm just by being near her, made her feel centered, focused, like she was actually in control of herself for the first time ever. It was a feeling she never wanted to go away. It gave her peace, and that was something she'd never had. "Talis?" she murmured.

"Yeah?"

"Did you really feel a connection with me when you saved me from falling at the concert?"

"No, I said I felt a connection with you the first time I saw you. Backstage, remember?"

"Oh, that's right! You were talking to Van!"

She felt him nod. "I was getting ready to tattoo Van and was talking to my sister-in-law at the same time. I saw you and couldn't even concentrate on what Evie was saying. You were the most amazingly beautiful thing I'd ever seen."

Cadence felt her cheeks turn warm and she grinned. "Really?"

He nodded again. "You didn't even care that I was standing there, and all I wanted to do was stare at you forever."

"And then afterwards I laughed right in your face." She rolled her eyes at her own childishness. "Geez, I don't know what's wrong with me sometimes."

His chuckle was a deep, throaty rumble that ignited her blood even further. "Don't worry about it, Cadence. That's done with now."

She shook her head. "No, Talis. It's not okay that I did that... And what's worse is that I kept doing it. Like my life is anything to brag about. I had no right to mock yours. When Olaf laughed at me today and told me I didn't stand a chance in the armored combat competition, it hurt. I have no idea why you've kept me around this long. I've been horrible to you."

He sighed. "Cadence—"

"Do you regret bringing me with you?" she interrupted.

"Not for a second."

"Why?" Why hadn't he kicked her out of his car when she'd gotten trashed in Vegas? Or when she'd laughed at him and mocked him time and time again? Or when she'd almost taken his friend's head off with an axe? Why did he continue to keep her around when chaos followed her every move and any other sane person would have ditched her long ago?

"Because I enjoy you, Cadence."

She shivered involuntarily at the sweeping, caressing timbre of his voice. She immediately covered it over by frowning. "What in the heck is that supposed to mean?

That's kind of vague. You enjoy me? That could mean any-thing!"

He chuckled. "Want me to elaborate?"

She gave a decisive nod. "Yes."

"Well, all right then. By saying I enjoy you I mean that I love the way you make me smile...and laugh." He ran one hand down her hair in a long, slow stroke. "I love how you always play and tease and don't let my teasing get the best of you."

Cadence smiled. They were on equal ground with that one. His sense of humor was what she loved the most about him.

"I love how you always smell like that brown sugar va-nilla lotion you use, and how you let me tuck your hair be-hind your ear when it's hanging in your face. And I love how you don't take anyone's crap. You're tough and strong and can hold your own, but you let me take care of you anyway." His lips drifted lazily along the side of her neck.

Cadence drew in a shaky breath and she leaned her head to the side, her eyes drifting closed. "My knight coming to rescue me," she whispered.

He chuckled softly and moved her hair aside so that he could nibble on her earlobe. "Most of all, I love how, every time you come into the room, I burn." He pulled away and shifted so that he could cup her cheek in his palm. Her eyes fluttered open and their gazes locked as the world around them seemed to slip away. His lips hovered extremely close to hers. "Is that answer satisfactory?"

Her smile was tremulous. She wasn't nervous around guys. Most of the time, she had them in the palm of her hand and she liked it that way, but she knew she wasn't in control when she was with Talis. She never had been. He had complete domination over her and it made her feel unsure of herself.

She nodded, unable to formulate any words when he was staring at her like he was. His light blue eyes were hypnotiz-ing her, weaving his magical spell over her. There had never been anything in her life she'd wanted more than his kiss.

For three heartbeats, time seemed to stop, and then both of them moved toward each other simultaneously. Talis' lips covered Cadence's and her entire world exploded and fell into place all at the same time. Perfection was a weak word.

There had to be something stronger to describe the delicious sensation of his full, supple lips against hers. Passion ignited inside her like a torch and she wrapped her arms around his neck, wanting him as close to her as humanly possible.

He pulled her up against him and tangled his fingers in her hair. He swept his tongue into her mouth and the fire that passed between them was insane and all consuming. Her fingers dug into his shoulders and pulled on the material of his shirt as she kissed him back with equal fervor. He growled and attacked her lips again, taking her face in his hands and exploring her mouth until she thought they would go up in flames and her heart would explode from how hard it was pumping.

When Talis finally pulled away, she was shaking. Her head spun like she'd drank too much tequila and her lips tingled. She brought a trembling hand to her mouth and let out a shuddering breath as Talis smoothed her hair and gazed down at her. "I'm dizzy," she murmured.

He smiled and lifted her chin to press a soft, lingering kiss to her mouth. He feathered his thumb over her bottom lip. "That was fantastic," he whispered. "Your mouth is perfection."

Her face turned hot. Fantastic was an understatement.

"Thank you," he murmured.

She gave a quizzical frown and looked up at him. "Why are you thanking me?"

His smile was gentle as he continued to touch her face. "Your affection is a gift, Cadence. You didn't have to give it to me. The fact that you did means a lot."

She swallowed hard because she suddenly wanted to cry. Her affection was a gift? No one had ever treated her like anything she gave was a gift. Men had always just taken from her, like they'd thought she owed it to them, like it was their right. She had never had someone view one of her kisses like a gift.

She looked down before Talis could see the tears burning in her eyes and she rested her head against his chest. She closed her eyes as she listened to his heartbeat and she realized that she never wanted to be anywhere but in his arms. It was the closest thing to paradise she had ever experienced.

Cadence couldn't keep her eyes off of Talis. She tried, but it was impossible. She loved watching the women belly dance. It was so mysterious and beguiling. She enjoyed watching the girls, but she loved watching Talis more. He looked so at ease as he strummed his acoustic guitar, producing haunting chords for the girls to dance to. She'd watched five shows so far and she wasn't tired of it at all. She had a feeling she could stare at him all day and never get enough.

They hadn't really talked about the intense kiss they'd shared the night before. They'd remained on the deck for a long while, silently enjoying being close to one another, and then it had been mutually decided that it would be best to go to bed since they had another full day of renfaire action ahead of them.

They'd slept, gotten up, eaten breakfast and headed out, but neither one had mentioned their kiss. She was kind of happy that they hadn't. It was a perfect moment in time and sometimes perfect moments were ruined if they were analyzed and discussed.

The audience applauded as the women finished up their show and Cadence grinned. She slid her gaze back over to Talis and found him staring back at her. He gave her a sensual smile and she felt her face turn hot. She bit her bottom lip shyly and looked down. What was with the shyness? She'd blushed more since meeting Talis than she had in her whole life.

"Screw this!"

Cadence looked up in surprise as she heard a crash on stage follow the sudden exclamation.

"I am sick to death of taking orders from you!"

One of the dancers had angrily knocked aside a stool that one of the other musicians sat on and she was flouncing off the stage in a whirl of bright colored scarves and veils. Heather chased after her, shouting at her to come back, but the woman slung some unsavory words back at her and continued out of the faire. Heather came back with her fingers tangled in her hair, looking distraught.

Talis met Heather on the stage and pulled her into his arms. Cadence stood and made her way to the stage, as it was obvious that Heather was crying.

"What am I supposed to do now?" she bawled into Talis' shirt. "She was our lead dancer!"

Talis sighed as he rubbed Heather's back in consolation. "You're better off without her. She was always causing problems and she drank all the time."

Heather sniffed. "I know, but we haven't been able to find someone to replace her. We're a trio, Talis! Not a duo. The whole show is going to be messed up next weekend! We can't find a dancer in a week's time!" She let out a little sob and buried her face against his chest.

"I'll do it," Cadence blurted. Her eyes widened because the words seemed to have flown out of their own volition.

Talis frowned and Heather lifted her head to look at her in confusion. "Are you a belly dancer?" she asked.

Cadence swallowed. A little voice in the back of her head was screaming, *What the crap are you doing?* but she tried to remain calm and look like she knew what she was talking about. "No, but I did ballet for years. I took belly dancing for a semester. I'm rusty, to say the least, but I'm a fast learner. If you showed me the routine, I'm sure I could have it down by next weekend."

Heather's face seemed to light up.

Talis raised an eyebrow. "Are you sure, Cadence? You haven't danced in a long time, and you have to practice for armored combat, too."

She scowled and folded her arms. "Do you doubt me?" she challenged.

His lips split into a grin and he let go of Heather to grab a hold of Cadence's arm and yank her close to him. He attacked her mouth, kissing her breathless before he pulled away and smiled down at her. "Never," he whispered.

Heather raised an eyebrow and cleared her throat.

Cadence stumbled when Talis released her and she desperately tried to remember what she had been doing. She looked at Heather and shook her head. "A-Anyway, yeah, I'm sure I could do it if you taught me the moves."

"Okay, I'll come by tomorrow and teach you the routine. We can do a quick rehearsal next Friday. Thanks a lot, Cadence. You're saving my butt."

Cadence grinned. "It's fine, Heather. I miss dancing. It'll be great to do some form of it again."

Heather smiled and left, probably to tell her other dancer what was taking place.

Talis turned back to Cadence and snaked his arm around her waist again. "You're turning into quite the little renfaire veteran, aren't you?"

She rolled her eyes. "Whatever, Talis. I'm just trying to help all you 'silly' people out." She grinned playfully. In truth, it was nice to feel like she was needed in some way, and she desperately wanted to dance again. Plus, she would be doing something responsible to help someone out for a change instead of just doing it to benefit herself.

"We'll have to get you a belly dancing outfit," Talis remarked with an evil smirk.

"Maybe I'll let you pick it out." She trailed her finger down the part of his chest the V in his shirt bared.

He made a purring noise and lowered his lips to hers again, making the kiss long, slow and torturous.

Cadence sighed and melted against him as he pulled back. "Am I going to be getting those on a regular basis now?" she whispered.

He smiled and rested his forehead against hers. "Would you like to be a subscriber?" he teased.

"A life subscription, if you don't mind."

He traced his finger along her bottom lip. "I think that can be arranged." He tipped her chin up so he could claim her lips again. "Your taste is addictive."

She giggled. "You like the taste of trouble?"

"No. I love the taste of fire." He kissed her again. "And with every kiss, a little more of me becomes yours."

A shiver of unease went up her spine at his confession, but she didn't have time to dwell on it. His lips seized hers again and she gave herself over to the passion she felt. She gave herself over to him.

Chapter Fifteen

Talis stood with his arms folded, leaning his hip against the rail of the deck as he watched Raven and Cadence spar in Julian's driveway. Tempyst had fit her for armor earlier that week and they'd hooked her up with the proper weaponry. Talis had worked with her a bit, but Raven had wanted most of the responsibility. It seemed that he'd taken a shine to Cadence after she'd shown him who was boss, and he was eager to take her on as a protégé.

Cadence was a ravenous learner of the craft. She picked up the skill like she had been born with a sword in her hand, and Talis was more than proud of her. Especially considering that belly dancing had been slightly more challenging than Cadence had originally thought. Heather had shown her the routine, but had been less than hopeful at the prospect of Cadence actually learning it in a week. Cadence assured her that it would be done, and she'd been practicing almost twenty-four hours a day.

Talis had never seen another living soul work as hard as Cadence had worked in the past week. He woke up and found her already up and stretching in the den, where she liked to practice her dancing. Throughout the day she took turns either sparring with Raven, or practicing the dance routine. It was surprising to see her so dedicated. For someone who had seemed so flip and flighty when he'd met her, Cadence was going above and beyond the call of duty for people she barely knew.

"She's really good," Julian remarked from behind Talis.

Talis nodded as Cadence let out a mighty yell and launched a mean attack against Raven. "She knows no limits. She gives it her all, holds nothing back. I've never seen anyone so wild."

Julian gave Talis a sidelong glance and a knowing smile. "We're not just talking about her fighting, are we?"

Talis looked at his brother and grinned. He shook his head. "No. Cadence is untamed in everything she does. She's like some sort of chaotic storm."

Julian leaned nonchalantly against the rail and chuckled. "Sounds like someone else I know."

"What's that supposed to mean?"

Julian shrugged one shoulder. "Well, you may be somewhat calmer now, but I distinctly remember a time when you resembled a chaotic storm."

Talis smiled as he thought about his rootless life. It was true. He'd lived on his whims for years. He did what he wanted, went where he pleased. Traevyn likened him to the wind. He wasn't so different from Cadence. He had known it from the start. The only difference was that he drifted where he went. She propelled herself with dynamite.

Almost too soon to suit Talis, the sparring match was over and Raven was patting Cadence on the back with a grin. He gave her some words of advice and the two of them headed into the house. Talis turned away from the rail with a sigh and frowned at Julian, who was giving him some sort of Cheshire cat grin. "What?" he muttered.

"You're smitten," he stated.

Talis rolled his eyes.

Julian chuckled. "Don't try to deny it, Tal. I know you two have been having wild make out sessions when you don't think I'm paying attention."

Talis actually felt his cheeks flush and he sighed. He hadn't been able to keep himself away from Cadence since they'd shared that kiss on the balcony. Every second he wasn't kissing her was a second he wanted to be kissing her and he stole those precious kisses every chance he got. "Nice, Julian. Do you have to bug me about it?"

"Of course. I'm your brother." He shook his head and laughed. "Traevyn is going to have a field day with this one."

Talis groaned. "I can't wait," he grumbled sarcastically.

"It's official," Raven announced as he came clanking up behind them in his armor. "I think Cadence may be better than all of us."

Talis turned and smiled. "Did she beat you again, Rave?"

Raven grinned. "Well, no, but I did have to step up my game a little. She's very good. She's going to surprise everyone tomorrow."

"I hope she knocks the stuffing out of Olaf," Talis remarked.

Raven chuckled. "You and me both."

Talis talked a bit more with Raven and Julian before Raven left to go rest up for the next day and Julian headed down to his office to work on something. Talis headed back inside, intent on finding Cadence and insisting that she take the night off. She had been working far too hard lately.

He stopped when he entered the den because Cadence was rehearsing and his eyes instantly riveted on the way her body moved to the music. She was wearing a black sport bra and a pair of tight black pants, and the way she was rolling her stomach at that exact moment was the sexiest thing he had ever seen. Belly dancing wasn't something foreign to him, but watching her do it was so much better.

He folded his arms and stood quietly by, knowing that she didn't know he was there. She was concentrating so hard, trying to get every step and movement down to perfection. He didn't know how she even had the energy to dance after fighting with Raven, but her exertion was evident in the beads of sweat that were running down the line of her spine.

Watching her dance was such a contradiction to watching her fight. When she fought, she hit like a Mack truck, attacking relentlessly and brutally. When she danced, her long legs and slender, shapely body made her the epitome of femininity. She was so regal and graceful, elegant in a way that made him burn inside. Only she could make him burn. His blood blazed for her.

The song Cadence had been practicing to ended, and she promptly sat down on the ground. Her shoulders slumped in exhaustion, and she labored for breath. Her beautiful hair hung in a limp, bedraggled ponytail with escaped strands of all colors in her face. She put her face in her hands and Talis walked over to her, intent on putting an end to her rigorous routine before she wore herself out and had no energy left for the next day.

"All right, that's it," he said as he approached her. "No more work for you today."

She looked up at him wearily and shook her head. "I have to practice one more time. Something's off and I have to fix it before tomorrow. I know Heather was disappointed at the rehearsal earlier today and I need to get my act together."

Talis frowned in disbelief. "Cadence, are you insane? Do you want to know what Heather said to me after the rehearsal? She said, 'holy cow, Talis. I thought maybe she'd be okay. I had no idea it would be like hiring a professional.'"

Cadence blinked up at him, uncomprehending. She shook her head. "Talis, this whole thing had been harder than I thought it would be. I really don't feel confident—"

"Cadence," he interrupted. "If you keep this pace up you're going to work yourself to death and you'll have nothing to give tomorrow. You need to stop. Trust me. Practice time is over. Come on." He held his hand out to her.

Her brow furrowed and she looked genuinely pained, as if the entire world was resting on her shoulders. "Talis, I have to get this right!" she insisted. "I really don't think—"

"Good lord, Cadence. When you decide to commit to something you do it all the way, don't you? You can't just go out and party in Vegas. You have to go party, get wasted, and try to leave with a stranger. When you decide to do armored combat, you decide you can't do it unless you're the champion and, when you decide to volunteer for Heather's dance show, you decide you can't do that unless you turn yourself into a Julliard graduate. Not to mention the fantastic way you royally ruined dinner last week."

She giggled, and it eased the lines of worry on her face.

He knelt down next to her with a smile. "Come on, enough practice for today. You look fantastic in both your combat and your dance. Come to town with me. We can hit Cabo Wabo in Harvey's casino."

She gave him a tired smile. "Thanks, Tal, but I think I'm just going to take a hot bath. My back hurts really bad, and I'm too tired to go out and party."

Talis briefly wanted to feel her forehead and make sure she didn't have a fever, but after all the work she'd been doing, he wasn't surprised that she wanted to do nothing. He smiled and smoothed her hair. "Go take your hot bath, beautiful."

She nodded, hoisted herself up off the ground, and wandered toward her bedroom.

Talis sighed, slightly disappointed that he would not be able to spend the evening with Cadence as he had planned, but he understood. The poor thing was exhausted beyond all belief. He frowned thoughtfully.

He wondered if Cadence had ever had someone do something genuinely nice for her. She had been working so hard and he was very impressed with the way she'd seemed to start turning around her life. She deserved to be rewarded somehow. She needed to know that she had made a good decision, and that all her hard work over the past week was not for nothing. He smiled and ran downstairs, shouting for Julian. He needed the kind of help only an older brother could provide.

Talis was satisfied with his plans for the next day. After a good deal of bullying, and after having to endure more ribbing than he would have liked, he had managed to convince Julian to help him with his project. He couldn't wait.

He sighed in contentment and stretched on his bed as he absently flipped through the TV channels. He smiled and reached down to scratch the head of a black cat, who was purring away next to him.

"Tal?"

His heart jumped at the sound of her voice. He looked up and saw Cadence standing in the doorway. She was all set for bed, even though it was still early, and dressed in a pair of plaid PJ pants and...one of his long sleeved AFI shirts. He frowned. "You're wearing my shirt," he stated.

She smiled and combed her fingers through her wet hair. She nodded. "I stole it from you when I saw it in the clean clothes pile." She walked quietly over to the bed and pulled the covers aside. She crawled beneath them, scooted the black cat aside, and snuggled against Talis with a sigh.

He couldn't breathe for a few glorious seconds, and he closed his eyes as he slipped his arm around her, pulling her closer. She rested her head on his chest and wrapped her arm around his waist with a yawn.

"I can hear your heart," she murmured. "It's beating

really fast."

He grinned and played with the damp ends of her hair. "Yes, well, what do you expect? You climb into my bed and drape that perfect body over mine...You're lucky you're so tired or you might be in trouble."

She giggled. "I like trouble, remember?" She sobered and closed her eyes. "You don't mind, do you? I just wanted to be close."

He shook his head. "No," he whispered. "No, I don't mind." He did, however, wonder just exactly what their relationship was. They hadn't really talked about the new development in the closeness department. Were they just very attracted to one another? Complete sexual chemistry? Friends with benefits? He knew that wasn't the way he felt... Not by a long shot. "Cadence?" His voice was raspy, betraying his emotions, and he frowned.

She shifted so that she could look at him. "Yeah?"

He swallowed hard. "What do you...?" He sighed. This was a lot more difficult than when he had asked her the question before, but that might have been greatly due to the fact that he hadn't really cared about her answer before. Her answer meant a great deal to him now. "Cadence, do you remember when I asked you before what you thought about me and you avoided the question?"

She smiled. "Yeah."

"Do you... Do you have an answer for me now?"

"What do I think about you?"

He nodded slowly, wanting, and at the same time dreading her answer. Maybe he was just a plaything to her, something to idly pass the time. He didn't think he'd be able to take that. Over the course of the last few weeks, he had grown to care for her more than he should have let himself. He couldn't help it. She was intoxicating.

Cadence smiled, obviously seeing the unease that he was trying to hide behind his eyes. "I think you're the best man I've ever known, Talis Whitelaw," she whispered. "The best stupid thing I've ever done is barrel in on you in that bathroom."

He smiled. "You really feel that way?"

She nodded, leaving out the part where he made her heart race and her body smolder. She didn't need to get too specific.

He frowned, apparently not satisfied with the conversation. "What do you... What do you think this thing between you and me is?"

She grinned, loving that he looked like a nervous teenager asking a girl out for the first time. She looped her finger around the chain on his neck and studied the dragon necklace that he wore constantly. "It's what you said it was before, Talis," she said quietly. "It's a connection."

"That's what you think, too?"

She met his eyes and nodded, all traces of teasing gone. "I've always felt a connection with you. It was so strong when you caught me at the concert that I had to turn away because it scared me."

That seemed to surprise him. "Really?"

She nodded, feeling awkward and shy. Only Talis ever made her feel that way. Her brows drew together. "It's like you're my weakness and my strength all at the same time," she confessed. "It's weird."

He grinned and traced the contours of her face with his fingertips. "Do you know what you are?"

She shook her head.

"Have you ever seen a wildfire? It's terrifying because of its intensity and you want to turn away because it's dangerous and you know that, if you're caught in its path, you'll be consumed. At the same time, all you want to do is stand there and watch it because it's mesmerizing. It's the most beautiful and volatile thing you've ever seen and you can't take your eyes off of it... That's what you are, Cadence. You're a wildfire that I know I should run from, but all I want to do is get closer to your heat."

She shivered at his words. No one had ever compared her to something like that before. It was romantic and beautiful and made her want to cry. Why did Talis always make her want to cry? It was like he could see every weak place in her heart, every bruise, every scar. He saw the wounds and he knew exactly what to do or say to soothe and heal them. "I think you're what fantasies are made of," she admitted.

He grinned and gave a soft chuckle. "Oh yeah?"

She smiled and nodded. "Every little girl's deepest fantasy come to life. A living man of myth and legend... And somehow, I'm the one who got lucky enough to find you..." She looked down as tears stung her eyes and her chest constricted painfully. "I just wonder how long I'll get to dream your dream before I have to let you go." Men like Talis were not meant to be with women like her. She knew being with him was only a beautiful moment in time. Beautiful moments didn't last. She, of all people, knew that sad truth.

Talis frowned and tucked back a strand of her hair. "Cadence," he whispered. "I'll stick around for as long as you want to keep dreaming. It can last forever if you want it to."

She squeezed her eyes shut and buried her face in his shirt as tears coursed down her cheeks. No. Nothing beautiful lasted forever. Not in her life. Beautiful things were flashed in front of her right before they were cruelly yanked away. She knew she could never stay with Talis. Sooner or later, she would mess it up like she messed everything up. It was only a matter of time.

Talis' arms tightened around her and he held her close. "What's wrong, sweetheart?"

Her heart felt like someone was squeezing it as she heard the term of endearment leave his lips, but she forced herself to laugh. "Oh, I don't know," she lied. "I think I'm just way too tired and overly emotional."

He smiled and stroked her hair. "I understand."

"Do you mind if I sleep here with you tonight?" she asked. She couldn't bear to be away from him. Not now.

He pressed a kiss to the top of her head. "No, of course I don't."

She held onto him tightly for a long time, trying to record everything about him in her memory. She knew she couldn't keep him, but she wanted to enjoy every second of him while he was with her. Sooner or later, the magical dream he had wrapped her in would disappear and, when that happened, she wanted to have all of her beautiful memories to hold on to. She knew that, no matter what else happened to her or where she ended up, the time she spent with Talis would be the best moments of her life and they would sustain her forever.

Chapter Sixteen

Applause sounded through the audience as the belly dancers finished up their second show of the day. Talis smiled because the entire area was packed with people. He had a feeling the word had gotten out about the hot new belly dancer because Heather, as lovely as she was, was petite and compact and the other dancer had a generous amount of belly to dance with. Cadence was tall and slender and gorgeous, and he could almost see the drool dripping from the many male spectators' mouths.

Cadence was fantastic. She captivated everyone and he was so proud of her that he felt like he would burst from it. He set his guitar aside as Heather went around collecting tips from the audience, and he grinned as Cadence came flying over to him looking frantic.

"Come on, Talis! I've got to go!" Heather had generously cut two shows out of their schedule so that Cadence could compete and she now had only fifteen minutes to run to the other side of the faire, get changed and beat the crap out of a bunch of guys.

Talis smiled and took her hand. "All right, let's run. Just try to go easy on me today, okay?" He winked at her as they took off sprinting.

Cadence grinned. She was kind of excited that she got to compete against Talis, but that wasn't what she was looking most forward to. All she wanted to do was beat that Olaf guy right into the ground.

It was an insane few minutes while Cadence changed out of her belly dancing costume and into her battle gear, but Raven helped her strap everything on and escorted her into the arena, where the first two competitors were already going at it.

Cadence's heart was up in her throat and she had to close her eyes and take a few deep, calming breaths. She felt like she'd been running a hundred miles an hour since she'd gotten there. She'd had no time to eat, or even breathe, for more than a few minutes. Her head was spinning, and she was a lot more nervous than she'd thought she would be.

Her first opponent was some guy with a French name that she barely understood and her stomach did several flips when they announced her name. She shoved her helmet on and gripped her sword, desperately hoping that she didn't end up humiliating herself. At least the guy was average in stature. He wasn't like Olaf, who was roughly the size of a barge. She could be grateful for small things.

Three matches later, Cadence was still swinging hard. Talis was still in the fight, as were Raven and Olaf. Olaf kept sneering every time they announced Cadence's name. She wanted to cream him. The guy needed to go down.

As the competition dwindled, Raven took out Talis before Cadence got a chance to, but she made it into the final three. It was down to her, Raven and Olaf, and she had to fight Olaf first. She was exhausted and so hot inside her armor that she was sure she had sweated off at least five pounds. Talis was standing on the sidelines with Ash, cheering her on, and even Tempyst had left his shop for a bit to come and watch her.

She closed her eyes and took a few deep breaths, trying to regroup, but she felt like she was going to die. She'd knocked four guys out of the competition and her arms felt like noodles. Her shoulders and back were screaming at her and she was so tired. Maybe Talis had been right about her working too hard because she didn't know if she could take one more step, let alone beat Olaf, beat Raven, and then go do about four more belly dancing shows.

"...Cadeyrn Wallace!"

She heard her warrior name announced and she stood straight, summoning every last bit of strength she had. She had to beat this guy. *She had to*.

Talis smiled as he watched Cadence strut out to meet Olaf. Cadeyrn Wallace... He loved it. Her last name had been Raven's idea. He'd said that, since she'd claimed to be fighting for freedom when they'd sparred, she should bear the same last name as William Wallace in *Braveheart*. Talis was just glad he hadn't painted her face blue and made her wear a kilt.

He shouted encouragement to her, as did Ash and Tempyst, and he waited in suspense as she and Olaf circled one another. He was easily twice her size and Talis knew that she had to be exhausted. He hoped she had enough stamina to stay in the fight. She had a good chance of winning if she did. He knew Raven was tired, as well.

Suddenly, all chaos broke loose as Olaf let out a monstrous, rage-filled shout and attacked Cadence with the force of a bull. She tried to move out of the way of his powerful swing, but she wasn't fast enough and his sword crashed into the side of her helmet, knocking her to the ground in one shot.

Talis' eyes widened and he ran to where Cadence was lying, afraid Olaf had managed to do some real damage. He glowered up at the man, who sneered down at them and chuckled evilly. "Cadence," Talis murmured as he helped her sit up. "Cadence, are you okay?"

She pulled off her helmet and shook her head, which was throbbing. She was glad her helmet had padding on the inside or she might be nursing a concussion. She rubbed at the sore spot on her head and nodded. "I'm fine... Just humiliated is all."

"I told you that you didn't belong here," Olaf growled. "Go back with the rest of the wenches." He spat on the ground where Cadence sat.

Enraged, Talis stood, looking prepared to knock his head right off, but Raven stepped casually out in front of him. "Let me handle it," he said confidently. He twirled his sword in his hand and grinned.

Talis glanced at Raven, then shot a deadly scowl at Olaf and helped Cadence stand. "Come on, let's get you some water."

Cadence hobbled over to where the others were, her pride hurting more than the rest of her. She'd wanted to take that guy down so badly and she hadn't even landed a blow. She'd gone down in the first two seconds. It was embarrassing.

"You did so well, Cadence!" Ash exclaimed as she approached. "You made it into the final three!"

She rolled her eyes. "And then promptly lost in a very ungraceful way," she grumbled.

Tempyst shook his head and unbuckled her gorget, removing it from around her neck. "Olaf is twice your size and you're exhausted," he said. "You shouldn't be ashamed. You fought four men larger than you and beat them all when you've never competed in armored combat before. That's impressive, Cadence. You should be proud."

"Besides," Ash said with a grin, pointing toward the arena, "Raven didn't let him win anyway. He avenged you."

Cadence looked up to see Raven holding his sword in the air in victory and parading in a circle like a peacock. Everyone cheered and Olaf angrily yanked off his helmet and stormed away. Pulling off his own helmet, Raven turned toward Cadence, smiled and bowed, blowing her a kiss. She grinned. At least Raven had beaten him. She would have been really bummed if the stupid oaf had won.

"No one's mopping up *anyone's* blood with me," Raven bragged as he strutted past everyone to go change. He threw a wink at Cadence as he passed.

Cadence smiled and looked down at her lap. She was happy Raven had won, but still downhearted. She'd wanted to win so badly. She'd trained so hard.

"Don't worry, Cadence," Talis encouraged. "There's always Big Sur. Olaf'll be there too. You'll get another chance."

Her mood brightened and she looked up at him. "Really?"

He nodded and kissed her on the nose. "Now come on, no time to waste. You have another show to do."

Cadence wanted to groan aloud, but she stifled it. After all, she was the one who had volunteered for the belly dancing. She hauled herself up off the ground and clanked wearily over to Tempyst's vendor stand to change. She sighed. The day was only half over and already she felt like she was going to pass out. It would be a miracle if she made it through the rest of the shows.

Cadence frowned at Talis as they stood outside Julian's house. Toward the end of the faire some nasty-looking clouds had rolled in and turned the otherwise pleasant day into miserable frigidness. The sky was white, the air was cold, and Talis was telling her she had to wait outside. She was not amused. She folded her aching arms and scowled. "Talis, what are you trying to do? Torture me? Everything hurts and I'm so tired I can barely stand. You're going to make me wait out here in cold, freezing my butt off?"

Talis gave her a boyish grin. "Just for a second. I have to do something. I promise I won't be long." He winked and disappeared into the house.

Cadence sighed. Not like she'd fought a battle or anything. It was cool. She'd wait. Sure, she'd danced her legs off and had been knocked in the head by a giant. No big deal. She'd just stand outside and shiver. She rolled her eyes and rocked back and forth on her heels. She was still wearing her belly dancing costume with just a black hoodie zipped up over it. The longer she stood out there, the more frozen she got. She couldn't feel her toes and was pretty sure that she could cut glass with her nipples if she wanted to.

The door opened back up suddenly and she flashed Talis an annoyed look.

He chuckled and reached out to take her hand. "Come on." He pulled her inside and led her to Julian's bedroom and bathroom.

Cadence gasped as she entered. There were candles everywhere and a bubble bath was waiting. Red rose petals stained the floor with splashes of color and one long-stemmed rose sat on the edge of the tub. She started to tremble for no reason and tears filled her eyes.

"Surprise," Talis whispered. He stood behind her and reached around to slowly unzip her hoodie. He eased it off of her shoulders and set it aside, placing a tender kiss to the nape of her neck.

Cadence shook her head and looked away, tears rolling down her cheeks.

Talis frowned and turned her to face him. "Cadence, what's wrong?" He reached out to catch her tears, gently caressing her cheeks with his fingertips.

"No one has ever done something like this for me," she murmured.

His smile was soft. "You worked yourself to death this week," he said, "and today, you were amazing. You saved Heather's show and managed to become the star in the process, and you fought like a warrior. A warrior of your caliber deserves to be treated like a queen upon her return. So..." He went to grab the long-stemmed rose, then knelt before her and presented it with his arms outstretched and his head bowed. "I am your servant for the evening, my lady. Whatever you wish will be yours."

Cadence stared at him, unmoving. She didn't know what to do, say, or think. Before, she would have found this display to be extremely ridiculous, but not now. She'd thought chivalry was dead when she'd met Talis, that a modern man's idea of romance was a cheap pick up line and a drink. Now she knew that men existed who lived and breathed the ancient code of romance and chivalry. It was as real to them as it had been in the days of Arthurian legend. And Talis was one of those men.

She'd never in all her life thought she would be on the receiving end of a gesture so romantic and kind. Her life was not romantic. It was a disaster. To have such a beautiful and well balanced man do something so selfless and heartfelt was overwhelming to her. She swallowed and reached out a trembling hand to take the rose Talis offered her. She breathed in its delicious fragrance and held it to her chest, as if doing so could lock the memory away in her heart for all time.

Talis glanced up at her, grinned, and stood. He reached out to cup her cheek in his palm. "Enjoy yourself, Cadence."

She closed her eyes and held onto his gentle touch. It was everything right in her life. "Thank you, Talis," she whispered.

He smiled and pressed an extremely tender kiss to her lips before he pulled away and left her to relax.

Chapter Seventeen

Julian's bathroom had an enormous window next to the tub and Cadence decided to draw back the curtains so she could look out at the evening. There weren't any houses directly behind the side Julian's bathroom was on so she wouldn't have to worry about anyone spying on her. She wanted to feel like she was part of the beautiful scenery outside without freezing to death.

She removed the maroon scrap of material that served as a shirt and her black skirt, complete with maroon hip scarf and belt with bells. She stepped into the hot water and shivered as it thawed her frozen body. She eased down into the tub and leaned back with a sigh. Everything ached, but the water soothed her tired muscles.

She looked over at the rose she had set back down on the side of the tub and she smiled. She picked it up and twirled it in her fingers. Talis was so unlike anyone she'd ever known. Everyone in her world was so harsh and selfish. Every man for himself. Protect yourself first and worry about others later. Talis was warm and tender and kind. He was always thinking about others, always thinking about her. She couldn't quite wrap her mind around it. She'd been basically alone her entire life. She'd always taken care of herself. Even Lance, who cared very much about her, had come along too late in her life to really do much good, and his attempts to overcompensate now were only making her crazy.

And she knew Tawny cared about her, but she'd never really felt like anyone understood her until Talis came along. Not really. They'd all seen her as the screw up she made herself out to be. Talis had seen her potential. Talis had seen *her*.

She sighed and set the rose back down, turning to gaze out the window at the thick evergreen trees and peaceful darkening sky. She blinked as she saw a flake of snow drift listlessly to the ground, and she grinned. She'd only ever seen snow when she was on tour in the cold European countries. She'd never seen it at a time when she'd been able to enjoy it. She was always rushing when she was on tour. Being a roadie was a twenty-four hour job when your brother was the bass player of the band.

She continued to watch out the window, and slowly, more flakes began to descend. She shook her head. It was crazy to know that it was snowing at the end of April. In Phoenix, the temperature was already in the eighties.

She sighed contentedly and sank deeper into the water. She felt more at home in Julian's house than she had anywhere in her life. She loved the thick forest and azure lake. She loved the beautiful house she was in and was saddened that they would be leaving in a few days. She enjoyed Julian's company, too. He was gentle, like Talis was. She wished she could stay there forever. Although, she was looking forward to meeting this infamous Traevyn and the sister-in-law Talis spoke so highly of.

Cadence watched the snow a little while longer, then decided she would get out before she wrinkled. She drained the tub, dried off, and smiled as she saw that Talis had laid out some clothes for her. She pulled them on and smelled her rose again like a twitterpated girl in some sappy love story.

She blew out the candles and headed out of Julian's room and down the hall. She frowned. Something smelled marvelous. She continued out into the front room and blinked in bewilderment.

More candles decorated every available surface and there was a fantastic fire in the fireplace. A bouquet of roses was in the middle of the coffee table and two plates of something that looked divine flanked it.

"Did you enjoy your bath?" Talis' voice came from behind her.

Cadence turned and stared at him. "Talis," she whispered, "I—" She shook her head. "What is all this?"

He smiled. "I made you a medieval dinner, my lady." He took her hand and led her over to the table.

All Cadence could do was stare. Each of them had a Cornish game hen on their plate that looked cooked to perfection, and two pewter goblets with dragons coiling up the stems were filled with red wine. "Did you make this?" she asked.

He nodded. "I didn't want to make you Italian food. That's your specialty." He flashed her a mischievous smile.

She rolled her eyes and sat down on the floor where one plate was. "Did the lords and ladies of old eat on the floor?" she grumbled playfully. "I thought that was only Asian people."

He chuckled. "My apologies, my lady. I left the royal throne in my other carriage."

She giggled and noticed that music was playing. She frowned as she listened to the familiar strains. "Is that The Cure?"

"Your favorite."

She looked up at him as he sat across from her. "You remembered?"

"Of course. Why wouldn't I?"

She shrugged and looked down. "I guess I'm just not used to people actually listening to me."

"I'm always listening."

His voice was soft and laced with so much sensuality that she shivered and her heart skipped a beat. She turned her attention back to the music and smiled. "Disintegration," she remarked. "My favorite album."

"Mine also," he stated. "You have good taste."

She grinned. "Did they have The Cure in the middle ages?" she teased.

He looked up and met her eyes, his own sparkling with the light from the candles and the fire. "If you want there to be Cure music in the middle ages, there will be. This is your night, Lady Cadence."

She felt her cheeks flush as she grinned and shook her head. She had to divert her attention to her plate because she was going to turn into a giggling idiot if she kept looking at him. He was so serious as he said that. *Lady Cadence*. She would have laughed at anyone else. She would have thought they were silly. Talis wasn't silly. Having him cook her a medieval dinner and call her "Lady Cadence" wasn't silly either. It was marvelous.

They shared pleasant conversation while they ate, discussing the day's events and talking about how Cadence was going to make Olaf regret beating her in the head once they got to Big Sur. By the time they had finished, Cadence felt much more relaxed and refreshed. Her muscles didn't hurt nearly as bad either. "Where's Julian anyway?" she commented absently.

Talis chuckled. "I kicked him out."

She raised her eyebrows. "You kicked him out of his own house?"

"Yeah. I made him help me and then told him he had to leave. Nice, huh?"

"You're horrible."

He shrugged. "Nah. He owed me."

"For what?"

"I don't know, but I'm sure he owed me for something."

She laughed.

Talis stood and walked over to her, offering her his hand. "Dance with me?"

She looked up at him and said nothing, but placed her hand in his and let him pull her into a standing position. He ran both of his hands briefly down her arms and slipped an arm around her waist, pulling her up close to him just as *The Same Deep Water As You* started to play. She let out a shaky breath as they started to sway gently to the music and Cadence smiled as she looked out the window at the steadily falling snow. It looked so serene and beautiful as the firelight cast shadow-shapes around the room.

She met Talis' mesmerizing eyes and sighed. Never in her wildest dreams would she have imagined such a beautiful moment. It was perfect. The dinner, the snow, the fire, the man... All of it was so much better than any fantasy she could conjure.

One line of the song suddenly seemed to ring out to Cadence clearer than all the others. It spoke of being together. It made her heart tremble. Dare she believe that she could actually hold on to something good? That maybe she wouldn't drive Talis away? That she could stay with him? Was it too much to hope for?

Before she could think too much about it, she willingly gave herself up to the magic in his eyes. She wanted nothing more in the world than to drown right there in those light blue depths that hypnotized her like nothing else could. His eyes, his lips, his touch...his heart and soul. She wanted it all.

Talis tightened his arms around Cadence and lowered his lips to hers in an unhurried movement. She closed her eyes at the velvet softness of his sinful mouth. Her world exploded again like it had that night on the balcony. It shattered in a way that made her quiver. She knew by the way he held onto her that his did, as well. Something about this kiss was so far beyond what they'd shared thus far that she felt the earth shift beneath them.

He reached his hands up to hold her face, tangling his fingers in her hair as he did so. His lips moved over hers gently, coaxing and caressing, making her lightheaded and unable to breathe. She held onto him for support and balance, kissing him back with everything she had in her, wanting him to see how she ached only for him. She had only ever ached for him. No other man had ever come close.

Talis was used to being in control. He was used to being calm and collected and he was used to knowing what step he was going to take next. This kiss destroyed all of that. He started to shake and he had to take his trembling fingers away from her face and wrap his arms around her body to stabilize himself.

Her lips were like satin wrapped flower petals. Soft, delicate, perfect, and so intoxicating he thought he might get drunk off of them. He deepened the kiss to taste her sweetness and it almost undid him. Her fingers twined in his hair, and he pulled back just enough to draw in a shuddering breath.

She breathed his name, pulling him back to her, and he indulged himself, kissing her until they were both breathless and on fire. Never had he felt such beauty, such sincere passion. Cadence seemed like everything wrong. She was bold, outspoken and, at first glance, selfish and childish. Who would know that underneath the brash, no-nonsense front she hid behind was an unsure, almost fragile girl who just wanted someone to treat her like she mattered? Talis felt privileged and honored that she had allowed him to see that part of her.

The primal man in him wanted to do just as Raven had suggested earlier. He wanted to gather her up in his arms and take her directly to his bedroom where he could explore her as he wanted and do wicked things that would make her gasp and moan. However, the gentleman in him overpowered his beast of lust and he gently broke the kiss, his chest heaving with the passion he felt. He closed his eyes and rested his forehead against hers, trying to get control of himself. Cadence was used to things in her life being wild and fast. He wanted to show her that good things could come out of being slow and responsible. Ripping off her clothes and ravaging her would contradict that in the worst way.

"Talis," Cadence gasped as she clutched at his shirt unconsciously, "I swear you're made of magic."

He smiled and pulled her body flush up against his. A burning tremor went through him at how soft she felt. He'd never wanted anyone as badly as he wanted her at that moment. "I think you've killed me," he whispered.

She grinned and nuzzled her nose against his neck. "I don't know what it is you've done to me, but I'm not me when you're around."

He frowned and raised his head so he could meet her eyes. "What do you mean?"

"This girl who fights with swords and belly dances at renaissance faires, and blushes when a man flirts with her... That's not me. I don't do responsible things. I don't succeed. I don't blush because I'm never caught off guard. I don't know what you do to me, but when you're around, I feel like you strip every kind of falseness away from me and leave me naked."

His brow furrowed in concern and he caressed her cheek. He concentrated on that concern so as to not concentrate on the image of her naked. "Cadence, I don't want to make you feel that way."

She shook her head. "No, you don't understand. I like it. I feel like someone's seeing *me* for the first time ever. It feels like freedom, Talis... Like you're setting me free. I don't ever want the feeling to go away."

He smiled softly. "I guess I'll just have to keep you around then."

She grinned and kissed him again, knowing in her heart that he was the only one whose kisses she could never get tired of. She'd never wonder what being with any other man would be like if she was with Talis. He was everything. The kind of man all girls dreamed about. She wanted and wished so badly that she could keep him for her own, but she was so afraid to hope. Was it really possible that her luck could change? That *she* could change?

Talis pulled away, took her hand, and started to lead her toward the front door, grabbing a blanket that was sitting on the couch. "Come on," he said.

Cadence giggled as she followed him outside, where he wrapped the blanket around the both of them and held her close as they watched the snow drift lazily to the ground. She sighed and closed her eyes, loving how silent and still everything was. It was the most peaceful moment of her life.

She smiled as snowflakes fell on her cheeks and caught in her eyelashes, and she rested her head back against Talis' warm shoulder. She was happy. Happier than she had ever been...and it terrified her.

Chapter Eighteen

Cadence had never seen a house like the one she currently stared at. And that's all she could bring herself to do. Stare. Lance had a beautiful home, but it was very modern. Van's was Gothic on the inside as far as decoration went, but the outside looked like any other beach house on the coast. This house... Holy crap. It was off a never-ending ride down Highway 1, then at the end of a dirt road that had taken them winding down a seaside cliff full of the most foreboding-looking trees she had ever seen. Now, sitting nestled in a grove of eucalyptus trees, she could swear she was staring at some manor from the reniassance.

It was dark in appearance, not tan or stucco like the homes she was used to seeing all the rich people in California have. It didn't have those obnoxious, enormous windows that gave the rooms an "open" feeling to them. It had wrought iron balconies and French doors.

"You gonna come get your duffle?" Talis asked as he shut the trunk of the car. "Or are you going to make me carry *all* of the luggage?"

She shook her head and snapped out of her trance. She cast a look back at Talis and raised an eyebrow. "Your brother lives here?" she squeaked in surprise.

Talis smiled and nudged her bag toward her with his foot as he picked up his two suitcases. "Yeah."

She continued to gape as she absently picked up her bag. "Dang, Talis. I thought Julian's house was nice. This is insane..."

He chuckled and led them up to the front door. He rang the doorbell with his elbow.

Cadence frowned as she heard two people shouting at

one another, then a lot of heavy footsteps and some incoherent grumbling. Moments later, the door was opened to
reveal a man who looked a little younger than Talis with
blonde dreadlocks tied back in a ponytail that went to his
shoulders. He was also wearing a sparkly tiara and a pink
ballet tutu over his tan cargo pants.

Talis raised his eyebrows. "Nice look, Seth. The tiara's a
good touch. Complements your eyes."

Seth rolled his eyes and folded his arms. "I'm a ballet in-
structor, *hello*," he muttered. "Besides, my sister is too
enormous to get here before the turn of the next century!"
He shouted it back over his shoulder so she would be sure to
hear his jibe.

Talis was not satisfied with the answer. "So, you decided
to change occupations then?" he continued to tease as he
pushed his way into the room. "I have to say, the tutu looks
exceptionally good on you."

He huffed and shut the door behind them. "I have to
wear the tutu," he stated.

"Yeah, Uncle Talis, he *has* to wear the tutu!"

Talis dropped his bags and spun just as a tiny girl with
the blackest, thickest head of hair Cadence had ever seen
came tearing into the room. "There's my favorite girl!" he
exclaimed as he knelt down to catch her in an embrace.

Cadence smiled. The little girl was wearing a pink leotard
and a tutu and tiara that matched Seth's. Cadence looked up
at Seth, who was still standing with his arms folded, and she
grinned. "I see whose fashion trends you seem to be following," she remarked.

"Being a live-in uncle is a full time job," he said with a
chuckle. He extended his hand. "I'm Seth."

"Cadence," she replied as she shook his hand. "Nice to
meet you."

Seth pointed to her Bleeding Passion sweatshirt. "Best
band ever," he stated.

"Yeah, Cadence is Lance Lawson's sister," Talis commented absently as he hoisted the little girl up onto his
shoulders and a petite, very pregnant woman came waddling
down the stairs.

Seth's jaw almost hit the floor and he stared at Cadence
in astonished wonder. "No way!"

Cadence giggled and nodded.

"You know that Van Marshall lives in Cambria, right?" he questioned. "That's not very far from here. Do you think you could get him to meet me?"

"Seth, stop being a stalker," the pregnant woman commanded. She grinned as she embraced Talis. "You look fantastic," she stated.

Talis smiled and turned to Cadence. "Evie, this is Cadence. She's my..." He paused for a moment, then cleared his throat. "She's my girlfriend."

Cadence felt the color drain from her face and her stomach did a somersault. Girlfriend... That word on his lips. It sounded so potent, so important. She looked up at him and her heart melted at the uncertainty on his handsome face. He seemed to be silently asking her, *Did I overstep? Is this okay?*

She gave him a warm smile. As if she would ever deny Talis. Not after the heated kisses they'd been sharing lately, and definitely not after the time he'd spent on her, talking with her, learning about her and understanding her. She would have moved heaven and earth for him if he'd asked her to. Being his girlfriend was a small request and a role she would gladly fill. It was a little scary, but she had done things much more risky in her lifetime.

"Hi, Cadence, it's nice to meet you. I'm Evie."

Cadence grinned as she shook the other woman's hand. She liked Evie instantly. She had that warm, gentle quality Julian had. She had to admit, though, that Evie was not what she had expected. Talis spoke so highly of her and her work that Cadence had expected her to be this extravagantly beautiful and eccentric woman with some sort of long, flowy gown on. Evie was petite and voluptuous with a wealth of dark hair highlighted with blonde. Her face was pretty and friendly and she wore a pair of black framed cat glasses. She wasn't unattractive at all, but she was the complete opposite of what Cadence had pictured. She felt at ease around her almost immediately.

"Seriously, can you get him to meet me?" Seth was still asking Cadence.

Cadence giggled. "I don't think they're home right now, Seth. They just finished touring, and Van and his wife went on vacation to Tahiti."

Seth's shoulders slumped in defeat and he sighed. "Foiled

again," he muttered. "Figures."

Evie rolled her eyes and pulled her daughter off of Talis' shoulders. "Don't mind Seth," she stated. "He goes down to Cambria at least once a month to stake out the poor man's house. He really is a stalker."

Seth gave his sister an indignant look. "I am *not* a stalker," he stated. "I am an admirer from afar. Besides, Evie could put an end to all of it if she really wanted to. One of her friends knows Van Marshall personally. Do you think she'd do something nice for her brother? Of course not." He folded his arms and scowled.

"Where's my brother?" Talis asked with a frown.

"He had to go into San Luis Obispo to deliver some paintings," Evie said. "He'll be back tonight."

He nodded. "All right, let me get this junk upstairs. Then I just want to sit and relax. I have been driving far too long."

Evie led the way up the stairs.

Cadence smiled as she saw Evie's daughter grab a hold of Talis' hand as he followed. He grinned down at her and she beamed back at him.

Cadence sighed and took a quick look around the dark, beautiful home with its black leather furniture, Celtic tapestries, huge fireplace and wrought iron chandelier hanging from the vaulted ceiling. And that was just the living room. All of the furniture that wasn't black leather was made of heavy, rich, dark wood. It was breathtaking. When she had first seen Julian's home, she hadn't thought any house could be as nice as his, but she had been mistaken. Julian's home had been warm and welcoming, but this home... For as ominous as it looked, she felt more at peace standing there in the foyer than she had in any home she'd ever lived in. Talis' family was enchanted. She was sure of it.

"So, Seth lives here?" Cadence asked from the bed as she watched Talis unpack his things. Since they were staying there for awhile, he wasn't bothering to leave his stuff in the suitcases.

He nodded. "He's your age. He's graduating from Cal Poly next year. He lives on campus during the week, but comes home every weekend."

"What's his major?"

Talis chuckled. "I have no idea. He's changed it three times, but I guess he's managing to graduate with some kind of degree. The dreadlocks are new."

"He seems really cool. Like my kind of person."

Talis turned and fixed her with a look. "You mean rootless, wild and crazy? Yeah, sounds about right."

She wrinkled her nose and flung a pillow at him.

He laughed as he dodged it.

"Your sister-in-law is really nice, and your niece is adorable."

"Evie is the best person I've ever known." He grinned. "Julia just loves me because I spoil her."

She giggled and pulled her knees up to her chest. "So... I'm your girlfriend now?" They had already shared a pleasant dinner with Talis' family and she had not yet had a chance to bring up the "G" word.

He paused in his unpacking and turned to face her. "I hope you didn't mind. I know we haven't really discussed it, but—"

She shook her head. "No, Talis. I don't mind." She gave him a beguiling smile. "I like the idea of belonging to you."

He smiled and reached out to touch her cheek. "You'll never belong to me, Cadence. That would be like trying to harness the wind."

She looked down shyly, her heart stuttering in her chest. But would he ever truly belong to her? How long would it be before she pushed him away and destroyed what they had like she had done with all the others? She tried not to think that way, tried to have hope, but she had a flawless record and the dark thought was always in her mind.

The only person who had ever kept coming back was Danny, and she guessed that was why she had kept letting him come back for so long. Out of everyone, he'd been the only one to ever just accept her for who she was. Regardless of how lazy and bumlike the man was, she had to give him credit for that.

"Hey."

Talis' soft voice brought her attention back to the present and she looked up at him. His eyes were warm and inviting and she couldn't help but smile. He returned the smile and leaned forward to kiss her gently. Cadence's heart melted and any troublesome thoughts disappeared. She sighed as he pulled away, relishing the feel of his kiss. For as long as she lived, she would never get tired of them.

"I'm thirsty," she stated. "I'm going to go get a drink of water in the kitchen, okay?"

He nodded and turned back to his unpacking.

Cadence left the room and quietly made her way down the stairs and into the kitchen. The hardwood floors were cold against her bare feet and she shivered. She poured herself a glass of water and leaned up against the kitchen counter, listening to the distant rhythm of the ocean waves while she drank.

She smiled and let her eyes travel around the large kitchen and dining room area. All the kitchen counters were black marble and the dining room table was a work of art in itself. Huge and mahogany with carved legs and high-backed chairs. She loved how everything in the house was so dark. It reminded her of the way she would imagine a vampire's castle, elegant and refined, but still so mysterious. It would probably seem foreboding to anyone else, but she toured with a Gothic metal band. This was right up her alley.

She sighed as she finished her water and set the glass in the sink. She switched off the light and made her way back to the stairs, yawning as she did so. She could never understand how sitting in a moving vehicle for hours could make a person tired. It's not like you were really doing anything.

She turned to ascend the staircase and got about halfway up it when she was made aware of a person coming down the opposite direction. All the lights in the house were off so she couldn't tell who it was, and she looked up so she could say excuse me and move out of the way, but the words lodged in her throat.

Her eyes widened because the person standing in front of her was the tallest man she had ever seen. She let her eyes travel slowly up his lean body and all she could see was a pair of menacing, black eyes staring down at her from a face that was highlighted eerily by the moonlight spilling in from the windows.

She screamed. She screamed because she thought that maybe a real vampire lived there, or that the house was haunted by one. She screamed with all her might because he was the most terrifying thing she had ever laid eyes on.

Then, suddenly, several lights were flicked on and her scream died. "...Oh wow," she whispered. The horrifying visage she had been staring at a moment ago disappeared with the light and was replaced by a gorgeous god of a man.

He had long, shining black hair that fell just past his waist and a face that was so beautifully sculpted it should have been a national treasure. The black eyes she had looked up into were not black at all, but a startling light green, and all she could bring herself to do was stare at him in much the same way she had stared at the house when she'd first seen it.

"Cadence, are you okay?"

Talis came running down the stairs just as Seth came flying up from his room in the basement. Evie followed close behind Talis, and the man on the stairs was wincing and rubbing at his ear. Cadence just continued to stare.

Talis chuckled and patted the man on the back. "She's got a good scream, doesn't she?"

He muttered something unintelligible.

"Uh oh," Seth said as he came to stand next to Cadence, "Traevyn's done it again."

Talis frowned. "What?"

Seth waved his hand in front of Cadence's still wide eyes. "He either scared the crap out of her and she's in a coma, or she's been stunned into shock by his studliness."

Talis laughed and took Cadence's hand. "Cadence, it's okay. This is just my brother, Traevyn."

Cadence squeaked as sense slowly returned to her. "S-Sorry," she stammered. "Y-you're really hot." Traevyn arched an eyebrow, several people chuckled, and her face turned molten. "Did I just say that out loud?" she whispered miserably.

Evie laughed as she wrapped an arm around her husband. "Don't worry, Cadence. I had much the same reaction when I first saw him."

Talis grinned. "Traevyn, this is my girlfriend, Cadence."

Traevyn had managed to recover from the assault on his eardrums and he smiled. He reached for Cadence's hand and brought it to his lips. "A pleasure to meet you, Cadence," he said. "Forgive me for startling you."

She shook her head, more than aware of the fact that

she was trembling still. "You didn't startle me," she corrected. "You gave me a heart attack."

"Mommy?" Julia's tiny, tired voice came from the top of
the stairs. "What's going on?" She was rubbing her eyes, but
her face lit up when she caught sight of Traevyn. "Daddy!"
she shouted. She flew down the stairs and promptly attached
herself to Traevyn's waist.

Traevyn grinned and knelt down to hug his daughter.
"Hey, princess," he murmured.

Cadence's heart softened as she watched the towering
man stroke the little girl's hair and kiss her on the cheek. Any
menacing qualities he had retained quickly disappeared.

"All right then," Seth said. "Now that we've all had our
excitement for the evening, I'm going back to bed."

Talis put his arm around Cadence's shoulders and kissed
her on the temple. "You all right?" he asked with a smile.

She blushed again as she stole another glance up at
Traevyn. "Yeah, I'm fine," she muttered.

Talis grinned, then looked up at his brother and laughed.
"Hey, Traevyn!" he teased. "Nice to see you!"

Traevyn chuckled and moved forward to embrace Talis.
"I didn't know you were still awake," he said. "Otherwise I
would have come and said hello when I got in."

"No biggie. Just stop skulking around in the night and
scaring the bejeezus out of my girl, huh?"

Traevyn smiled. "I'll do my best."

Talis maneuvered past Traevyn, Evie and Julia, pulling
Cadence along behind him up the stairs. "See you guys tomorrow," he yawned. "I'm gonna hit the sack. I'm beat."

"Good night, Talis," Evie called. "You guys sleep well."

"Sorry Traevyn scared you to death," Talis said to Cadence as they reached his room. "I should have warned you
about him."

Cadence rolled her eyes. "Warned me that he's the most
intimidating man on the planet, or that he's the best looking
man on the planet?"

Talis turned and faced her with a frown. "Excuse me?"

She giggled playfully and wrapped her arms around his
neck. "Awww, what's wrong? Are you insecure?"

He snorted. "Well, when my girlfriend laughs in my face
the first time she sees me, and then tells my brother he's
really hot the first time she sees *him*..."

She pulled back and slapped him playfully on the arm. "Gimme a break, Talis! That was so embarrassing!"

He laughed and pulled her back into his arms. "Don't worry. I'm sure everyone will make a point to taunt you about it in the morning."

She groaned and buried her face against his shoulder.

He chuckled. "It's pretty crazy around here most of the time, but I love staying here."

She sighed, looking up at him. "And we're here for the duration of the renaissance faire?"

"The rest of the summer. We'll be here during the week, but camp at the site on the weekends. The rest of the guys will be there too." He combed his fingers through her hair and sighed as she rested her head against his chest. "Sleep in here tonight?" he whispered.

She smiled and snuggled against him. "Okay." In the back of her mind, she wondered why Talis hadn't made a move to sleep with her yet. In was weird to her because most of the guys she'd dated before seemed to only ever want that.

Talis seemed content to hold her and kiss her and cuddle. He slept beside her and held her close, but never tried to cross the line. Even during some of their more intense make out sessions, he'd always retained his control. It was strange, but she had an amazing amount of respect for him because of it. She wanted Talis with every fiber of her being. She wanted to touch and explore every inch of his beautiful body until she committed him to memory, but she was enjoying taking things slow. It was a change from the way she usually lived her life and it fit with every other change Talis had brought to her. He was slowly but surely altering her entire lifestyle, and she was grateful for it.

And to think, she had been so willing to just write him off when she'd talked to him after the concert. She was such an idiot. If she hadn't run into him at the Salt River in Globe by blind, ridiculous chance, she would have missed out on the best thing to ever happen to her. She couldn't imagine not being with Talis now. She didn't want to. It was far too painful.

Chapter Nineteen

Cadence woke up by herself again. No matter when she got up, Talis was always up before her. She didn't know how he did it. The only time she'd ever been awake before him had been the night after her spectacular drunken display in Las Vegas. She figured that probably had something to do with the fact that he'd been so pissed at her. He'd probably stayed up half the night fuming and, as a result, slept later than usual. She loved going to sleep in Talis' arms, but she wished that, just once, she could wake up there as well.

With a yawn, Cadence rolled herself out of bed, stretched, and pulled her hoodie on over the T-shirt she had worn to bed. She combed her fingers through her disheveled hair and made her way into the hall. She frowned because she heard an awful lot of voices coming from downstairs, and she thought it was strange considering it was nine o'clock in the morning.

"Good morning, Cadence!" Evie's cheerful voice greeted.

Cadence looked up at her as their paths met at the top of the staircase. She smiled. "Good morning."

"Did you sleep well?"

Cadence nodded, stuffing her hands in the pockets of her hoodie and shivering against the chilly morning air.

"I hope you didn't freeze. The fog off the ocean makes this house so cold sometimes. Especially because we have mostly hardwood floors."

Cadence shook her head. "It's fine. Nothing could be colder than Julian's house. It snowed while we were there." She frowned as a loud burst of laughter sounded from the kitchen area. "What's going on down there anyway?"

Evie rolled her eyes. "Go see for yourself. There's far too

much testosterone in there for one person to handle."

Cadence giggled and descended the staircase. She was taken aback as she entered the kitchen and saw Traevyn making some sort of food, Julia swinging her legs on the kitchen counter as she watched him, and Talis tattooing Seth at the dining room table while all of the renfaire guys sat around drinking coffee and shooting the breeze.

"Told you," Evie said as she made her way into the kitchen behind Cadence.

Several of the guys looked up as Cadence and Evie entered, and Raven grinned. "Lady Cadence!" he exclaimed. "You look ravishing this morn!"

She rolled her eyes and headed for the coffee pot. "What in the world are all of you doing here this early?" she grumbled.

"Having a war council meeting," Ash replied.

She frowned. "I beg your pardon?"

Talis chuckled. "We're just trying to get everything organized. Figure out who's competing in what this year, what events are going on. That kind of thing."

She shot them all a scowl. "Thanks a lot for including me, guys. Last time I checked, I was part of your roguish band of warriors also. At least, I think that was me who made it into the final three at that last battle in Tahoe."

All of the guys went silent and exchanged surprised looks.

"Cadence, you're absolutely right," Tempyst finally said. "We should have waited for you."

"We didn't think," Raven continued. "It's been just the six of us for a long time."

Her eyes narrowed. "I forgive you guys," she stated, "but I don't forgive *him*." She stabbed her finger at Talis.

Talis winced and tried to hide behind Seth while he continued to work.

Cadence smirked, finished her coffee, and went to the seat next to Raven. "So, what's up then?" she asked. "Fill me in. How did you all get here at the same time anyway?" She turned the chair sideways and sat down, leaning back in it and stretching her legs across Raven's lap.

"Devlyn here lives in Reno," Draco supplied. "After the renfaire in Tahoe we went down there and hijacked his RV."

"Are you going to compete, Cadence?" Raven asked as

he absently started to rub her bare feet.

Talis noticed and frowned disapprovingly, which made Cadence smile. Raven was such a ladies' man that he even flirted with his friends' girlfriends without meaning to. "Of course I am," she stated. "Like I'm really going to let Olaf bludgeon me in the head and get away with it."

Raven grinned. "That's what I like to hear. All right, there are combat demonstrations every weekend at this renfaire, but only three competitions. Ash and Talis are going to be doing some of the joust demonstrations and some of the armored combat demonstrations, but are only competing in the melee battle."

"The what?" Cadence asked.

"Melee," Devlyn said. "It's a big, free for all battle where everyone fights everybody else. It's like if you were fighting in an actual battle."

She nodded. "Gotcha." She looked back at Raven. "Are you competing in that also?"

"Please," he said with a snort. "I'm fighting in them all."

She smirked.

"There's an archery demonstration and competition that Devlyn's taking part in, and Draco and Tempyst are being good girls and sticking to their crafts while the real men do the fighting."

Draco scowled and Tempyst rolled his eyes.

Cadence giggled. "So, I guess sign me up for all three competitions then."

"All three?" Ash questioned.

She looked over at him. "Yeah. Three chances to kick the crap out of Olaf. Given the fact that he knocked me out in the first two seconds the last time I fought him, I need all the chances I can get."

Raven chuckled and patted her ankles. "That's my girl." He threw a wink her direction.

"No," Talis corrected, "that's *my* girl." He shot Raven a deadly glower.

Cadence giggled and pulled her legs off of Raven. She stood and went over to where Talis was working, watching as he finished up the tribal arm band Seth was getting. "Nice," she said. "Does that mean anything, or do you just like it?"

Seth looked up at her. "Just like it." He grinned. "Love me the ink."

Cadence smiled and caught Traevyn rolling his eyes as he stirred whatever was in the skillet. "Do you have any tattoos, Traevyn?" she asked.

Talis chuckled and Traevyn shuddered. "No, thank you, and I don't plan on getting any either."

"Traevyn is terrified of needles," Evie remarked from where she was playing patty cake with Julia.

"I'm not terrified," he grumbled.

"No, not at all," Talis said. "He only screamed a *little* bit like a baby when he had to get a tetanus shot." He looked up and gave his brother a wicked grin as chuckles went around the room.

Cadence smiled. "Aw, come on. Evie, don't you think your husband would look sexy with a tattoo? All men look sexy with tattoos."

Evie smiled at her husband and swaggered over to him. "Hmmm...I dunno. Maybe one of those Celtic shoulder pieces." Traevyn looked down at her as if he feared for her sanity and she giggled.

Cadence retained her grin as she watched Talis finish up Seth's tattoo, then rub ointment on it and cover it over. She went to rinse out her coffee cup with a yawn. "All right, time to hit the shower. You guys gonna hang around for awhile?"

Everyone nodded and she made her way back into the living room. She stopped short in front of the fireplace because the sunlight was coming in through the front room window and shining right on a gorgeous painting she hadn't noticed before. She stared at it in awe.

In it was a man with long, black hair sitting on the ground, his face sad and mournful. Behind him stood a woman in an exquisite turquoise gown with an aura of fire and a pair of white wings that were wrapped around the man in front of her. "Holy cow," she murmured.

"Do you like that?"

She glanced over her shoulder and saw Traevyn enter the room carrying his breakfast. He gave her a friendly smile. "I love it," she said. "Did you paint this?"

He nodded as he came to stand beside her.

"Is that you?" She pointed to the man in the painting.

He nodded again. "And Evie."

"That is the most beautiful thing I have ever seen."

He smiled. "That's because she inspired it."

"She looks like an angel."

His smile morphed into a grin. "Exactly. My angel... Are you familiar with any of my work? Or Evie's?"

She felt her cheeks flush and she looked down. She had about as much culture as a banana slug. "No, I'm not. I know of you, but I've never seen your work... I'm sorry."

He chuckled. "No need to apologize. You're either into art, or you're not." He stole a sidelong glance at her. "You must like it a little, or you wouldn't be interested in Talis."

"Oh, I love art," she said. "I just never had the opportunity to learn much about it."

"Well, you'll learn about it if you stick around long enough in this family."

He continued over to the couch and Cadence went on up the stairs, but his words echoed in her mind. She wanted to stick around. She really did. She felt like she fit in more with Talis' eccentric family and group of friends than she had anywhere else she'd ever been.

There wasn't much time to fool around after all of the guys had shown up, and the first week of Cadence's stay in Big Sur was spent running to and from the renaissance faire location making needed preparations. They needed to stake out a campsite, set up vendor stands, get everyone registered, and figure out the schedule of events.

Most of the guys hung out at Traevyn's house every night and that made for a crazy free-for-all, which usually sent Traevyn upstairs where no one saw him until things quieted down. Cadence really didn't blame him. The first night Raven and Talis had broken out into an impromptu duel right in the middle of the living room and, considering how many priceless pieces of art and expensive decorations were in there, Cadence could understand why Traevyn headed for the hills.

The melee battle was the first competition and it was scheduled for Opening Weekend. Cadence was also still dancing with the belly dancers, but luckily for her, they shared the stage with another group of belly dancers so they didn't have to adhere to such a rigorous schedule. That gave her time to practice her combat, relax a little and, most importantly, be with Talis.

The Saturday of Opening Weekend was insane and cha-otic. Because this renaissance faire was so much larger than the one in Tahoe, it took twice as long to run from the belly dancing stage to the combat arena. Not to mention that Tempyst's blacksmith shop was on the complete opposite end of the grounds so no one could use that as a convenient changing station anymore. Cadence had to change into her battle armor backstage after the belly dancing show and then proceed to clank her way across the grounds to the arena. The only thing that saved her was the fact that the shows weren't scheduled back to back like they'd been before so at least she had a considerable amount of time to get where she needed to go.

Cadence did okay in the melee battle, but not as well as she would have liked. She had her legs hacked off by some wiry little dude halfway through and had to lie on the battle-field for what seemed a million years pretending to be dead while Raven methodically picked everyone else off one at a time. She was beginning to think that Raven really was un-beatable and that she may have actually been better *before* he'd taught her all the techniques. It seemed that what had enabled her to beat Raven before had been sheer determina-tion and emotional response to the things he'd said to her.

He'd told her after that battle that nothing was more dangerous than a warrior who had something to fight for. She didn't know what she was fighting for anymore. She didn't feel as wrathful as when she'd first met them all. Talis had brought her a certain amount of peace and, while it made her everyday life much easier to live, it was doing nothing for her combat.

They were all camping at the faire grounds that night, like they would be doing every weekend until the renfaire was over. Seth was hanging out with them too, considering he was away at school all week and only got to go home on the weekends. He claimed that he wanted to visit with Talis and didn't want to miss out on the excitement, but Cadence got the distinct feeling that he was just trying to come up with excuses to not study for the finals he had coming up in a few weeks.

It surprised Cadence just how much the entire camp re-sembled a band of wandering gypsies. The tents and gear were modern, but the atmosphere was definitely that of a different time. Most everyone was still in their garb and were sitting around fire pits talking and laughing.

The faire grounds were located in the middle of a bunch of the same kind of foreboding trees that surrounded Traevyn's home and the fog had come in, cloaking everything in mystery, but no one's spirits were dampened by it. The belly dancers that shared the stage with Heather's group could be heard shouting like *Xena* a few camp sites away as they danced to booming drums. Every time a song ended, raucous applause and cheers would crescendo over the camp. Cadence smiled as she listened. A measure of tranquility descended on her and she sighed, her thoughts drifting to Lance.

She wondered what he was doing. He had stopped calling her and, when Cadence had last spoken to Tawny, she'd said that he'd claimed he'd given up on Cadence and that if she wanted to ruin her life, it was her own business. He couldn't be bothered by her anymore. Bothered. Was that really how he viewed her? As a burden? A wayward child who needed to be given tough love?

With a heavy sigh, Cadence stood and left the camp site, the momentary tranquility she had felt dissipating as her troubled thoughts took over. Talis was with Ash, Seth and Devlyn in Devlyn's very unauthentic RV, and she didn't feel like joining the group right now. She pulled her cell phone out of her pocket as she walked listlessly through the fog and trees, and she contemplated calling her brother. What would he think when she told him about what she'd been doing? Would he be proud of her, or would he laugh at her? Would he think she was just being ridiculous?

She chewed on her bottom lip and stabbed his number into the phone, hitting send before she lost her courage. He was the only brother she had. She couldn't let their relationship dissolve just because she was stubborn. Not after seeing how close Talis was with his family. She needed Lance in her life. She needed him to know that. She had never been against him. She just needed him to realize she was a grown woman. If she made a mistake, it was her own doing. It wasn't his responsibility to keep watch over her. She wanted a brother, not another father.

Her heart sank when she heard his voice mail and she

sighed softly, stopping in her pointless wandering. She shivered against the chilly fog and wrapped her arms around herself as she waited for the beep. "Hey, Lance," she said, "it's me... Look, Tawny told me what you said and I appreciate you backing off, but I don't want you to think you have to ditch out of my life. I haven't gotten into any trouble. I've actually been doing really well. The guy I'm with is really cool, Lance. He's been helping me sort out my issues..." She took a deep breath. "Anyway, this is gonna sound kind of crazy, but I've been traveling with this bunch of people who travel with renaissance faires and they kind of got me involved in sword fighting." She laughed. "I have two fights coming up. One in about two weeks and the other one is the weekend after. It's kind of important to me. We're in Big Sur if..." She shook her head, feeling foolish. "I dunno, like maybe if you wanted to come and see me or something. No big deal. Just thought I should let you know." She rushed through the end, her voice picking up its usual flippant note. She hung up and shoved her phone back into her pocket, feeling strangely alone and not knowing why. It hurt, resting on her chest like a heavy weight.

"Stop it, Raven. Just leave me alone."

Cadence frowned and her head shot up as she heard the voice close by. She turned and the wisping fog parted to show Raven and Heather standing in a clearing close by. They didn't see her and Cadence stepped back behind the nearest tree so they wouldn't think she had been purposely spying.

Heather was trying to walk away from Raven, but he had a hold of her hand and was trying to pull her back to him. "Heather, please, listen to me," he begged. "I didn't know you felt that way. You never told me."

She whirled angrily. She was still dressed in her gypsy clothing and the bells around her ankles and waist jangled underneath her black cloak. "I shouldn't have had to tell you, Raven! If you'd stopped to pay attention to me long enough, you would have known!"

He looked flabbergasted. "Heather, I'm not a psychic! Your demeanor toward me was a complete contrast to the way you claim you felt. What was I supposed to think when every time I tried to get close to you, or touch you, you pushed me away?"

"I was afraid!" she cried. "I was afraid of letting you too close because I knew you'd hurt me!" She snorted and jerked her hand out of his grasp. "Guess what? I was right. What a surprise." She scowled and turned back around, heading for the camp.

Raven extended his arm after her in a halfhearted attempt to stop her, but he sighed in defeat and lowered his head, rubbing his fingers across his forehead as if trying to rid himself of a headache.

Cadence watched him silently for a moment, wondering if she should just disappear and pretend she hadn't seen any of that. She started to leave, but stopped when she saw him unsheathe the sword he still wore lovingly strapped to his back and hold it up in front of him. She frowned thoughtfully. He looked just like a medieval painting, dressed in his red and black tunic and black cloak, his sword gleaming in the moonlight, surrounded by fog. He looked like a knight of old, preparing to do battle with some unseen and terrible foe.

With fluid grace and elegance, Raven began to practice through a sequence of battle moves, as if he was a real life warrior training in the lists. He did it with his eyes closed, all of his concentration on the movement of his sword. Cadence could only stare. He was so beautiful... Devastatingly so. His face was calm, placid, and she couldn't mistake how rapturous he looked. It was like his mind had gone to a different place...a different time.

"Raven," she called quietly, afraid that speaking too loud would destroy the beauty of the scene.

He stopped, startled by her presence, and turned to face her. "Cadence," he whispered. "What are you doing out here?"

She grinned as she approached him, her hands stuffed in her modern sweatshirt. She knew that she should be dressed like everyone else was, and she had been for awhile, but once the fog rolled in, she'd refused to freeze to death just so that she could put on a show. She was the only one in camp in jeans and a sweatshirt other than Seth.

"Pretending not to eavesdrop," she said with a giggle.

Raven's lips split into his magnificent smile and he chuckled, but there was sadness in his handsome face.

Cadence sighed. "So do you always practice sword fighting when you're having girl trouble?"

"I practice my sword fighting whenever I can." He looked up at her. "It's what I'm good at..." He shrugged. "It's all I'm good at. Have to keep it up or else I'll have nothing."

Cadence blinked, taken aback by his words. She had never once heard him say anything that wasn't completely laced in arrogance. She frowned. "Whatever, Raven. Don't be ridiculous."

He snorted. "I'm not being ridiculous; I'm being truthful. Why do you think I do this, Cadence? Why do you think I devote myself to this craft? I have nothing else. During the renfaire off season, do you know what I do?" He shook his head. "I'm a friggin' waiter."

He sounded so disgusted with himself that she felt like she had to say something humorous to cheer him up. It was the only way she knew how. "Hey, I bet you get really awesome tips though."

He met her eyes and gave her a small smile, but sighed. "That's the thing, Cadence. I do get good tips. I get good tips and I get compliments from the staff and my co-workers, and everywhere I go I get girls throwing themselves at me, but what good is that? What good does that do me when I mess up every potential relationship I have? I am horrible at relationships." He shook his head in frustration. "I just don't get it."

Cadence sighed, hating how dejected he looked. She wasn't used to seeing him that way and it bothered her. She smirked. "Raven, you are talking to the queen of relationship disasters," she said. "I'm horrible at them too."

He rolled his eyes. "Please. Talis would lie down in the mud and kiss your boots if you asked him to."

"Yeah, but that's because Talis is more resilient than most. I've put him through his fair share. He just refuses to give up on me." Her heart warmed at that realization. He was the first person who had stuck with her through everything. He hadn't bailed on her when she'd gotten too intense. He had never given up on her. She shrugged. "What happened with Heather anyway?"

He heaved a sigh. "We dated for awhile. I was totally in love with her, but I always felt like she kept me at a distance. After awhile it got to be too much for me so I broke up with her. It's not in my nature to stay alone for long..." He slid his gaze over to her and gave her a slightly pained expression. "That's just one of my many issues."

She gave him a sympathetic smile.

"I started dating this other girl, even though I was still stuck on Heather. Heather thought I had cheated on her or something." He shook his head. "Sometimes I'm just all messed up in my head and have no idea what I'm doing. I just don't like to be alone. Women like me, they make me feel chivalrous and sexy and...I don't know, worth something?"

She frowned in contemplation. "You don't feel worth anything unless you're with a woman?"

He looked back down at the ground. "I don't know... I'm just stupid sometimes."

She cracked a smile and put her hand on his shoulder. "Raven, we're human. We are all stupid most of the time."

He chuckled and met her gaze again. "Yeah, I guess you're right."

"For what it's worth, you matter very much to all of your friends back at camp. You matter to Talis, and I'm pretty sure you matter to a lot of other people too. You are worth something, but take it from me, other people can't convince you of that. You have to learn it yourself."

He raised an eyebrow and some of the mischief returned to his eyes as he sheathed his sword and turned to face her. "Have you learned that?"

She laughed. "I'm working on it."

He grinned and took her hand, bringing it to his lips and kissing her fingers tenderly. "Thank you for talking with me, Cadence. You didn't have to."

She shrugged. "You're my friend, Raven. You've helped me out a lot. I couldn't just let you stand all alone in the fog."

He shook his head and let his eyes appraise her face. "Oh, Lady Cadence," he murmured, "if you didn't belong to Talis..." He grinned wickedly and pulled her close to him so that his mouth was whispering against her ear. "The things we could do together."

It was a sensual, magnetic purr and she shivered in spite of herself. *Holy cow...* She cleared her throat and gave a nervous laugh, taking a step back. "Glad to see you're feeling better, Raven."

He grinned again, his smile gleaming white and devilish.

It was different than Talis'. Talis' grin was taunting and sexy. Raven looked like he wanted to devour her. Man, whoever ended up taming Raven would have to be one heck of a woman.

"What is going on over here?" Talis' voice came. He approached, glancing suspiciously at the two of them.

Cadence grinned and loved how Talis immediately put his arm possessively around her shoulders. "Raven was having girl problems," she explained. "I was trying to help."

Talis' eyes narrowed at his friend and he stared at him for a long minute. "I don't like the way you're grinning, Raven. Were you thinking of brushing up your skills on *my* girl?"

Raven shrugged flippantly, all of his arrogant charm restored. "Well, since you refuse to do it, I was thinking of taking her back to my tent and claiming her the way you should be doing."

Cadence's face flamed and she had to look away.

Talis did not look amused. "I'm glad you think you're funny," he grumbled.

Raven fell to his knees dramatically in front of Talis. "Forgive me, my brother," he pleaded, adopting an English accent. "I meant no wrong." He unsheathed his sword again and lay it down in front of him, bowing over it. "I lay my sword at your feet and vow to never touch the silken skin of your radiant woman ever again." He glanced up at Talis with devilish mirth. "Except, of course, when your back is turned."

Cadence laughed and Talis rolled his eyes. His hand trailed down her arm and twined their fingers. He started to turn away, shaking his head. "Good lord, Raven. You missed your calling. You should have been an actor, I swear."

Cadence giggled again and looked back over her shoulder at Raven as Talis led her away. "I'll come find you when Talis is asleep," she whispered, more than loud enough for Talis to hear. She gave him an innocent expression as he glared down at her, and she grinned as she heard Raven erupt into laughter.

Talis shook his head and muttered something unintelligible as he continued back toward camp.

She fell into step with him, enjoying the laughter Talis and his friends had brought into her life. Going with him was the best rash decision she had ever made.

Chapter Twenty

Talis was watching her sleep. He couldn't help it. She was so fascinating when she was awake, so passionate and fiery. The only time he ever saw her calm and tranquil was when she was sleeping. It was the only time she ever looked at peace. During the day he knew her mind was always spinning a hundred miles an hour.

He sighed and reached out to push back a tendril of her hair. She'd fallen asleep by the fire, curled up in her sleeping bag. She hadn't wanted to miss any of the conversation that the guys had been sharing. Now, everyone else had gone to sleep in their trusty RV, leaving the two of them by the fireside.

He smiled as he remembered camping with Cadence in the Pinals. They'd been nothing short of complete strangers, yet he'd felt so drawn to her. He'd felt drawn to her from the minute he'd seen her. What was it about her? What was it that constantly pulled him in?

"I caught you," Seth's taunting voice came.

Talis looked up and saw him coming down the RV steps, grinning. He chuckled. "Come on, I have a beautiful woman sleeping in front of me. Can you blame me?"

Seth grinned. "Not at all, man." He took a seat next to Talis and sighed. "You did manage to find yourself a serious hottie. I'll give you credit for that. She seems cool, too. All wild and free like you are."

Talis smiled and shook his head. "She's like a wild horse. Completely untamable."

Seth wrinkled his nose. "You wouldn't want a tame woman, Tal. She'd bore you to death. Honestly, can you see yourself settling down with a woman like my sister? Sure,

Evie's spunky and has a pretty scorching temper, but she's basically domestic. She loves cooking and taking care of her family and having babies. Can you see yourself with a woman like that?"

Talis found the very idea more than distasteful. He loved his sister-in-law, but he could never be with a woman like her. She was perfect for Traevyn. He was intense, violently so. She balanced him out, complemented him. They fit. Talis would feel stifled and stuck if he was with a woman who was a homebody. He loved to wander, loved to feel free. Cadence fed that craving in him for she craved it as well.

No...Seth was right. He would never want Cadence to be tame. It was her wildness that fed his desire for her, the desire that threatened to consume him more and more every day.

It was strange for Talis to find himself so attached to a woman. He'd had relationships before, but he'd always managed to stay somewhat detached. He'd watched his brother fall so desperately in love with a woman that, when he had lost her, he'd crumbled. Traevyn didn't know how to love halfway and Talis knew that he was the same in that sense. Because he knew that about himself, he had always remained somewhat guarded. He didn't want to risk losing his heart to someone who would obliterate it.

It seemed like he couldn't help his feelings for Cadence. His heart gave him no choice in the matter. It was odd and foreign, and half the time he didn't know what to do with it. It made him fiercely possessive, which was something he was not familiar with. All he knew was that he couldn't stand the way Cadence flirted with Raven, even though he knew it was all in good fun. The thought of her showing attention to another man grated on his nerves.

He heaved a sigh and ran his fingers through his hair.

Seth raised an eyebrow as he slowly demolished an entire box of mini chocolate chip cookies. "What's the matter?"

Talis gave him a weary expression. "I'm beginning to realize that I'm a little more like Traevyn than I ever thought."

Seth winced. "Man, that's tough. One is hard enough to deal with."

Talis chuckled. True, Traevyn was not the easiest person to live with, but he had found Evie, and she loved him. He was happy. He'd had his heart decimated and stomped on, yet he'd found the strength to give all of himself to another person and, truthfully, Talis had never seen him so happy. Maybe letting go and loving all the way wasn't such a bad thing. Maybe it was worth the risk.

He glanced down at Cadence's angelic face again and his gaze traced her delectably soft lips. She was so reckless, so dangerous... A slow smile curved his lips and a deep kind of satisfaction wrapped around his heart. She was exactly what he needed and he knew it.

"Cadence, you need to pay attention!"

The snap of Raven's voice brought her out of her reverie and she looked up into his disapproving face.

"What are you doing? Are you even here? You need to bring your head back into the game if you want to win. You've only fought one person and you barely got through that one. How do you expect to beat Olaf if you're daydreaming?"

She sighed and looked down. She knew Raven was right. She needed to get her head screwed on straight, but she couldn't when all she kept doing was looking for Lance. He hadn't returned her call, but she'd really thought he might show up. Just to see. Out of curiosity, if nothing else. It stabbed at her heart to know that maybe he really had given up on her. Maybe he no longer cared. Perhaps, in all her selfishness, she had pushed him away as well. It was what she did best. She wouldn't be surprised. Tears stung her eyes and her shoulders slumped.

"Cadence! Hello! Are you even listening?" Raven knocked on her helmet and she scowled up at him.

"Raven, knock it off!" Talis chided. He frowned and shoved him aside as he came to stand in front of Cadence. He placed his hands comfortingly on her shoulders. "Baby, what's wrong?"

Cadence met Talis' eyes and she couldn't stop the tears from coming. She wasn't an idiot. She had barely made it through that first fight. She'd looked like a first timer. Like someone had shoved her out there with no clue as to how she was supposed to fight. The only reason she'd won had been because of luck. Pure and simple. She was off-balance and distracted. "He didn't show up," she murmured.

He frowned. "Who?"

"My brother." She looked at the ground as tears trickled down her cheeks. "I called my brother and told him about my fight. I wanted him to come see me... He didn't."

Talis blinked in stunned silence for a moment before he sighed and pulled her into his arms. "I'm sorry," he said softly.

"Cadence, you have to go!" Raven shouted. "You're up!"

Cadence wrenched herself out of Talis' arms and tried to find some sort of focal point, but her thoughts were scattered and it was next to impossible to see from the tears in her eyes. And to make matters worse, she was up against Olaf. Already.

Raven all but shoved her into the combat arena and she desperately tried to pull her mind back to the task at hand, but she couldn't. Not when the only person who had ever given a crap about her no longer cared at all. What was the matter with her? It was her own fault. She had told him to back off, to stop pestering her. She had ignored his many calls when she had run off with Talis. She had pushed her own brother right out of her life. She had no one to blame but herself. It was her pattern, the black mark she left behind. She destroyed. No matter what. No matter how hard she tried to do otherwise, she always destroyed what she loved.

Olaf leered at her as he circled her with malice, and she heard Talis shouting encouragement while Raven shouted commands, but she really didn't register anything. She shook her head to try and clear her thoughts as she raised her weapon in preparation. Olaf swung hard, like he had done before, but she was expecting it and she dodged. It gave her a tiny bit of satisfaction.

They danced around a bit, dodging one another and making swings that were more threat than anything else. Cadence kept glancing past him to the onlookers, hoping to see a glimpse of Lance, but he was nowhere around. He really had ditched out on her. He honestly didn't care.

Suddenly, Cadence found herself on her back, unable to breathe. The wind was knocked from her lungs and all she could do was lie there for several seconds of agony while her body tried to remember how it was supposed to function. The world spun in a threatening manner for a moment before she took a deep, gasping breath and everything became clear again. Olaf stood over her, and he snarled hideously.

"How many times do I have to tell you, wench?" he hissed. "Go back to where you belong!"

Her eyes widened and she could only stare in horror as he raised his sword and prepared to swing down at her again. She squeezed her eyes shut and braced herself for the blow, but it never came. A great crashing sound echoed through the arena and she opened her eyes to see Raven standing protectively over her, his sword keeping Olaf's from making contact with her.

"Disqualified!" one of the officials shouted frantically. "You, sir! You are disqualified from this competition! Unsportsmanlike conduct!"

Olaf spat several nasty swear words at Raven and gave him a deadly glower.

"You call yourself a warrior?" Raven growled. "You're nothing but a big bully playing with a stick. No warrior of any value strikes a man when he's down. No human of any value, for that matter. You may be disqualified from today's event, but you mark my words, I'll be looking for you next weekend. And I'm gonna knock your ugly head off."

The way Olaf glared at Raven as he stalked off made Cadence's stomach churn, but it didn't seem to faze Raven in the least. He knelt immediately and helped Cadence into a sitting position, along with Talis who she could hear from behind her. They were both asking her if she was all right and she could hear the concern in Talis' voice. It broke her heart because he shouldn't be concerned for her. He shouldn't care at all. Not for her. She brought nothing but pain to people.

People like Raven and Talis...

They were like beautiful stars to her, untouchable in their splendor, and for some reason, they wanted to bestow their radiance on her. She couldn't understand it, and it made her feel sick and unworthy. She didn't deserve beautiful stars. She was like the sludge on the bottom of a lake, the stuff only the toads touched. She deserved toads, not princely knights who protected and defended her. At that moment it seemed very wrong for her to be where she was.

Feeling confused and heartbroken, she yanked her helmet off and pushed away from both Talis and Raven. She stood, threw her helmet aside, and started to stalk off.

"Cadence!" Talis shouted, running after her. "Where are you going?"

"Away," she spat. She didn't stop. She couldn't. She couldn't even look up into his gorgeous blue eyes and remain sane. She would lose it.

Talis frowned. "Where? Cadence, stop. Talk to me."

Tears still burned behind her eyes, but she refused to let them come. Tears were humiliating. She ignored Talis and kept walking.

He let out a frustrated sigh. He grabbed hold of her elbow and yanked her around so that she faced him. "Cadence!" he snapped.

She jerked her elbow out of his grasp and scowled up at him. "What, Talis?" she cried. "What do you want? For me to fall in your arms and have you make it all better? Don't you understand? No one can make it all better! I've done all this to myself! You told me to take responsibility for my actions. Well, here you go. This is me taking responsibility."

"No, this is you running away," he grumbled. "No warrior ever ran away from a problem."

"Newsflash, I'm not a warrior! You're a warrior! Raven is a warrior! You're noble and honest and you know how to fight your way through things with poise and dignity. I claw my way through problems. I claw and I slash and I run. I hide in corners and hope the thing chasing me goes away. I don't even deserve to be in the presence of men like you. You protect and help people. All I know how to do is tear them down and destroy them." She shook her head as the tears surfaced. "I'm the complete opposite of you. I'm what men like you fought in ancient times. If you had any brain in your head at all you would turn your back on me and forget you ever met me. It's only a matter of time until I destroy you too." She spun and started to run before he could see her tears.

She heard him shout for her to come back, but she didn't stop. She felt so out of control. It was a feeling she hadn't had since she'd found Talis, but it was back with a vengeance.

As she ran toward the camp, she saw Seth headed through the parking lot toward his car and she called after him. "Are you going back to Traevyn's house?" she asked as she ran up to him.

He nodded.

"Can you take me with you?"

He frowned. "Well...okay. What about Talis?"

"Just take me, please?"

He raised an eyebrow, but shrugged and motioned for her to get in.

Chapter Twenty-One

Cadence sighed as she let her eyes roam over the many works of literature in Traevyn's office. She had never seen so many books in her life. At least not in someone's house. She couldn't even imagine reading that much. She could barely read a magazine without getting bored. Her mind was always on other things, thinking ahead to the next thing she should be doing. Unfortunately, the things she always thought about doing were never conducive to a productive lifestyle.

"What are you doing back without Talis?"

Cadence started badly and let out a startled shriek as she spun to see Traevyn standing in the doorway. She let her breath out in a rush and put her hand over her heart. "Traevyn...good lord."

He chuckled. "Forgive me. I seem to do that a lot. I scared the wits out of my wife once in the exact same manner."

"You already scared me to death once. Isn't that enough for you?"

He smirked and wandered leisurely into the room. "You like literature?" he questioned, indicating his bookshelf.

Cadence glanced at all the books and shrugged. "Not really."

He arched an eyebrow. "You're perusing my bookshelf just because?"

She giggled and shrugged again out of nervous habit. "I'm not very well read." She glanced up at him. "I'm not smart like that. I'm just looking."

The corners of his mouth twitched as if he thought about smiling for a moment, but never quite made up his mind. "Cadence, just because you aren't well read doesn't mean you're not intelligent. I somehow doubt my brother would be dating a moron."

At the mention of Talis, her heart twisted and she looked down. "Talis is the moron for even thinking about getting involved with me," she murmured.

Traevyn frowned and braced one hand against the bookcase, shifting his weight so that he was standing close to her, but not crowding her. "Why are you back without him anyway?"

She felt the threatening sting of tears again and hated it with everything in her. "I ran away like a coward," she whispered.

He gave a small sigh. "Because...?"

"Because I'm cursed!" she spat vehemently, looking up at him for a brief moment.

He raised both of his eyebrows in surprise. "Cursed, are you?" He smirked. "Which voodoo priestess did you manage to piss off?"

She gave him a halfhearted scowl.

He chuckled. "Tell me why you're cursed, Cadence," he coaxed.

She sighed in defeat and shook her head, wondering why he even cared. He had absolutely no ties to her whatsoever. What did it matter to him what was bothering her?

She glanced up at him. His shining ebony hair fell freely around his shoulders, thick and gorgeous, and he stared down at her with those penetrating light green eyes, waiting patiently for her response. Good lord, he was unnerving. She felt like she was being interrogated when he wasn't pressing her at all, and for some reason, she wanted to talk to him. Traevyn was the kind of man you wanted to tell all your secrets to because he looked like he had a wealth of his own and wouldn't judge you for your problems.

She sighed and let her shoulders slump. "I invited my brother to come see my fight," she admitted quietly. "He didn't come..." She swallowed as the tears burned. "It's just typical. I pushed him too far. This whole time I've been with Talis, he's been calling me and I've been putting him off, ignoring him, telling him to leave me alone and let me live my own life. Now it's too late. He doesn't care anymore. I pushed him away... I push everyone away."

Traevyn watched her for a moment before folded his

arms. "Why do you say that?"

"Because it's true!" she cried. "Everyone or anything I've ever cared about I've destroyed! It's what I do. That's why—" She squeezed her eyes shut as tears leaked out from between her lids and slid down her cheeks. "That's why I can't be with Talis. I know that, sooner or later, I'll just destroy him too. I don't deserve a man like him. He's so good and so noble. I'm just a screw up. Even when I try not to be. He deserves someone who isn't going to make him worry. Someone who he can depend on. I'm reckless; I'm irrational. Half the time I'm crazy!"

"And you're the one he chose," Traevyn interrupted smoothly.

Cadence stopped before she could form her next sentence and stared up at him in bewilderment.

Traevyn smiled gently. "Cadence, I know my brother. He's not one to just give his heart away. I watch him with you and he's different around you than he's ever been with another girl. Talis is always calm, always controlled. You bring out a fire in him. I can see it."

She gave him a pained look. "That's not necessarily a good thing."

"Yes, it is. Talis loves life. He loves everything about being alive, but you bring a certain passion to him that makes it that much better." He gave her a pointed expression. "Trust me. I know my brother."

She sighed, shook her head, and turned to absently play with the pages of a book. This conversation was making her amazingly uncomfortable. "I think you're crazy," she stated.

He chuckled and reached out to take the book from her hands. He closed it gently and placed it back on the shelf, then took her by the shoulders and turned her back to face him. "As for you being cursed," he continued, "that's nonsense."

"You haven't lived my life," she muttered miserably.

He looked away for a second and sighed. "Cadence, sometimes life has a way of dealing us some nasty blows. It's not because of anything we've done, and it's not because we're cursed. It just happens. All we can do is try to get through it, move past it, learn from it, and grow." He smiled. "My wife taught me that."

She met his eyes and gave him a small smile in return.

"Maybe you haven't had the greatest luck," he continued, "but that doesn't mean you're going to screw up everything in your life. Don't discard Talis because you're afraid, and don't write off your brother. There could be a good reason behind his not showing up. Most importantly," —he lifted her chin so she had no choice but to look at him—"don't give up on yourself. The second you do, that's when you're really cursed. Cursed to your own self-made prison. Trust me on this."

Her heart shivered at his words and the intensity with which his velvet voice delivered them. She nodded, some of her chaotic emotions calming for the moment.

"Here," Traevyn said, "remember this:
"Out of the night that covers me,
Black as the Pit from pole to pole,
I thank whatever gods may be
For my unconquerable soul.

In the fell clutch of circumstance
I have not winced nor cried aloud.
Under the bludgeonings of chance
My head is bloody, but unbowed.

Beyond this place of wrath and tears
Looms but the horror of the shade,
And yet the menace of the years
Finds, and shall find me, unafraid.

It matters not how strait the gate,
How charged with punishments the scroll,
I am the master of my fate;
I am the captain of my soul."

A tremor worked along her spine and she stared up at him. "That was the most amazing thing I've ever heard," she whispered. "It sounded like a battle song."

"It's a poem by William Ernest Henley called *Invictus*. It means 'unconquered' in Latin. Just remember it when you start to feel cursed." He gave a playful smile. "You decide your fate, Cadence. No one else. No spirits from the great beyond. No old crone with a crystal ball." She giggled and his smile grew. "You and only you. You are the captain of your soul. Remember that."

She looked up at him and smiled, loving him more than any other person on the planet at that moment. For some reason she couldn't explain, Talis and his family seemed to understand her without even trying. She shook her head and laughed. "How is it that you knew exactly what to say to me to make me feel better?"

He smiled just a little. "There is a lot about you that reminds me of Seth, and I've spent a lot of time around him over the years." His eyes softened. "And there is a lot of Talis in you, as well."

She shook her head and looked down wearily. "Somehow I can't imagine Talis ever feeling as completely helpless and out of control as I do."

"Talis is never out of control, but Seth is. Seth doesn't know what he's doing from minute to minute, much less have any clue what he's going to do with the rest of his life. He has the same lost look in his eyes that you do. You are like Talis because you're not the type of person who can be tied down or chained to one place. You need to be wild and free and that is the complete spirit of my brother. That's why he likes you. And you fit because he does know where he's going. He shows you the way; you wander free together. It works, you see?" He gave her a playful wink.

Cadence grinned, liking how Traevyn's words filled her with hope. Maybe she really could have some sort of future with Talis. Traevyn wouldn't say things like that to her just to make her feel better. He had no reason to. He had to be telling her the truth, and that made her otherwise bleak outlook on life just a bit brighter.

Suddenly, the sound of the front door banging open reverberated through the house, startling both of them.

"Cadence!" Talis' voice echoed, making Cadence jump and Traevyn raise his eyebrows in surprise.

Cadence ran from the office and down the hall. She came to an abrupt halt at the top of the staircase and her heart skipped a beat as she drew her breath in with a small gasp.

He stood in the living room, still in his medieval attire. His sword was strapped to his back, his black cloak elegantly swathing his broad, strong shoulders. He looked so dangerous that she could barely breathe. His black hair framed his face in brilliant, dark waves and he stared up at her with stark possession in his stormy eyes. She had never seen him look that way before and it made her mouth go dry with a twinge of exhilarating apprehension. He was always so mellow, so easy going. Now she felt like she really was staring at a warrior of old, a man dark and powerful, so dangerous that it made her heart pound with the sheer sexuality of it. And she thought, for the briefest of moments, that he looked exactly like his brother.

He started to ascend the staircase, his eyes never leaving her face. Her heart hammered against her ribcage, but she couldn't look away. Her eyes followed him as he slowly stalked up the stairs, taking his time and looking absolutely predatory. He didn't pause in his stride as he came up to her and lifted her into his arms.

Cadence closed her eyes and her arms went around his neck immediately while the breath left her body at the dominant way in which he behaved. No one she'd ever dated had been dominant. She'd always been the one in control. She knew she couldn't have controlled Talis in that moment if she'd tried.

She buried her face against his shoulder as he carried her past Traevyn and Evie—who had emerged from her studio to see what all the noise was about—and down the hallway.

"You're not related or anything, are you?" Cadence heard Evie mutter to her husband.

At any other time, she would have smiled, but her heart was pounding, and it continued to do so when Talis kicked open the door to his bedroom and set her roughly down on the end of the bed. He remained silent as he stepped back and slowly unhooked the baldric from around his chest, setting his sword aside. He removed his cloak in the same unhurried manner, keeping his eyes riveted to hers.

She couldn't breathe and she dare not speak. Every muscle in his body rippled with power and sensuality and it made her ache for him in a way she had never felt before. Desire was not something foreign to her, but the inferno Talis evoked in her body was overwhelming.

He approached her and pushed her down so that she was lying on her back, easing himself on top of her as he did so. Cadence's breath hitched and she closed her eyes as he trailed his fingertips down her throat.

"You, woman, are going to drive me out of my mind," he

all but growled. "Do you know how infuriating you are?" He whispered it in her ear, nipping her earlobe and making her gasp. She had changed out of her medieval costume, and he slid his hand up her shirt so that his fingers were spanning her stomach. "I am coming to realize that I don't like it when you run out on me, and I don't like it when you talk down to yourself." He grazed her neck with his teeth and grinned in satisfaction at the way she shivered. "I am through chasing you, Cadence. The next time you run out on me, I'm not coming after you. Do you understand me?"

She nodded breathlessly as he continued to trail his palm across the bare skin of her stomach, dipping just the tips of his fingers below the waistband of her pants in a teasing caress that nearly killed her. He brushed his lips along her neck and the column of her throat, all of his movements an aching taunt. He was stirring the fire within her so much that she thought she might burst into flames at any moment and incinerate everything in the room.

"I mean it," he continued, lightly biting her bottom lip. "I have been chasing after you since I met you and I am through with it. I know you have terrible self esteem, but there comes a time when you have to face what you fear and realize that *you* have control over your life. I am tired of you running from me. If you really want to be with me, you will stay with me."

His lips hovered over hers, teasing her to the point of madness, but somewhere in all of the insane passion he was bringing to life in her, a small shred of sanity slipped in. She opened her eyes and gazed up into his, feeling those hated, familiar tears behind her eyes. He really did want her, like Traevyn had said. He was asking her to commit to him. She wasn't just a temporary fling to him, someone he could pass the time with. He was asking for commitment, for her allegiance. He was asking her to be his.

She reached up and caressed her hands across his cheeks, tangling her fingers in his ebony hair. She smiled softly as she felt some of his predatory dominance slip at her gentle gesture. "I do want to be with you," she whispered. In truth, she had never wanted anything more in her life. "I'm sorry I ran from you. I'm sorry I keep running from you."

"No more," he stated. "I mean it. I won't chase you again."

She nodded. "I know. I understand. You won't have to." She pulled him back down so that she could seal the promise with a kiss and, suddenly, nothing else in her world mattered. Not her sordid past, or her awful self doubt. The only thing that mattered to her was the fact that an extraordinary man like Talis, a man she did not rightly deserve, actually wanted to be with her. She'd never imagined something like that for herself.

She was supposed to end up with a guy like Danny. Some loser with no future. She'd never thought knights in shining armor really existed, and she'd definitely never thought that she would stumble upon one in a bathroom stall. It made her think that maybe she had actually managed to do something right amidst all of her mistakes. Something had made Talis want to stay with her, had made him hang in there and not give up on her. It was enough to make her think that maybe she really did have enough good in her to be able to change her life and be accepted by a wonderful family like the Whitelaws. "'I am the master of my fate,'" she whispered against Talis' lips. "'I am the captain of my soul.'"

Talis pulled back and frowned down at her. "What in the heck are you talking about?"

She giggled, loving how absolutely confused and frustrated he looked. It was adorable to her. "Nothing," she stated.

He sighed and rolled his eyes. He flipped over onto his back and huffed as he stared up at the ceiling. "You do realize that you're going to be the death of me, right?" he grumbled.

She bit her bottom lip, still burning from his touches and kisses. She got up from where she had been lying and sat down on top of him, straddling his hips and making his eyes all but bulge out.

"Oh right, that makes things so much better," he almost groaned.

She grinned and ran her palms up his chest. "Talis," she whispered.

He met her eyes with a slightly pained expression, as if fearing what her next words were going to be.

She swallowed hard, but forced out the words, forced herself to make the leap into the unknown. "I love you," she whispered.

He stared at her for several heartbeats, looking completely stunned, before he reached up and gently pulled her down so that she was lying across him. He sighed and wrapped her in his arms, holding her close. "Cadence," he whispered, "you are unlike any woman I have ever known. You never cease to surprise me." He smiled and tangled his fingers in her hair. "Lucky for you, I like surprises."

She glanced up at him. "Really?"

He smiled. "Yeah. Come here." He pulled her up so that he could kiss her again, letting his mind repeat her words over and over again. Having her admit that she loved him was huge. It showed vulnerability and she didn't like to show that. It showed him that she was finally trusting him. Trusting him with her heart, and that meant everything to him.

Chapter Twenty-Two

"So, you attacked Ash because he was flirting with Evie before you were even dating?" Cadence laughed. She was sitting on the ground in front of the fire and she situated herself so that she was in a more comfortable position as she looked up at Traevyn. The whole family had decided to camp out with them at the faire grounds to support her big fight the next day, and it warmed her heart like nothing else ever had.

"I did not attack him," Traevyn grumbled indignantly.

Evie rolled her eyes. "He was a barbarian," she muttered.

Traevyn slid a gaze over to his wife. "If I remember correctly, you called me that right to my face."

She met his eyes and thought for a moment. "No, I think the actual term used was caveman."

Everyone laughed, and Seth shook his head. "You guys were both being idiots," he stated. He turned to Cadence and the others who hadn't heard the story yet. "Evie was like, 'Oh, he'll never like me. I'm not pretty enough, blah, blah, blah.'"

Evie blushed and looked away, but Traevyn smiled and reached out to stroke her hair.

"And Traevyn was like, 'Oh I can't like Evie because I'm her mentor, and I'm an old man, and I'm jaded, and I know she only thinks of me as a friend, blah, blah, blah.'"

Traevyn scowled at Seth. "I distinctly remember that differently," he muttered.

Seth rolled his eyes. "Whatever. The point is, they were both being stupid. Evie had no clue Traevyn liked her and I actually think that, at that point, Traevyn didn't even know that he liked her. So Ash is, like, completely innocent in this whole thing and he asks Evie out. Next thing you know Traevyn is—"

"Scaring the crap out of me," Ash supplied dryly.

Chuckles went through everyone and Talis shook his head. "I thought I was going to have to find a new roommate."

Traevyn snorted. "Oh come on, I'm not that frightening."

Cadence and Evie both stared at him in shock. "Are you out of your mind?" Cadence cried. "The first time I saw you, I almost had a heart attack!"

"I second that," Evie put in.

He rolled his eyes and folded his arms.

"I don't think you're scary, Daddy." Julia, who had been playing with Draco, turned her attention to Traevyn and went to stand beside him with a big grin on her face.

Traevyn's expression softened and he reached down to lift his daughter onto his lap. "Well, that's all that matters then, doesn't it, sweetheart?" He kissed the top of her head and she snuggled against his chest with a smile.

"That's all right," Cadence giggled. "The first time Ash met me, my friend broke his nose."

"And almost castrated me," he grumbled miserably.

"Yeah, and the next day I was trying to teach Cadence how to throw missile weapons and she almost took his head off with an axe," Talis said.

Evie's eyes bulged. "Oh my gosh! That's horrible!"

Ash sighed and shrugged. "Just my luck, I guess."

"Um...excuse me?"

Cadence turned to look up at the new voice and she froze.

"Is this guy one of yours?"

She wasn't sure what she reacted more strongly to. The fact that her brother was standing right there when she had been so convinced that he didn't care one iota about her, or the fact that he was practically holding up a bleeding and very battered Raven.

"Raven!" Talis shouted. He jumped up and went to him immediately, helping him ease into the nearest camp chair.

There was a moment of chaos as all of Raven's friends jumped out of their chairs and started to talk at once, asking him what had happened and if he was all right.

"Guys, give him some space," Cadence commanded, not unkindly. She glanced up at Lance, who looked bewildered and completely lost. She wanted to fling her arms around him and cry, but she needed to find out if Raven was all right first. "Lance, what happened?"

He shrugged helplessly. "I found him in the parking lot."

"Raven, what happened?" Talis repeated.

"I got the crap kicked out of me, that's what," Raven grumbled. He groaned and leaned his head back against the chair.

Cadence felt sick as she looked at him. His nose and his lip were bleeding and he had a gash across his cheek also. He was holding his hand to the left side of his ribcage and she reached out and touched his arm consolingly. "We should get you to the hospital," she suggested.

He shook his head. "Nah, I'm fine."

She snorted. "Yeah, you look real fine, Raven."

He shook his head again. "I've been beat up before. No need to drive who knows how long to a hospital that will tell me I have a cracked rib and a few gashes on my face and then slap me with a couple thousand dollars in bills. I'll be fine."

"What happened?" Devlyn persisted.

"I got jumped. Attacked when my back was turned. I didn't even get a chance to defend myself. Nice, huh?"

"By who?" Cadence screeched.

"Someone who doesn't want me competing tomorrow."

There was a moment of silence before Talis' face grew deadly. "You think Olaf did this to you?"

Raven sighed. "There's no proof. He had his face covered. But I know the guy's stature. It had to have been him."

All of the renaissance men suddenly became very irate and the level of logic in the group dropped as the level of testosterone rose. Everyone started to talk at once about how they were going to find where he was camping, give him what-for, etc.

Cadence rolled her eyes. "You guys!" she shouted. "What's that going to accomplish, really? The only thing finding him and beating the tar out of him will do is get us all kicked out, which would make Olaf all the more ecstatic. Sit down, all of you."

Draco, Devlyn, and Ash, who had been the ones spearheading the idea of retaliation, stopped and stared at her like she had lost her mind.

"Sit down!" She commanded again. "This is not friggin' *West Side Story*! Do you really want to go off like a bunch of brutes and beat someone to death when there is a little girl in our camp? What kind of an example would that be setting? Would a bunch of medieval knights go charging into battle immediately after one of their own had been wronged? With no kind of plan whatsoever? I somehow doubt it. Trust me on this one, acting on pure instinct causes nothing but trouble. *Sit down.*"

They stared at her a moment longer, then all grumbled incoherently and grudgingly obeyed. Cadence shook her head, unable to wrap her mind around the fact that Olaf would actually go to such great lengths to get Raven out of the competition. "I can't believe this," she muttered. "Why would he do something like this? It's just a game!"

Raven snorted. "Just a game? To ninety-five percent of the competitors, yeah, but you know there's always someone who takes it to the next level, who borders on obsession. Olaf's hated me for the longest time. He's never been able to beat me. I guess he finally got sick of it." He winced as he tried to shift in the chair.

"Are you sure you don't want to go to the hospital?" Cadence persisted.

He gave her a pained smile. "No, I'm fine, Cade. I promise. Just, somebody get me something to clean my face up with and give me some extra strength pain killer."

"Come on, Rave," Devlyn said, helping him out of the chair. "Let's get you in the RV so you can lie down."

Cadence watched as they toted Raven inside and she ran her fingers through her hair in agitation. She couldn't even begin to comprehend the kind of brutality Olaf had just displayed. She had gotten in her fair share of fights in the past, but she never would have attacked an unsuspecting person while their back was turned. That was just low.

Her eyes narrowed menacingly and she squared her shoulders in a determined sort of way. He may have been able to keep himself in the competition by not showing his face when he attacked Raven, but he was going to be one sorry jerk after she got through with him.

"I know that look, Cade. What kind of damage are you planning on doing?"

Cadence whirled at the sound of Lance's voice and, for a moment, her anger and hatred dissolved and she flung her arms around him. "I can't believe you're here!" she cried.

Lance smiled and returned her embrace. "Yeah, I'm sorry I couldn't come last weekend. We were in the middle of this PR thing and I didn't even get your message until it was too late."

She shook her head, tears stinging behind her eyes. He hadn't forgotten about her. Traevyn had been right. She swallowed and looked down at the ground. "I just thought you'd gotten sick of me. I figured I'd pushed you too far."

He frowned and snorted. "Gimme a break, Cade. You're my sister. Granted, I was not happy with you ditching out on me and going AWOL, but Rochelle made me get a clue after awhile. I called your friend, Tawny, and was really pissed so I told her I couldn't be bothered with you anymore, but I think I was more hurt than anything. Rochelle made me realize that I was probably completely smothering you so I just backed off." He stuffed his hands in his pockets and shrugged. "I didn't mean to stifle you, Cadence. I just wanted to protect you."

She arched an eyebrow. "You didn't mean to stifle me?" She smirked. "Lance, you went searching through the desert looking for me. You even looked in the men's room, for crying out loud."

He frowned and his eyes snapped to meet hers. "How do you know that?"

She grinned wickedly. "'Cause I was hiding in one of the stalls."

His eyes widened. "You were not! Oh my gosh, Cadence! Do you know the tongue lashing I got from Rochelle because of that? And you were in there the whole time!"

She laughed. "Talis was hiding me."

He frowned disapprovingly. "Yeah, who is this Talis guy anyway?"

Suddenly, Seth came flying out of the RV, all but falling down the steps. He tried to gather himself and look dignified, but Cadence wanted to laugh out loud at the look on his face as he approached. Talis followed, grinning.

"Lance Lawson," Seth breathed in a kind of reverent awe.

Cadence giggled. "Yeah, Seth, this is my brother Lance. Lance, this is Seth."

Seth held his hand out, but his eyes didn't leave Lance's face as he shook the rock star's hand. "Holy friggin' crap," he murmured. "Seriously, dude, you're the best bass player alive."

Evie rolled her eyes. "Seth..."

He scowled at her over his shoulder. "Shut up, Evie. Just because you have no musical knowledge..."

Lance chuckled and glanced over at Evie. He did a double take of Traevyn and frowned thoughtfully. "Hey, isn't that...?"

"Traevyn Whitelaw," Cadence supplied. "And his wife—"

"Evelina Whitelaw," Lance finished. He strode over to them with a wide grin on his lips. "Van loves their art. He has tons of it in his house, Cadence. Didn't you ever notice?"

Cadence looked down self-consciously as Lance started to talk to them. Of course she hadn't noticed. Every time she'd been at Van's house it had been for some kind of party and every party she'd ever gone to, she'd gotten trashed at. Like in the midst of her drunken splendor she'd taken the time to study Van's art?

She felt an arm slip around her waist and she smiled as she was pulled up against Talis' chest. He pressed a kiss to the base of her neck and squeezed her gently. "Your brother is here," he stated.

She leaned back into his embrace. "I noticed."

Lance glanced up from his conversation with Evie and Traevyn and his smile turned into a frown when he saw Talis holding onto Cadence. He immediately headed back over to her, but before he could get any words out, Talis pulled away and extended his hand to Lance in greeting.

"It's good to finally meet you in person," Talis said. "I'm Talis Whitelaw."

Lance eyed him suspiciously for a moment before slowly shaking his hand. "Whitelaw, you say?"

Talis sighed and smirked. "Yeah. I'm Traevyn's brother. I was also the tattoo artist who did Van's tattoo the night of your concert in Phoenix."

"Really? Sorry, I don't remember you." He shot a glower in Cadence's direction. "I was too busy trying to figure out where my fugitive sister had run off to."

Cadence rolled her eyes.

"Well, if it makes you feel any better, I had no hand in helping Cadence escape that night. I actually tried very hard to engage her in conversation and make her think I was interesting, but she ended up laughing right in my face and calling me silly." He raised a taunting eyebrow at her.

Cadence huffed. "Do you have to tell that to everyone

you meet?" She folded her arms in agitation.

Lance chuckled, easing the tension of the situation. "So, how did you end up with her then?"

"I told you," Cadence spat. "He hid me in the bathroom. But he only agreed to do that because he gave me an ultimatum."

"An ultimatum?"

"He told me that he'd only hide me if I agreed to travel with him and be his squire for the summer."

Lance raised his eyebrows. "What? Cadence, are you out of your mind? You agreed to run off with a complete stranger just to avoid me?"

"Compared to the lecture I knew you'd be flinging my direction if you found me, yeah."

Lance scowled, but he looked vaguely hurt underneath his disapproval.

Talis sighed and briefly thought that Cadence hurling accusations at her brother was not a good way to make things right between the two of them. Even if it was true, she didn't need to start launching an attack the second her brother walked into camp.

"All right, stop it," he said calmly. He glanced over at Cadence, not wanting to embarrass her, but wanting her to get the point. "You guys haven't seen each other in awhile. You have all weekend to dig into one another. You don't need to do it all tonight."

Cadence blushed and looked down.

Lance sighed and scratched at the back of his head as if he was thinking over several things to say before deciding which one would actually come out of his mouth. "So, how did you get involved in sword fighting, anyway?" he finally asked.

Cadence shrugged. "I was watching Talis and Raven battle and Raven challenged me afterward. He had been bragging all kinds about how he was unbeatable and he pissed me off so I decided to do it."

Talis chuckled. "Beat him into the ground too." He reached over and stroked Cadence's hair in a gesture of affection and comfort. He could see that her defenses were up, despite the fact that she had really wanted to see her brother. She was talking with that flip note in her voice and she stood with her arms folded, looking for all the world like she was going to punch something if anyone even glanced at her funny.

Cadence eased at Talis' touch. She hated that, after the brief moment of jubilation she had felt at seeing Lance, her guard had immediately gone up. She wanted to laugh and talk and tell him all the things that she had been doing since meeting Talis, but she couldn't help but think that he was going to talk down to her or lecture her. It was what he did. He was good at it. It was hard to throw that aside and try to give him the benefit of the doubt, even when she was sure that her being flippant and snide was not helping.

Lance glanced from Talis to Cadence and back again as if trying to assess the situation. He cleared his throat and folded his arms. "So, how did you guys hook up? I mean, are you dating, or what?"

Cadence huffed in irritation, but before she could formulate a venomous response, Talis smiled politely and put his arm around her shoulders, dragging her close to him. "We are," he stated simply. "We just started dating, actually. We have gone most of the journey just being friends." He met Lance's eyes. "It was next to impossible to not fall for her," he said. "Seeing her kick the ever-loving crap out of a bunch of guys twice her size and with ten times more experience was a real turn on." He squeezed her playfully and grinned down at her.

Cadence rolled her eyes and blushed, but was surprised when Lance chuckled. "At least you finally found an outlet for all that rage, Katydid."

She looked up at him in shock at hearing his nickname for her. He hadn't called her that in ages. She smiled when she saw he was being genuine, and some of her tension melted away.

"Dude." Seth was back and had apparently decided that he had been ignored long enough. He was tugging on Lance's sleeve like a little kid who wanted something from his mommy and staring up at him with the same wide-eyed, revered expression he'd worn earlier. "Seriously, I hate to break up the family reunion and all, but I have pretty much been waiting my entire life to meet you so..."

"Seth!" Evie scolded. "For crying out loud! Can't you leave the poor man alone?"

He glared at his sister. "Look, what would you do if Monet was suddenly standing in front of you?" She opened her mouth to respond, but he cut her off. "You'd crap your pants, that's what you'd do. And you'd follow him around asking him all sorts of dumb art questions about landscapes and impressionism. So shut it and let me have my moment, would you?"

Traevyn chuckled and Evie rolled her eyes.

Lance grinned. "It's cool. I don't mind," he assured.

Cadence smiled as Seth started to volley questions at Lance, and she pulled gently out of Talis' embrace. "I'm going to go talk to Raven, okay?"

He nodded and kissed her on the forehead.

All of the guys were still talking about retaliation at the kitchen table when she entered the RV. She smirked and let them continue with their rambling as she made her way into the back where Raven was lying down. He looked awful, and she sighed as she sat down on the bed next to him. His eyes opened and he turned his head to look at her. She smiled and brushed some of his hair off of his forehead. "Hey," she said softly. "How are you doing?"

"Terrible," he groaned. "I don't know what hurts worse. My body or my pride."

She shook her head. "You were attacked from behind, Raven. You couldn't defend yourself. There is no dishonor in that."

"I guess every undefeated champion has to fall sometime, right?"

She hated the self-loathing she heard in his voice and rage churned inside of her at the thought of Olaf attacking her friend while his back was turned.

She felt a fierce kind of loyalty toward Raven and she couldn't put her finger on why. She had a feeling it had something to do with the fact that he had treated her vehemence with respect and admiration. He hadn't looked down on her, hadn't frowned and pointed a finger and told her that it was bad. He'd shoved a stick of rattan in her hand and told her to go at it. He'd praised her and she'd had very little of that in her lifetime.

The rest of the guys had proven very supportive, and she had grown to care for each one of them as well, but Raven was different. She felt like Raven understood her on some kind of deeper level. Maybe it was because he hid like she did. He hid beneath a front of arrogance and charm while she hid beneath a careless attitude and sarcasm. They both felt like they were worthless, like they had nothing to offer. They both had terrible self esteem, but no one would ever know it. Raven was kindred to her, and having someone hurt him felt like a direct personal assault. In a way, she couldn't help but wonder if it was because of her that Raven had been attacked.

He'd fought Olaf before, lots of times, but no act of violence had been made until Cadence had entered the picture. Both fights Cadence had participated in, Raven had beaten Olaf after Olaf had whooped on her. And because Raven was a performer in every sense of the word, he had bragged to a lot of people in camp about how he had defended the valiant Cadeyrn Wallace against the underhanded assaults of Olaf the Ogre, or Olaf the Enormous, or whatever else Raven had decided to call him at the time.

Cadence distinctly felt like she had played a part in Raven getting hurt, and she hated herself for it.

Raven frowned as he watched her. "What's going on inside your head, Cadence?" he asked. "Your mind is always turning."

She gave him a meager smile. "Nothing, Raven," she assured him. "Though I will say one thing. When Talis first introduced me to all of you, I had no idea what words like 'honor' and 'chivalry' meant. To me, things like that were only found in fairy tales. You have all shown me that those things still exist in a corrupted world. I can't allow that to be damaged." She met his eyes. "There are a thousand Olafs in the world I come from, Raven. People who only want to hurt and stomp on others to get where they want. I have been victimized by them my whole life. I refuse to allow one of their trashy kind into the sanctuary I have found with all of you. I'm not a gutter rat anymore. I'm not the strung out drunk you find sleeping in the alley. Maybe that's what I used to be, but not anymore. I'm a warrior now. Made that way in spirit by trial and circumstance. Made that way in form by you. You've trained me well physically. Life has trained me mentally. I have no intention of letting this injustice stand. I am tired of watching people I care about get hurt. I can do something about this and, come tomorrow, I promise you, I intend to do just that."

Chapter Twenty-Three

News about Raven's assault spread through the renfaire camp like wildfire and, by the next day, the story had gotten so warped and twisted that some people said he had been mugged by a deviant and others swore that he had fended off up to ten attackers while trying to save a helpless woman from terrible dishonor.

Cadence couldn't believe the tales that some people could come up with just to make things sound more interesting, but she imagined that Raven preferred the dramatic tales over the truth. At least the stories made him sound brave and heroic.

Some people did, however, stick to the truth, and the crowd around the armored combat arena was the largest Cadence had ever seen. Raven had a lot of friends and a lot of fans. Those who were loyal to him wanted to see Olaf go down as badly as she and the rest of the guys did.

Plus, Draco had a big mouth and, since Cadence wouldn't let them all murder Olaf in his sleep, he had gone around telling everyone that Cadence was going to put him in his grave at the next competition. She rolled her eyes as she shoved on her helmet and tried to get into warrior mode. Yeah. Cool. No pressure.

She glanced around at the onlookers as she tried to get in her zone, and she let out a slow breath. Talis stood off to her right, smiling like he was the proudest thing on the planet. All of the other guys flanked him. Even Draco and Tempyst had closed up their shops for a few hours so they wouldn't miss the fight. Traevyn, Seth and Evie stood together while Julia huddled close to Evie and eyeballed all of the strange-looking people who were surrounding her. Next to them was Lance, and her heart warmed at seeing him. He was there to see her, to support her. It was one of the best things that could have happened. Having him there gave her the drive to want to do that much better. She needed to prove to Lance that she could be good at something.

But the best motivation of all came in the form of Raven, who sat in a chair next to all of his friends. His handsome face was marred with bruises and he was favoring the left side of his body where his injured rib was. He looked pale and sad and it made something inside of Cadence grow steely and calm. All of the chaos that usually took up space in her brain quieted, and all she could hear was the rhythm of her own heartbeat. She felt her spine grow rigid and her shoulders square as she turned to face her first opponent. She couldn't let anyone beat her. She had to make it to Olaf. Failure was not an option at this point.

As the battles went on, Cadence methodically knocked everyone out of her way. Talis watched her as she attacked with agile strength and deadly precision. He couldn't tear his eyes from her. It was like she had transformed over night. And, even though she had been remarkable to watch when she'd first fought Raven, all wild and impulsive, it was nothing compared to how it was to watch her now. She was skilled, accurate and graceful in a way he had never seen a fighter. It was the dancer in her that caused it, and watching her bulldoze the competition was just like watching a morbid dance. He had never seen her mind so set, so devoted to the task at hand.

As bad luck would have it, Cadence had to fight everyone else before she got to Olaf, but Talis was surprised at how she was handling herself. After every fight she walked back to him, where she removed her helmet, doused her head in water, and took a long drink. The exertion was apparent in the way her chest heaved and how flushed and sweaty her face was, but she retained a grim, undeterred focus, and when she had finished re-hydrating, she shoved her helmet back on and marched back into the arena with just as much stamina and determination as before.

It amazed him because, the other men she was fighting had to knock out their own share of the competition to rise in the ranks and, where they looked winded and exhausted, she only looked mildly tired.

He joined the others in cheering for her, but all of them stared in awestruck silence more than they shouted. It couldn't be helped. In the entire time they had been part of the SCA and the other events like this faire, none of them had ever seen a woman fight the way Cadence was. She was meticulous, a machine. She had an objective, and she wasn't going to give herself any other option but winning.

As the fighters dwindled and Cadence faced the final fight against Olaf, she turned back to the others and pulled her helmet off, preparing to take her drink of water and ready herself for the battle. The excitement and apprehension was thick in the air and even Lance seemed nervous.

"You're doing amazing, Cadence," Talis said softly as she approached. He gave her an encouraging smile.

She met his eyes and cracked a small smile, but didn't allow her affection for him to distract her. She drank her water, shoved her helmet back on, and turned to the arena. This was it. The two last to compete. The two best warriors out of the eight total who were fighting. They'd both beaten three opponents. Now, they fought one another.

"Cadence!"

She turned at the sound of Raven's voice and went over to him.

He shook his head in amazement. "Where have you been hiding this champion?" he asked with a proud grin.

Her heart softened and she smiled just a little. "I guess I just needed something to fight for." She turned and saw Olaf already in the arena, swinging his sword back and forth in a menacing fashion. Her eyes narrowed, she squared her shoulders, and marched toward him without fear. This guy was going down.

Raven blinked as he watched her and frowned up at Talis, who had come to stand next to him. "What's she fighting for?" he questioned.

Talis looked at him and smiled. "Vengeance, Raven," he answered. "She's avenging you."

He looked shocked for a moment before he turned his attention back to the fight.

There was nobody outside of Olaf to Cadence. He was the only thing in her world at the moment. Him and all of his cold, ruthless, underhanded arrogance. Talis didn't exist, her brother didn't exist, the guys didn't exist and her troublesome thoughts of worthlessness didn't exist. She didn't need to second guess herself on this one. She had this and she knew it in the very core of her being. This victory was all hers. This was for the man who had seen potential in her, her trainer. This was for the man who validated her, her brother in arms. Most of all, this was for the man who understood her, her friend. Raven. This was all his.

Her sword met Olaf's with a thunderous crack that went splitting through the arena. Her eyes locked with his through the face plates of their helmets, and he sneered at her evilly. She smirked, anticipated his next move, and blocked it, causing a lot of onlookers to gasp in surprise. He stepped back to regroup, and she twirled her sword in her hand with a cocky grin, much like the way Raven did when he fought. She realized he wasn't really all that intimidating. He was just a man. A childish, stupid moron who never grew up. A soldier wannabe who'd never had the cajones to actually make it in the military. "Invictus," she whispered to herself. "Invictus... Unconquered... Here we go."

She struck. She launched her attack so quickly that she must have looked like a mere blur of motion, all of her moves precise and deadly. He may have brawn, but she had speed, and she had a reason. Before Olaf could even figure out what she was doing, she had killed him three times over and, just for good measure, she finished with a nice, clean wallop to the side of the head. He fell to his knees.

There was a moment of dead silence before everyone around broke into the most resounding cheer she had ever heard in her life. Olaf yanked off his helmet and flung it aside, hurling several nasty swear words at Cadence in the process.

She looked down at him, deftly removed her helmet, and smirked. "Guess I finally found my place, huh?" she asked. "Staring down at you while you're on your knees in front of me." He snarled and started to rise, but she stabbed the point of her rattan sword into his chest and scowled at him. "Don't you ever touch my friend again," she hissed. "If you do, I'll be sure that the next time I beat the stuffing out of you, I do it when you aren't armored." Her eyes narrowed. "Don't believe me? I have the criminal record to back me up." She pulled her sword away and stabbed it up into the air, causing further cheering from the onlookers.

Pride like she had never known filled Cadence as she made her way back to her friends. Talis and Draco came running at her and she laughed as Talis hoisted her up into his arms and spun her around.

"You were fabulous!" Ash shouted as he joined them. "That was the best fight I've ever seen!"

"The whack to the head was a nice touch," Draco commented. "Especially after you'd already eliminated both of his legs and his gut."

Devlyn laughed. "No kidding. When you decide to kill someone, you make sure you do it right."

She laughed and her eyes fell on Raven, who was sitting in his chair, grinning. He met her gaze and dipped his head in a very medieval gesture of respect. She sighed and her heart softened as she looked at him. She gently pushed her way out of the circle of guys, who were still all raving about her moves, and went to stand in front of him. She bowed, held her sword out to him, and knelt, laying the sword at his feet in much the same way Raven had done to Talis the night he'd been teasing him. She looked up at him with a soft smile and leaned up to press a gentle kiss to his forehead. He blinked, pulled back, and looked so bewildered that she couldn't help but give a warm grin.

"You do matter," she stated. "Don't ever think you don't."

He stared at her for a long moment, tears hovering just behind his eyes. He blinked them back and nodded, but still looked visibly shaken by her actions.

She stood, touched him lightly on the shoulder as she went by, and turned to Lance with a grin.

"Katydid!" he shouted with a laugh. "On my gosh! Where did you learn to fight like that?" He didn't give her a chance to respond before he gathered her in his arms and squeezed her hard. "That was incredible! I am so proud of you!"

Cadence swore her heart stopped at those words. She couldn't even remember the last time Lance had said he was proud of her.

"Man, I wish Rochelle could have seen this!" he continued. "We're staying at Van's right now. I invited her, but I think she wanted me to come on my own so that we could do 'our thing.'" He rolled his eyes as he pulled away. "Kat would have loved to see it, too. We all know how much she loves to beat up on things."

Cadence laughed and pushed some of her sweaty hair behind her ears.

"We need to celebrate!" Draco shouted. He slung an arm around Cadence's shoulders and grinned. "I say we all head back to Traevyn's."

Traevyn raised an eyebrow and muttered something that no one but Evie heard. She laughed. "Everyone is more than welcome!" she exclaimed, which made Traevyn wince.

"We should get pizza!" Seth suggested.

"I need to put all my valuable possessions away," Traevyn grumbled.

Talis chuckled. "All right, let's figure this out then. I'll take Traevyn home so he can warrior-proof his house. Who wants to get the pizza?"

"I will," Cadence volunteered, "but I'll need to borrow a car."

"Take mine," Talis said. "I'll take Traevyn's."

She nodded.

"Hey, I'll go with you," Seth said to Cadence. "Evie and I know where the best pizza place in Monterey is." He grinned at his sister. "Don't we?"

Evie giggled. "I think we know where all of the pizza places in Monterey are. Julia and I will go with you guys too."

Talis nodded. "All right, I don't need to do anything else here today. The rest of the guys have some other stuff they need to do and will probably follow later, but do you want to head out now?"

Cadence shrugged. "Sure."

"Hey, Cade?"

She turned to look at her brother.

Lance sighed and looked apologetic. "I would love to celebrate with you, but I really have to get back. Van's trying to get this new album written and he needs my help with a lot of stuff. I'm kinda swamped."

She shook her head. "No, it's okay. I understand." She hugged him. "Thank you so much for coming, Lance."

He smiled and held her close for a moment. "No problem. I'm proud of you, Katydid. I really am. You did good this time." He pulled away and winked at her.

She grinned, feeling like she was on top of the world. She watched as her brother bade goodbye to everyone and headed out while all the others tried to sort out who was going to ride with whom and when everyone else was going to show up.

She sighed blissfully. For the first time in too long she felt like she deserved all the joy she was experiencing. She had fought long and hard to turn her life around and get where she was. She deserved this. These friends, Talis, all of it. Maybe she really did. Maybe Traevyn was right and she wasn't cursed after all. Maybe, from here on out, things would be better, she would be better. For the first time in her jaded life, she actually believed that might be possible.

Chapter Twenty-Four

"I still can't believe the way you eliminated that guy in only about three minutes," Seth ranted as they made their way down Highway 1 out of Monterey and back to Traevyn's house.

Cadence grinned and glanced at him in the passenger seat, but quickly turned her attention back to the road. Fog had started to roll in while they were at the pizza parlor and it was getting steadily worse. Navigating the twisting highway was difficult, especially for someone who had lived in cities and desert her whole life. She was trying to seem placid and calm about the whole thing, but she gripped the steering wheel so hard that her knuckles were turning white.

"I was definitely impressed," Evie said from the back seat. She groaned. "Fog," she muttered. "Always with the fog. I'm beginning to hate fog."

Seth chuckled. "Yeah, no kidding. It makes driving impossible. There's been a lot of times that I thought for sure I was gonna bite it driving back to Traevyn's from campus. Maybe you should pull over, Cade," he suggested.

"Are you nuts?" Evie protested. "Then we'll be stuck here all night long. It's only going to get worse. Just turn on the fog lights and we'll be fine. I've driven in worse than this."

Cadence swallowed hard because it really was getting next to impossible to see. She fumbled for the fog lights with trembling fingers and, when she finally succeeded in turning them on, her heart leapt into her throat as the milky expanse in front of her parted to reveal a deer standing right in the middle of the road.

"Cadence, watch out!" Seth shouted.

She screamed and slammed on her breaks, but she

swerved as she did so, swearing on everything that she held dear that she saw something like headlights flash in the corner of her left eye. She screamed louder and tried to maneuver the car past the deer, but she had jerked the wheel hard to the right and she didn't have time to correct it. The tires squealed shrilly and horribly on the asphalt and the worst kind of panic flashed through her as the car went off the road and into a gully flanking the highway.

Everything was deadly silent for an agonizing moment as Cadence trembled and stared out the window in horrified shock at the way the driver's side wheel was still spinning even though it was off the ground. She pried her fingers off of the wheel, amazed that she seemed to be completely unharmed aside from the fact that her chest hurt from where the seatbelt had bit into her on impact. "Oh my gosh," she whispered. "I-Is everyone okay?" Panic took over her shock and she whipped around to look at Seth. "Seth, are you all right?"

He groaned and winced as he clutched his shoulder. "My shoulder's jacked up," he rasped. "Check Evie."

Cadence frantically shut off the engine, unbuckled her seatbelt and turned in her seat. "Evie, Julia? Are you all right?"

"Mommy!" Julia started shrieking. "Mommy! Wake up!"

Blind, all-consuming terror gripped at Cadence's chest as Julia's hysterical screams filled her ears. Evie and Seth had both been on the side of the car that had gotten most of the impact. The car hadn't rolled completely, but it was lying at a forty-five degree angle on its right side.

"Evie!" Seth started to shout. He ignored his own injuries and climbed out of his seat so that he could get to his sister. She was lying motionless with her head up against the window. "Evie!"

Evie groaned and her eyes opened slowly. She winced and raised her head.

"Evie, are you all right?" Seth prodded. "Are you hurt?"

She blinked rapidly and reached out to her daughter, who was still crying hysterically. "I'm all right," she mumbled. "I just blacked out." She touched her temple, which was bleeding, and frowned. "What happened?"

Seth turned all of his attention to Cadence, his blue eyes blazing with angry fire. "What *did* happen, Cadence?" he exclaimed. "What in the world were you doing?"

Cadence was shaking uncontrollably now and she felt sick to her stomach. "There was a deer—"

"I saw the deer!" he continued to yell. "But what made you decide to take a trip into the ditch?"

"I thought I saw—"

"You thought you saw what, Cadence?" he bellowed. "A leprechaun? A nice, shiny UFO? There was nothing there! I told you to pull over! Why didn't you listen to me? You could have killed us all! My sister is pregnant!"

"Seth!" Evie interjected. "Seth, stop it! This isn't her fault!"

"Not her fault? It's all her fault!"

Tears slipped silently down Cadence's cheeks as she continued to listen to Seth's harsh, angry words. She couldn't even bring herself to react. All she could do was sit there and take it. Evie kept trying to interrupt, telling him he didn't know what he was talking about, but he ignored her. Julia was still crying and screaming. She felt numb and cold and all she could do was sit there, praying and wishing with all her might that she would wake up in a second and all of this would have been a nightmare.

She jumped as she heard a loud rap on her window, and she turned to see a man in uniform shining a light into the car.

"Is everyone all right?" he called.

Relief flooded Cadence and she pushed the door open, climbing out to meet the Highway Patrol officer. "Oh, thank goodness!" she cried. "There's a pregnant woman in here! And a little girl. And I think that his shoulder is hurt." She pointed to Seth and dragged her shaking fingers through her hair. "There was a deer and then I thought I saw..."

She squeezed her eyes shut and shook her head. What had she thought she'd seen? Had she really seen anything at all, or had she been so freaked over the deer that she had imagined the other object? Her trembling increased and she continued to cry.

This was her fault. All her fault. In one act of carelessness she could have killed Traevyn's entire family. She could have taken everything that mattered away from him... For the second time. Her stomach roiled and her legs gave out as the impact of her actions hit her fully.

"Miss? Miss!" The officer knelt and put his hand on her shoulder. "Are you hurt?"

"I'm fine," she whispered. "Please, help them." She couldn't believe that a police officer had gotten to them so quickly. Had he seen the accident? How had he just miraculously shown up? It didn't matter. So long as he got Evie to a hospital.

She trembled quietly in the twilight. Just a few hours ago everything had been perfect. Her life had been beautiful for a second. Now, it was all gone. And she had done it to herself. Just like she always had. Seth had told her to pull over. She should have listened. Even though Evie had said to keep going, she should have pulled over and let Seth drive. He was used to driving in the fog. She wasn't. She'd never driven in fog in her life. Her tears slid unheeded down her cheeks and fell to the ground.

"Miss?"

She looked blankly back up at the officer.

"I'm going to need you to give me your statement. An ambulance is on the way."

"Where did you come from?" she murmured.

He sighed and smoothed his bushy, brown mustache. "I was on duty not far up the highway, doing radar speed checks. I heard the tires squeal and I drove until I found the skid marks. Are you sure you're all right?"

She nodded numbly and forced herself to stand. "I'm fine. You said you needed my statement?"

Traevyn was visibly frantic as he and Talis followed the nurse down the corridor of the hospital. It seemed like the longest corridor ever created. And it was too white. White and sterile and awful. Traevyn all but bulldozed the nurse as they stopped at a room, and he shoved his way inside, paying next to no attention to Talis, who trailed behind him. "Evie!" he cried.

She sat on the edge of a hospital bed, looking much too small and fragile in that moment.

Evie looked up as she heard her husband's voice and she held her arms out to him as he flew over to her. "Traevyn," she murmured. He caught her in his arms and held onto her tightly. She closed her eyes and sighed.

"Evie," he whispered again, her name sounding like it ached to speak it.

Talis held back and watched as his brother shut his eyes and rocked her gently back and forth. The call he'd gotten on his cell phone as he and Talis had been driving home... Talis would never forget the panic, the blind terror he'd heard in Traevyn's voice after he'd received the message. His family was all that mattered to him in the world. His heart was not strong like some. It had been obliterated once before.

If Talis didn't know any better, he would have sworn that he hadn't breathed the entire drive due to the overwhelming fear he had over what would happen to Traevyn if the news at the hospital was less than positive. It had been the longest and most agonizing ride of his life.

"I'm okay," Evie reassured him gently. "I just whacked my head." She pulled back and attempted to ease the terrible worry that was etched into every line of his face. "Luckily, I have a pretty hard noggin. The doctor said I don't even have a concussion." She gave him a wobbly smile.

"The baby—"

"The baby is fine," she said. "And Julia is fine too. She's with Seth. He dislocated his shoulder and is in the room next door."

Traevyn let out a long, relieved breath and suddenly looked very tired. He closed his eyes and bent to rest his forehead against Evie's. "I was so scared," he whispered. "I thought—"

"It doesn't matter," she interrupted, reaching up to tangle her fingers in his hair. "We're all fine."

"Where's Cadence?" Talis interrupted. He was trying to give his brother and sister-in-law the time they needed, but someone else he cared a great deal about had been in the accident too. He knew she was not hurt because she had been the one to call Traevyn, but it made him extremely uneasy to see that she wasn't anywhere around.

And she hadn't called him. She'd called Traevyn, but she hadn't called him. That made his blood run cold.

Evie pulled away from Traevyn and gave Talis an apologetic look. "I don't know where she is, Talis. We were brought to the hospital. She stayed behind to talk to the police and I haven't seen her." She shook her head and looked from Talis back up to Traevyn. "It wasn't her fault. Seth started shouting all these terrible accusations at her after the accident. He was just scared and upset. He didn't know what he was saying. It wasn't her fault. There was a lot of fog and there was a deer in the road. She swerved to avoid the deer and then, out of nowhere, this other car comes barreling at us."

Traevyn frowned. "Other car?"

She gave an emphatic nod. "No one else saw it but me. Seth was too focused on the deer to notice. It looked like it was pulling off of one of those look out spots along the highway and it just came right at us. Probably didn't even see us at first because of the fog. Somehow, even while she was trying not to hit the deer, Cadence saw it. We went into the ditch because she swerved just in time." She looked back to Talis as if trying to drive home the importance of what she was saying. "Maybe we ended up in a ditch, but if she hadn't seen that car, it would have broad-sided us and we'd probably all be dead."

Talis felt his heart sink like a cold, dead weight. He had a terrible feeling about this. "But Cadence doesn't know that it wasn't her fault?"

Evie shook her head. "That jerk of a driver who almost hit us just kept on going and Seth didn't see him. He was so angry and panicked and I was disoriented. I didn't get a chance to tell Cadence that she hadn't imagined it. She thinks that she was careless, that she almost drove us to our death."

Talis felt sick. She would run. He knew it. Deep in his heart, he knew she would run. She hadn't called him. She hadn't trusted him to comfort her, hadn't confided in him. She would be determined to go it alone like she did with everything in her life. She would go back to thinking that she was cursed and nothing but poison to those she cared about. She would abandon him, run out on him again.

He eased himself down into the chair that was across from the bed and heaved a weary sigh. He pulled out his cell phone and dialed her number once, twice, four, five and six times. All he got was her voice mail.

Cadence didn't feel the cold as she walked. The fog was dense and all encompassing and it would have chilled her to the bone normally, but she didn't feel anything. The police officer had driven her back to Traevyn's home after they had finished at the scene of the accident and she had spent a good deal of time just staring up at the painting Traevyn had over his fireplace. The painting of Evie, his wife, his angel... His life...

Traevyn. He had been so very kind to her. He'd let her stay in his home, extended a hand of friendship and welcomed her into his family when Talis said that he didn't like to let anyone in. He had taken a chance on her because Talis cared for her.

And she had repaid him by almost taking away everything that mattered in his world. Because she had been reckless, she had endangered the lives of his wife, his daughter, his unborn son and his brother-in-law, who may as well have been blood related by the bond they shared. She single-handedly had almost destroyed Talis' family. And for what? Because on some crazy, last minute whim she thought she'd seen something out the corner of her eye that could have been a threat? Was she out of her ever-loving mind?

She stuffed her hands deeper into the pockets of her black sweatshirt and felt her tears running hot tracks down her cheeks. She had been an idiot to think that her life could be different. She had condemned herself the moment she had considered that possibility. When she'd been in that arena, after winning the fight with Olaf, and everyone around her had been hugging her and praising her, she'd felt like she deserved it. Like for the first time in her life she was worthy of the praise. She had done something right. She had made a good decision.

She'd told Talis that she wouldn't run from him again. She'd decided to trust that maybe things really could be different, that she could know something beautiful. She'd been so stupid. She'd let her guard down. She'd let herself believe. Only terrible things happened when she let herself believe that she was better than she was. Life had a cruel way of reminding her of where her place in the world truly was.

She knew that she was turning her back on Talis by running from him, and that was why she knew she had to do it. It was the only choice she had, and the only good decision she had ever made. In order to protect him, she had to leave him. She left because she loved him. She would never love another human in the world like she loved Talis, and that was the reason she knew she had to go.

She couldn't stay and taint him. He was too good, too pure and divine and beautiful. She was nothing but mire and rot. She brought destruction wherever she went and he did not deserve that. He shouldn't have to spend the rest of his life looking out for her because she was incapable of doing it herself. He deserved so much more than she could ever give him.

So she walked. Walked along the side of the highway in the fog with only her duffel bag. She'd left him a note so he would know why she'd done what she had. He would be hurt. He would be upset. He would never come after her and she knew that. It was what she intended. Maybe, one day far from now, he would look back and see that it was an act of love and not an act of cowardice... And it killed her inside.

Knowing she was walking out on the only man who had ever stuck with her, taken the time to understand her insanity. He had cared for her when everyone else would have given up. Knowing that she would never again look into those light blue eyes of his, or feel the touch of his sinful lips, or go to sleep listening to the comforting rhythm of his heart. It killed her. What she did was no easy way out. She just hoped he realized that one day.

She frowned as she heard the sound of a car approaching and she turned, sticking her thumb out hopefully. She knew the chance of a driver actually seeing her on the side of the road in fog this bad was slim to none, but she had to try. She couldn't walk alone on the highway forever.

To her surprise, the car passed her, but then slowly backed up. The passenger window rolled down to reveal a middle-aged woman in a freakishly bizarre crocheted hat and glasses that took up most of her face. "Where you headed, honey?" she asked.

"Arizona," she replied, "but I'll go as far as you can take me."

"I can get you to L.A."

She nodded. "That's perfect. Thank you." She could catch

a plane or a bus there and head back to Tawny. She got in the car and closed the door. The slamming of it made a lump of grief rise in her throat and she squeezed her eyes shut.

"You all right?" the woman asked her. "It's dangerous to be walking all alone in fog like this. What happened to you?"

Cadence shook her head, unable and unwilling to speak. The only man she'd ever loved was far behind her and all she wanted to do was feel his arms around her again, but she couldn't go back. She had to move forward. He had done so much for her. He had given her a taste of something beautiful, something perfect. He had given her a fairy tale. This was the least she could do for him.

She leaned her head back against the seat and sighed. She closed her eyes, just hoping the trip went quickly.

Talis stared at the note in his hand, his heart aching in his chest. She really had left him. She was gone... He had no idea where she was, if she was all right, or safe, or anything. He'd called her at least twenty times, but she was avoiding his calls the same way she'd avoided Lance's when he'd first met her. She was gone.

Her note claimed that she'd left because she loved him, but he had a hard time wrapping his mind around that one. If she loved him, she wouldn't have robbed him of his right to make his own decision. It was his choice to make whether or not he wanted to be with her. She claimed she was poison and destroyed everything. Well, it was his choice to make whether he agreed with her or not. *His* choice.

She had never been poison. Reckless? Yes. Careless? Maybe. But she had been making good choices for the last several months. She had been turning her life around. The accident hadn't been her fault, but he couldn't even tell her that because she wouldn't give him the chance.

With a heavy sigh, he picked up his cell phone and stared at it for a long moment. He would call her one last time. If she picked up, he would tell her the accident had not been her fault, that she had actually saved everyone's life by her hasty decision to swerve the car, but if she didn't, he would stop calling her. He would let her go. He had to. If she wasn't willing to let him make up his own mind about her, he wasn't willing to beg her to come back. He was a Whitelaw and, despite how different they all were, the one thing all the Whitelaw men had in abundance was pride. He wouldn't chase after her again. He had told her that. She had known that when she'd gone.

He took a deep breath and dialed her number, everything inside of him screaming to the point of agony in hopes that she would pick up the phone. She didn't. He closed his eyes and slowly pressed the end button, thinking it was sickeningly symbolic. He pulled his knees to his chest and stared blankly ahead at the wall in his bedroom.

He felt empty, like his heart was a desolate chasm. He felt dark. Dark and sullen and cold like his brother. For the first time in his life, he felt completely and utterly alone.

Chapter Twenty-Five

Cadence was at the kitchen table, blindly flipping through a magazine. She wished Tawny would stop staring at her the way she was. Like she was afraid she was gonna slit her wrists or something. It was stupid. She was depressed. So what? She didn't need a babysitter. She just wanted to be left alone.

"Cade?" Tawny called softly as she walked over to her. "What are you doing?"

Cadence looked up at her. "Just looking through this magazine."

"Again? You've read it twice already."

Cadence shrugged, closed it and sat back in the chair, wrapping her arms around herself like she was cold, even though she was anything but in Tawny's stifling house.

"It's a hundred degrees outside," Tawny commented with a frown. "Why are you wearing long sleeves?"

"I like this shirt," Cadence replied. She ran her hand up the sleeve self-consciously. It was an AFI shirt.

Tawny sighed and sat down across from her friend. "It was his, wasn't it?"

Cadence met her eyes for a brief moment, hugged her arms tighter around herself, and looked down.

"Why don't you call him?"

"I can't, Tawny. That would defeat the purpose. I left for a reason."

"But shouldn't you let Talis be the judge of whether or not he wants to be with you?"

She shook her head emphatically. "Not this time."

"But, Cadence, you're miserable."

"I deserve to be miserable!" she snapped. "I almost killed

half of his family, Tawny!" Tears welled up in her eyes. "I deserve to be miserable forever and he needs to be far, far away from me."

Tawny sighed again, and Cadence bristled at the concern reflected in her eyes.

When she had shown up at Tawny's door a week ago, her friend had been surprised and, when she'd told her that she'd hitchhiked half the journey, she'd been outraged and had been ready to fire a lecture off at her. Apparently, the look on Cadence's face had halted the words she would have said, but instead of yelling at her, she'd been giving her that pathetic, worried look ever since.

A knock sounded on the door, and Tawny got up to answer it. Cadence glanced over to try and see who it was, and she blinked in bewilderment. A tall, slender man with shaggy brown hair and a goatee stood on the other side, and Tawny raised her eyebrow.

The man smiled. "Hey, Tawn," he greeted. "I'm amazed I remembered where you lived. Is Cadence with you by chance?"

Tawny frowned and folded her arms, trying to block Cadence's view of the door. "What are you doing here?" she spat.

"I have something important I'm doing here this weekend. I've been trying to track Cadence down, but she must have changed her number or something—"

"Yeah, changed it to get rid of you," Tawny interrupted venomously.

Cadence stood with haste, almost turning the chair over.

The man gave a polite smile despite Tawny's rude remark. "Listen, I just need to ask her something. It's important to me."

Cadence shoved Tawny aside and ignored her protests. She frowned. "Danny? What are you doing here?"

His face lit up when he saw her. "Hey, honey!" he exclaimed. "You look fantastic!"

She smiled, but she knew it came off rather dismal.

"I just took a chance and came here," he explained. "I figured, if you weren't here, Tawny would at least know where I could find you."

"Like I would have told you," Tawny grumbled.

Cadence shot a scathing look over her shoulder at her

friend and opened the door. "Come in," she invited. Tawny muttered something incoherent and left the room, but Cadence welcomed the familiar embrace of her ex-boyfriend. He was something from her world, something she understood, and no matter how messed up it was, she was grateful to have him standing there at that moment. He was a reality she could cope with.

"You look really fantastic, Cadence," he repeated.

She smiled. "Thanks, you look good, too. Nice goatee."

He grinned and stroked it dramatically. "Thank you. It fits in nicely with my new job."

She frowned. "Your what?" She did notice that, even though he was still kind of shaggy-looking, he didn't look nearly as white trash as he had the last time she'd seen him. He wasn't wearing a holey, white wife beater and ripped jeans, and he didn't stink like old onions. Not to mention his teeth were clean, which was really a pleasant surprise. He was dressed in a sort of beatnik style and looked like he would be right at home sitting in a coffee shop, typing on a laptop and drinking a latte.

He grinned. "I got a job, Cadey!" he exclaimed. "Like a real one!"

She giggled in spite of herself at his enthusiasm. It was something she had always loved about him, his zest for life. "You mean no more gas station?"

He grimaced and shook his head. "No, check it out. I started working at this guitar shop last year in Phoenix, right after we broke up. It's a family owned store, but they started doing really well in sales so they decided to open up another one in Tempe. Guess who they asked to be the manager?" He put his hands on his hips and stuck his chest out with pride.

She couldn't hide her shock. "Really?"

"Yeah!" He chuckled. "Surprised?"

She shrugged. "I can't say I'm not, Danny."

"I know, I know. Look, that's one of the reasons I'm here, Cadey. You may think that the two years you spent with me didn't mean that much to me, but they really did. I was a jerk, I was a scab, and you still somehow managed to see some sort of good in me. I leeched off of you and you always saw my potential when no one else did. That's what got me where I am. You got me where I am, Cadence."

She stared at him, fighting the sting of tears. She was so sick of tears. What he had just said... He felt for her the same way she felt about...Talis.

"You are always gonna mean more to me than half the people in this world," he continued. "Which is the main reason I'm here. I need to ask you something..."

Talis could barely handle all of the noise in the RV as Devlyn drove him from the renfaire camp to Traevyn's house. The last place on earth he wanted to be was around a lot of people, but here he was, amidst all of his laughing, shouting friends. It couldn't be helped. His car was out of commission and he had no way of getting to and from the faire grounds. He just wished his friends would have stayed back at the camp instead of coming with him. Devlyn could have driven him by himself. There was no need for everyone else to pile in. He knew they were trying to make him feel better, that they were worried about him, but he really couldn't take being around everyone. He wanted to be alone.

It was bad enough that he had to stay with Traevyn and Evie, who constantly harped on him to call Cadence, or go after her. Traevyn had been surprisingly relentless, saying that Talis had lost his mind and that he was more stubborn than him and Julian put together. Talis wouldn't be swayed. Cadence had chosen to leave. She had robbed him of his decision, had ripped the choice from him and made it on her own. He couldn't keep chasing her. It was exhausting. And he couldn't be with someone who refused to trust him. He couldn't spend his life reassuring her. He did miss her laugh, though. And the way she smelled... And the way her body felt against his...

It was Saturday and they should all be camping at the faire grounds, but Talis had decided to take Sunday off. He didn't really have anything to do and he wanted some time to himself... At least that's what he had planned. Now it looked like he was going to be stuck with the renfaire posse whether he liked it or not.

He sighed as they pulled up to Traevyn's house and he escaped the RV as soon as possible. Maybe if he ran, he could find some dark corner to hide in.

"Talis!"

He groaned aloud. No such luck. Seth was already bounding out the front door. Did he plan on starting in on him already? Talis was beginning to contemplate making a schedule and posting it throughout the house. No lecturing until after six p.m. Then they could all have at him for about an hour. At least then he'd get it all at once and not have to get it from his family while he was home and the guys while he was at the faire.

Raven was probably worse than most everyone else and Talis didn't know how long he could take being made to feel about two feet tall. Couldn't anyone see where he was coming from?

Wearily, Talis turned to face Seth as the other guys began to file out of the RV.

"Dude, your phone has been blaring," he said. "It's driving us all nuts and no one recognizes the number." He held the cell phone out to Talis.

Talis snatched it from Seth and opened it up. He dialed his voicemail and took a few steps away from everyone. At least he could pretend he had a semblance of privacy while he checked his messages.

"Hey, how's he doing?" Seth whispered to Raven.

Raven rolled his eyes. "Terrible. He's miserable, but he won't call her because he's too prideful and too stubborn."

Talis glowered and pretended that he couldn't hear their conversation.

"No kidding. He's being impossible. I think he may actually be worse than Traevyn."

Raven sucked his breath in like he was in pain.

"Yeah," Seth said. "At least Traevyn figured it out eventually that he wanted to be with Evie and he went after it. Talis is just being hard headed."

"Seth?" Evie called. She came out the door, followed by Traevyn and Julia. "We were going to go down to the beach for a picnic. You wanna come? Oh, I didn't know everyone was coming back tonight."

Talis' eyes bulged suddenly and he fumbled with his phone to end his voicemail and dial just about everybody he could think of who might know how to get a hold of Lance. When no one picked up, he whirled to grab Seth by the arm.

He yanked him around to face him. "Did you get Lance's number?" he snapped.

Seth blinked in bewilderment. "Uh...no." He frowned. "I should have, though. How stupid am I?"

Talis gave him a shake. "You know where Van lives, right?"

"Yeah..."

"I need you to take me there, right now."

Seth stared at him in complete confusion. "What? Why?"

"Because I don't have his number either, no one who does is answering their friggin' phone, and I have to get to Arizona! Now!"

"Whoa, whoa, whoa," Seth said, waving his hands in front of him. "Time out. What the crap is going on?"

Talis shoved the phone in Seth's hand and pressed a button. "Listen to that."

Seth raised the phone to his ear with a puzzled frown. The message was loud enough that Talis could hear the whole awful thing over again while Seth listened.

"Hey, Talis... This is Tawny. Cadence's friend, remember? I—well, you gave me your number before and I kind of took it upon myself to call you.... Look, I'm not entirely sure what's going on between you guys, but Cadence really needs you. She's never going to tell you that because she's got it in her head that she's doing you a favor by staying away from you..."

There was a horrible crackle of static that made Seth wince for a moment.

"...Look, Danny showed up. He came looking for Cadence and asked her if she would...." There was a long pause. "...Marry him. She said she would do it. They're going to be down at the Elk's Lodge tomorrow at noon. She wants me to be there so I'm going to be with them, against my better judgment... Anyway, I don't know if this even matters to you, but I just really don't think she's okay. I've never seen her this way. She was doing so well when she was with you. She was happy. I was just hoping... But I'll let you go. I probably sound like a babbling idiot anyway."

Seth stared straight ahead for a moment, then frowned. "Well...she sounded awfully nonchalant about all of that..."

Raven frowned. "What? What's going on?"

Talis snatched his phone back. "Cadence is getting married," he snapped.

Everyone immediately stopped any kind of conversation they were having and all stared at him.

"What?" Evie cried.

"Look, I need to get to Van's! I have to find Lance! Seth, can you please get me there?"

He shook his head as if sense was slowly returning to him. "Uh...yeah. Sure. Get in the car."

"Hold on!" Evie shouted. "I'm going too!" She started for her own car.

"What?" Traevyn cried. "Evie, have you lost your mind?"

She shot a deadly scowl at him. "Don't even, Traevyn. I'm going."

He opened his mouth to protest, but he ended up sighing in defeat and going to the car with her.

"Where are we going?" Julia questioned.

"We're going on a little trip, baby," Evie explained.

"All right everyone, back in the RV!" Raven shouted. "We're going to see a rock star about a bride!"

Talis blinked rapidly for a minute, his mind refusing to compute what was currently happening. "Wait, you guys are coming too?"

Raven turned and looked at him as if he couldn't believe Talis would even ask him that question. "Um...yeah," he stated simply.

"You're all nuts!" Talis cried. "We can't all just pile up to Van's house! We'll all be arrested! It'll be a miracle if we can get through security as it is!"

"That's true," Seth put in. "They have a gate out front and you have to buzz an intercom. Some dude asks you if you know the password and if you don't, you can't come in."

Talis groaned.

"How do you know that?" Raven asked.

Seth gave him an innocent expression.

Talis rolled his eyes. "Okay. Seth, drive. I'll keep trying to call Jerry. He's my tattoo partner. He should have Lance's number. He's a regular client of his."

"We'll just park up the street and wait," Raven suggested. "That way it won't look like an ambush."

Talis waved his hand. It was ridiculous that everyone was going with him. What good was it going to do to have a caravan? If everyone wanted information, he would gladly call them when he knew what was going on. He saw absolutely no point in all of them trekking down to Cambria when they would just have to turn around and go back home again, but whatever. He didn't have time to argue with his friends and family right now. He had to get to Cadence before she messed up her entire life. "Whatever. Come on, Seth. Let's go."

Seth ran to his car and Talis leapt in, his heart hammering against his rib cage with adrenaline and horror. How could she do this to herself? She had told him that Danny had been no good for her. How could she go back with him? How could she just decide to marry him?

He whacked the side of his head against the window a few times, hating himself. Why did he have to be so prideful? Why did he have to be so stubborn? He could have prevented this. He could have gone after her. He could have left her a voicemail saying that the accident hadn't been her fault. Why hadn't he? Because he'd been pissed? Nice.

Well, now she was self destructing and it was all his doing. He was the biggest idiot on the planet. He should have listened to his family and friends. He should have listened to his heart. He'd always lived his life by listening to his heart. Why had he decided to throw all of that out the window just because she'd hurt his pride? He knew Cadence had a hard time trusting. He knew she had no self respect. Why did he think that she would do anything differently than what she had done just because he had been with her for a few months? Did he think that he could change an entire lifetime's worth of thinking patterns just by being around for awhile?

The truth of the matter was, he had abandoned her. He had left her to her own devices because she'd injured his self esteem. What kind of selfish moron did that? He closed his eyes and leaned his head back against the seat as Seth tore down the highway. He felt like the biggest jerk in existence.

Chapter Twenty-Six

Seth pushed the button on the intercom at the wrought iron gate outside of Van's home and waited. Talis was still trying to call Jerry, but no one was picking up. Everyone else was parked in a pod up the street.

"You again," a thick, French accent drawled over the intercom suddenly. "How many times do I have to tell you? You are not welcome here, you leettle stalker! You come here again and I'm going to call zee cops!"

Seth stared at the intercom with an affronted expression. "I am not a stalker!" he insisted. "I am an admirer from afar! Besides, that doesn't matter! I need to talk to Lance Lawson! It's important!"

"Right, like I am zupposed to believe zhat. No passwaerd, no entry. You know zee way it works."

Talis frowned at the intercom voice and looked at Seth. "That guy is *really* French."

Seth nodded. "I totally picture him like the chef in *The Little Mermaid*."

Talis decided he would give it a try and pressed the button. "Excuse me, my name is Talis Whitelaw. Can you tell either Mr. Marshall or Mr. Lawson that I am here? They know me. I'm dating Lance's sister and I did Van's latest tattoo."

"Do you know zee passwaerd?" the French guy repeated, sounding greatly irritated.

Talis sighed. "No, but—"

"No passwaerd, no entry! Au revoir!"

Talis let out a snarl and stabbed Jerry's number into the phone again. "I don't have time for this," he grumbled.

Seth studied the gate. "I wonder..." He closed his eyes, seemed to steel his resolve, and threw his shoulders back.

"All right, Tal," he said. "If Van's wife comes out and kills me, I want my headstone to read that I was an exceptional brother-in-law."

Talis frowned at him. "What are you talking about?"

Seth sucked in a breath like he was preparing for battle. "This is my fault. If I hadn't run my mouth, Cadence wouldn't have run off. I'm taking one for the team, Tal."

Talis stared at him in confusion and his eyes bulged as Seth blew out the breath he'd taken, drew in another one, and launched himself at the gate. "What are you doing?" he shouted.

"While they're beating the crap out of me, you go find Lance!" he shouted back down at him as he pulled himself up and over the gate.

"Seth!" Talis cried. "Are you insane? You're gonna get arrested!" The French guy started to shout something over the intercom about cops right as Talis finally heard Jerry's voice on the other end of the phone. "Hello!" he screamed, his voice hinting at hysteria. "Jerry? Where have you been?"

Seth somehow managed to haul himself over the gate, but lost his grip and fell to the ground on the other side in a heap. He groaned and sat up slowly. "My butt..." he grumbled. "I think I broke it." He blinked as he looked up and saw nothing impeding his progress to the front door. "I'm in," he murmured in awe.

The front door opened and Talis recognized Kat as she came blazing out into the yard. "Wait!" he exclaimed, flailing his arms wildly and holding out his phone. "Don't kill him!" He knew he should be grateful that it was only Kat and not a troop of armed guards, but he knew that Kat was the head of security for the entire band and she could probably inflict more damage than most. They had only a gate man for a reason. Van didn't need any more security when his wife was a lethal weapon.

Kat glanced from Seth to Talis and frowned.

"Please!" Talis cried. "I'm the guy who did Van's tattoo! Talis! Remember? I know Cadence!"

Kat's frown deepened and she looked down at Seth. "And you are?"

"Seth," he stated.

Talis snorted. "That's my idiot brother-in-law," he supplied. "Please don't arrest him. Look, I have Jerry on the phone. Jerry, the tattoo artist who does Lance's tattoos. He has the password. Lance gave him the password."

Kat folded her arms. "The password changes monthly."

Talis sighed. "Well, just give me a minute then and Jerry will give me Lance's number. I'll call him myself. I need to talk to him about his sister!"

"What about my sister?" Lance emerged with Van and Rochelle following behind him.

Talis let out a visible sigh of relief. "Oh thank goodness," he breathed. He hung up on Jerry without bothering to explain and grabbed hold of the bars on the gate, afraid that if he didn't, his legs would give out on him.

Lance looked down at Seth and frowned. "Hey dude, how'd you get in here?"

"He climbed the gate," Kat replied. "Scared the ever-loving crap out of Pierre."

Lance chuckled and extended his hand to help Seth up. "It's okay, I know these guys. Let Talis in, would you?"

Kat pushed a combination of keys on the gate and it opened slowly to admit Talis.

"What's going on?" Lance prodded.

"I need your help," Talis said. "There was this accident last week and Cadence thinks it's her fault. Look, I don't have time to explain, but she ran off and now she's marrying Danny tomorrow at noon."

Lance's eyes widened. "She's what?"

"We need to get to Arizona," Talis stated.

"Take the plane," Van volunteered. He glanced at Seth, who was just staring at him in mesmerized silence. He frowned, looking slightly uncomfortable. "Is he okay?" he questioned.

Talis rolled his eyes. "He's fine."

"We can take you to the airport," Van continued, trying his hardest to ignore the way Seth was looking at him.

"Thank you," Talis murmured. "You have no idea what this means to me."

Van smirked. "You might want to take the sword off though," he commented. "I don't think you're going to get past security with that on."

Talis frowned and looked down, realizing for the first time that he still had his medieval garb on and his sword strapped to his hip. He rolled his eyes and unbuckled his belt.

"I'm going with you," Rochelle stated.

Lance nodded.

"Me too," Kat put in.

Van frowned down at her in question.

"What?" she asked. "Cadence is my friend too."

Van shrugged. "All right, we all go then."

Talis nodded. "Seth, go tell the others that we're going to the airport. Maybe they'll go home now."

"Others?" Lance questioned as Seth tore himself away from Van and went to do as Talis ordered.

"Yeah, I have a posse full of people down the street all waiting to see what's going to happen. It's ridiculous."

"Not ridiculous," Kat countered with a smirk. "That's sweet. Cadence must have a lot of people who care about her."

Talis sighed. Except she didn't know that. She thought that she didn't matter to anyone. His heart seized in his chest and he looked down. When he got to Cadence he would make sure that she never left him again. She mattered so much to so many. She mattered so much to him. He loved her. He loved her in a way that made him ache inside.

"They all insist on following us to the airport," Seth replied as he came jaunting back.

Talis frowned. "What? Why?"

"I don't know," he said with a helpless shrug.

Talis shook his head and waved his arms in frustration. "You know what? Whatever. I don't have time to try and figure it out. Let's go."

Van nodded. "Let me get the keys and we'll head out."

Talis couldn't take the waiting. They were all in the airport, where they had been for the last four hours. It was ten o'clock at night and all Talis could do was watch the time tick away. One more hour that brought him closer and closer to failure. They had been stuck there because of the fog. All of the planes were grounded and everybody was spread out in the airport lobby, waiting. He didn't know why everyone was still there. There was nothing they could do, but it was too foggy to go back home now anyway.

Rochelle, Lance and Kat were all talking to Seth, who had practically attached himself to them. Van was off talking to one of the airport officials to see if they could tell him when the planes would be cleared for takeoff. Julia slept in Raven's lap while he read a book and Evie was dozing against Traevyn's shoulder. All the rest of the guys were playing card games on the floor.

Talis was restless and he kept pacing. He knew it was doing no good, but the more he sat still, the worse he felt. He just kept going over and over in his mind everything he had done wrong. He hated himself for abandoning Cadence. He hated himself for being too stubborn when everyone around him had told him he was acting stupid. He was going to lose her. She was going to marry that bum of an ex-boyfriend because she thought it was what she deserved. He was going to lose her, the one woman he had ever loved, and he had no one to blame but himself. It made him feel sick inside.

He loved Cadence. He really and truly did. And he'd never really had a chance to tell her how much because he thought he had all the time in the world. He'd blown it. He'd blown his only chance with the only girl who'd ever made him feel the way Cadence did. He was a supreme idiot.

"I have bad news," Van announced suddenly.

Talis spun to face him.

Van sighed. "It doesn't look like anyone's going anywhere for the rest of the night."

Talis let out a frustrated, pain-laden roar that made everyone jump and startled Evie awake. It was torn from the very depths of his soul and he tangled his fingers in his hair, feeling like his entire world was crashing down around him. "This is my fault!" he shouted. "I'm going to lose her!"

Traevyn stared at him for a moment with a look of shock on his face. Talis had never lost control in front of his brothers. Not once. He was always calm and reasonable. He always had it together.

Traevyn propelled himself out of his chair and across the room. "Talis." He took him forcefully by the shoulders.

Talis gasped for breath, the horrendous torrent of emotion too much for him to handle. He shook his head. "I'm going to lose her, Traevyn!"

Traevyn shook his head. "No, you're not. Listen to me."

"This is all my fault!"

"Talis!" He gave him a shake. "Listen to me! You're not going to lose her! I'll drive you. I'll drive you myself. I'll get you there. I promise."

"Dude, that's like a ten hour drive," Seth remarked.

"Then we'd better leave now," Traevyn said. "I'll drive through the night."

"I'm going with you," Seth declared. "This entire thing is my fault. I have to apologize to her."

"I'm going too," Evie stated.

Traevyn turned to her. "Evie, darling, I don't think—"

"Just try and stop me, Traevyn. I dare you." She stared him down in a way that let everyone in the room know she meant her words.

"Hey, don't mess with the pregnant lady," Seth said.

Traevyn sighed. "Fine."

"We're going too," Lance said, indicating him and Rochelle. "She's my sister."

"So are we," Kat put in. "Cadence is as much of a sister to Van and me as she is to Lance. She's one of the best people on our crew. She needs to know that we care."

Traevyn blinked in bewilderment.

"And don't even think about leaving us behind," Raven said. "Cadence is one of us. Warriors don't abandon one another."

Traevyn frowned. "That's fine, but...you're not all going to fit in my car."

"We'll follow in Van's car," Lance said.

Raven nodded. "And we have the RV."

"That thing goes like two miles an hour," Talis remarked dismally.

"So we'll get there after you! At least we'll be there! Cadence doesn't think that anyone cares about her! She thinks she's worthless and doesn't matter! She needs to see that we all care about what she does with her life! She needs to see that we're all there for her! We're a band of brothers, Talis. We always have been. Cadence knocked a six-foot-four, massive guy down to the ground for me! She's the kind of friend most people spend their lives wishing they could find. I am not going to turn my back on her right now!"

"None of us are," Draco added. "We all love her. We all go."

Talis stared in shocked awe at everyone for a moment,

unable to believe how much Cadence had affected everyone around her. She thought of herself as nothing, as poison, but all of these people were willing to risk their lives and drive through the fog in the middle of the night just to prevent her from making the biggest mistake of her life, just to get Talis to her in time. It warmed his heart to know that the both of them had such amazing and loyal friends. It was something to be cherished.

He gave a decisive nod. "Right, let's go."

Chapter Twenty-Seven

"I can't believe this," Talis groaned as he stared at the long line of bumper to bumper traffic clogging up Highway 60 through Globe. "You've got to be kidding me!" He raked his fingers angrily through his hair and glanced over at Traevyn, who had pretty much been living off of coffee and pure adrenaline all night long.

Miraculously, the RV had managed to keep up and was pretty close behind them, but now they were stuck in a traffic jam that had them at a complete standstill. It was eleven-thirty and Talis' heart hammered relentlessly. He was running out of time! In a half an hour Cadence was going to ruin her entire life! His brother had not driven him through the desert all night long with his pregnant wife in the back seat just to have him fail!

He growled miserably and put his head in his hand. Unfortunately, there was no way around this one. They were stuck and didn't look like they would be going anywhere for awhile.

"It looks like there must have been a pretty big accident," Traevyn commented as he inched up gradually. "I see police cars all over the place."

"Dude!" Seth exclaimed suddenly.

Talis jumped at the shrillness in his voice and he frowned.

Seth let out a hearty laugh. "Oh my gosh! Check it out! That's the best thing I have ever seen!" He jabbed his finger toward the parking lot of the Wal-Mart they were driving past.

Talis squinted at where Seth pointed and raised an eyebrow as he spotted a tan horse, all decked out in saddle, bags, and the whole nine yards, tethered to the handicapped parking space sign and standing placidly between the lines.

Seth laughed again. "What kind of town is this? Hicksville, USA?"

Evie smiled and sat back from where she had been craning her neck to look. "That's definitely something you don't see every day."

"'Hey Earl, that's a nice vehicle you got there,'" Seth mocked, adopting a very Western accent. "'How much horse power's that thing got?' 'I dunno, JimmyBob. Only about one.'" Seth dissolved into laughter, cracking himself up with his own joke.

Talis smirked in spite of himself, unable to remain straight faced. It was an interesting thing to see. He sighed. Well...the person who owned that horse had the right idea. At least they wouldn't be stuck in traffic...

His eyes widened and he sat up straight in his seat. "That's it," he muttered. He opened up the car door.

"What are you doing?" Traevyn shouted.

"I'm going to get my girl!" Talis cried. "Seth, call Ash! He'll tell Traevyn how to get to the Elk's Lodge!" He slammed the door and started to sprint to the Wal-Mart parking lot.

Seth sat back in his seat and frowned thoughtfully. "How many laws have we broken in the last twenty-four hours, do you think?" he asked.

"Well," Evie said, "you broke into Van's house, trespassed on private property..."

Seth started to count on his fingers. "I'm pretty sure Traevyn broke the land/speed record in getting us here on time and now Talis is stealing a horse."

"And I think Devlyn ran a few red lights in that RV trying to keep up with us," Evie added.

Seth looked down at his hand and nodded.

"Talis strapped his sword back on," Traevyn said. "Does that count as a concealed weapon?"

Seth frowned and looked at Evie. "I don't know. What do you think?"

She shrugged.

"Hm... Well, we'll say five point five then."

Traevyn nodded, completely over any ability to be surprised. He was tired, starving, and was pretty much convinced that his brother had lost his mind. Nothing fazed him at this point.

"Not bad," Seth remarked.

Evie looked down at Julia. "Don't ever do any of this, sweetheart," she ordered.

Julia just giggled.

Cadence sighed and absently fumbled with the bouquet in her hands. The minister was droning on endlessly and she just wished he would get it over with. The dress she had on was hot and she was tired. She just wanted to get the ceremony done with so she could put all of this insanity behind her and get on with some semblance of a normal life.

In the back of her mind she wondered if she would ever really know what a "normal" life was. It seemed to be a word that wasn't in her vocabulary.

"Do you, Daniel Sutter, take this woman to be your lawfully wedded wife?"

She sighed. Oh thank goodness. The minister had finally gotten around to asking the vows. She glanced up at Danny, who grinned broadly, and she smiled. She'd never seen him look so happy...

Cadence, as well as everyone else in the room, jumped as the doors burst open with a tremendous crash, and the echo of booted feet could be heard rapidly coming through the corridor. Cadence turned toward the approaching sound and her eyes bulged. She swore her jaw actually hit the floor as she watched Talis, dressed in all his medieval finery, stride purposefully through the room. The look on his face was grim, dark and determined, and her heart stuttered like a faltering engine.

He pulled his sword clear of its sheath in one fluid movement and pointed it directly at Danny's throat without even breaking his stride. Everyone screamed and Danny jumped back in horror, holding his hands up in the air.

"Talis!" Cadence shouted. "Oh my gosh! What are you doing?"

"Cadence," he said calmly, never taking his eyes off of Danny, "you cannot marry this man."

She blinked rapidly and frowned. "Talis!" she spat, anger

replacing her utter shock. "Grow a brain for a second and look around! Does it look like I'm getting married to you?"

Her words startled Talis out of his tunnel vision and he glanced around him. Cadence was standing next to a woman in white... Wait, that wasn't right. There was a woman standing in white next to the guy he was pointing the sword at and Cadence was standing next to her...wearing blue? He frowned.

"Talis!" Cadence barked. "Put down the friggin' sword! Are you out of your mind?"

He lowered it a bit, but not completely. "I thought Danny was getting married," he rasped. He suddenly felt really cold and really hot all at the same time and had no idea what that meant. He was pretty sure it was the red haze of humiliation gradually taking over his cold, determined focus.

"Danny *is* getting married!" she cried. She pointed to the terrified woman standing next to her. "To Olivia!"

Talis blinked. "...Olivia?" His throat went very dry.

"Put down the sword!" she demanded again.

He jumped and quickly sheathed his weapon. He looked up at Danny, who was shaking and had a fine sheen of sweat decorating his forehead. Olivia's bottom lip quivered and she had huge tears in her eyes. "I—I am so sorry," he whispered. He felt like his mind was turning slowly, as if it was refusing to process any of this new information. "Tawny said—" He pointed in no particular direction, trying to convey what his thoughts were. "Tawny said—"

"Tawny said what, Talis?" Cadence prodded. She looked irritated and outraged and appalled. He couldn't blame her, really. She was probably embarrassed beyond all belief.

"Tawny said that you were marrying Danny."

"No, I didn't!" Tawny protested, standing up.

Talis scowled and yanked his cell phone out of his pocket. "Look, I'll prove it!" He felt like a complete imbecile. He had just crashed some stranger's wedding and held a sword at the groom's throat. He would be lucky if he didn't end up in jail. He sure as heck wasn't going to go down looking like an idiot. Tawny had said that Cadence was getting married and he was going to show everybody!

He called his voicemail, and when Tawny's message came on, he put it on speaker phone so everyone could hear.

Cadence felt her face flame at Tawny's words. She felt

betrayed knowing that Tawny had called Talis behind her back. She'd had no right to do that! Why didn't anyone ever let her make her own decisions? She'd had a good reason for leaving Talis! It was not Tawny's right to interfere!

She frowned as she heard the part of the message where Tawny seemingly said that Cadence had agreed to marry Danny, and she turned a confused expression to her friend.

Talis snapped his phone shut with satisfaction. "See?" he said. "I'm not insane."

A few of the guests started to chuckle amongst themselves.

"Talis..." Tawny closed her eyes and heaved a sigh. "Oh my gosh, this is horrible." She passed her hands over her face for a minute. "There was a really bad storm when I called you. The phone must have cut out. What I really said was, 'Danny asked Cadence if she would be a bridesmaid in his wedding. I guess he found some girl who actually wants to marry him...'" She held her hands out helplessly.

Talis stared. It seemed to be all he could bring himself to do. He suddenly felt very, very tired. He shook his head. "Y—You're not getting married?" he asked Cadence.

She shook her head emphatically, darting her gaze around at all the eyes that were on them. "No, I'm not."

He pointed to Danny. "But he is?"

"Yeah."

"To Olivia?" He pointed to the woman in white.

Cadence wished someone would just come in and shoot her. "Yes."

Talis rubbed his hand over his face and groaned. "I stole a horse!" he exclaimed.

She raised an eyebrow. "You stole a horse?"

He shook his head and turned back to Danny and Olivia. "I am so sorry," he apologized as he slowly backed his way down the aisle. "Please, continue." He looked at Cadence. "Our stuff can wait."

She raised both her eyebrows. "Can it? Great. Sit down." She turned her back on him and squeezed her eyes shut, wishing that she could just disappear. That had to have been the worst, most humiliating moment of her—

"Stop the wedding!"

She flinched. Scratch that.

Seth flew into the room and came to a screeching halt as

Talis stood from where he'd sat down and started waving his hands frantically to signal "no."

Seth recoiled as he looked around the room, and held his hands up. "Oh, my bad," he said. "My bad." He turned just in time to catch Traevyn and Evie and motioned them to sit down.

Cadence's chest constricted. She wondered what having a heart attack felt like. Could abject humiliation and horror bring on a heart attack? She looked up at Danny and shook her head. "Danny, I'm so sorry," she grumbled.

As if she hadn't suffered enough, she heard the sound of more thundering footsteps and she groaned. Had he brought the entire friggin' army with him? She turned slowly just to see her brother, Rochelle, Van, his wife, and all of the ren-faire guys bottlenecking at the door as they all bumped into one another trying to stop. Seth waved them down, trying to tell them to sit, and Cadence sighed. "Anyone else coming?" she asked miserably.

"Van Marshall...at my wedding," Danny murmured. "Dang..."

"Uh...we're the last," Ash said with a nervous laugh. "Just...uh...carry on."

She turned her back on them stiffly and gave a tremulous smile to Danny and Olivia. The minister was visibly shaken and his voice trembled as he rushed through the last part of the ceremony. Actually, everyone was visibly shaken. The bride, the groom, all the guests... Cadence really felt like she was living a nightmare that wouldn't end.

As she followed the wedding party out of the room, she flung her bouquet down and sat down on a small step outside. She glanced off to her right as she spotted a tan horse swishing his tail in boredom. She frowned.

Danny came up and touched her shoulder, making her look up at him and groan. "I am so sorry."

He smiled and knelt down next to her. "Cadey," he said softly, "what's going on with you? What in the world was all of that about? Because it looks to me like you've got a guy who really doesn't want you getting married and a whole passel of other people who share his sentiments."

She let out a ragged, frustrated breath and stabbed her fingers through her hair. "I told him to leave me alone!" she cried. Sudden, unwelcome tears flooded her eyes and she looked down, unable to stop them. "I told them all to leave me alone. I don't deserve to be around them! All I bring is destruction and mayhem! Look what I did to your wedding!"

He chuckled and rubbed her shoulders. "Cadence, listen to me. I don't know if my opinion means anything to you at all, but you've always been completely full of crap when it came to that statement."

She frowned and looked up at him.

He smiled and wiped at her tears. "Destruction and mayhem don't follow you anymore than it follows anyone else. Maybe you have a few out of the ordinary things happen to you, but that just means your life is interesting. You're not cursed. You just think you are because you were made to feel worthless your whole life."

She shook her head. "You don't understand. I've done bad things—"

He laughed. "I don't understand?" he cried. "Look who you're talking to, Cadence! I was much worse off than you were! Have you forgotten who you spent two years of your life with?"

Her lip trembled, but she said nothing.

He sighed. "The past defines us, but it's the future that makes us what we are. Every day we are given chances to make choices. Some of the choices we make are good, some of them are bad, but you know what the beautiful thing about it is?" He tucked a strand of hair behind her ear. "Every day that passes gives us a new opportunity to start over. The present becomes your past so that you can have a future. Make sense?"

She gave him a quizzical frown, but strangely, she understood him. For a moment, she wondered when the scraggly, deadbeat guy she had been with had become so wise. Maybe it was true that people could change. Maybe this whole time she hadn't been running from her "curse." She'd been running from herself because all she knew how to be was one way. It was easy to run, easy to cut people out of her life under the guise of protecting them. It was easier than letting them in and taking the chance of being disappointed, or being abandoned, or being hurt.

"Stop living in your past, Cadey," he murmured. "You're not that beat down little girl anymore. Your mom isn't around the corner waiting to hurl insults your direction just because she can. You're strong now. Strong and independent."

"I'm a warrior," she whispered. She closed her eyes and thought of Raven and how she'd beat Olaf. The smallest of smiles touched her lips as she remembered how everyone had stood by her.

"You always have been," Danny assured. "Now go inside and, for crying out loud, listen to whatever it is that guy has to say. Because, I don't know about you, but if I'd just pulled a sword on someone only to find out that the entire situation had been a misunderstanding, I'd be feeling kinda ill." She laughed, which made him grin. "I think he deserves to at least be listened to."

She nodded and stood, embracing her longtime friend. She was so grateful to have him there at that moment, grateful to see that they could both move past the worst part of their lives and start over. Danny gave her hope; he made her see. He made her see when no one else could because he had lived the same life she had... And he had come out okay. He had found Olivia, who loved him. It made her realize that she could be okay, too. She really could be. She took a deep breath and prepared herself, then pushed open the door and went back inside.

Chapter Twenty-Eight

Cadence couldn't believe how many people were actually there as she made her way back into the building. Van and Kat, of all people... And all of the renfaire guys were still in their fricking garb. But what caught her attention was Talis. He was sitting forward in a chair with his elbows braced on his knees. His fingers were tangled in his mass of black hair and he stared down at the ground.

Her heart went out to him and all she wanted to do was go to him and hold him, but she held back. Mainly because Traevyn was making his way toward her and she couldn't bear to look up into his penetrating green eyes. The night of the accident came flooding back to her in vivid clarity and it was made ten times worse as she heard Julia let out a loud peal of laughter at something Raven had said to her.

Tears burned her eyes and she retreated. She shouldn't be there. Good lord, she should be far away from all of these people.

"Cadence."

Traevyn's voice was soft, not harsh and accusatory like it should have been. She turned, not able to look up at him. She had almost squelched that carefree laughter. She had almost taken everything from him and she did not deserve his soft voice. Not by a long shot.

"Cadence." He was firmer this time, reaching out and taking her shoulders to stop her from running away. "You stubborn, cowardly woman. Stay put and listen to what I have to say."

She bristled at him calling her a coward, but she stiffly obeyed his command. She deserved whatever he was going to fling at her. She could take it.

"It wasn't your fault," he stated.

She blinked. Okay, she could take anything but that. Her tears overflowed and spilled down her cheeks. "Of course it was my fault!" she cried. "I drove your family into a ditch!"

He shook his head emphatically and lifted her chin, forcing her to look at him. "No, you don't understand. There was another car, Cadence."

She blinked in bewilderment and frowned. "What?"

"I didn't see it," Seth said as he ran over to them. "Evie did. I guess there really was another car. It shot out and almost hit us. You didn't imagine it." He shook his head. "I was such a jerk, Cadence. I'm so sorry."

She stared at Seth and then looked back up at Traevyn with a puzzled expression.

He nodded at her. "Evie told me that if you hadn't swerved and gone into that ditch, you would have been broad-sided and probably all would have been killed. Cadence, your good decision saved my entire family."

She continued to stare at him as the words sunk in. Good decision…. She had made a *good* decision? Her actions had *saved* Traevyn's family? That thing she had seen flash out of the corner of her eye hadn't been a hallucination after all?

Seth sighed. "I'm so sorry, Cadence. This was all my fault."

She shook her head and forced a smile, even though her mind was reeling from the sudden realization that she hadn't done something unforgivable after all. "No, Seth. You were upset. It's okay. I'm not mad at you."

He winced. "Sorry I totally barged in on your friend's wedding also."

She laughed. "Well, you weren't the first and you weren't the last so don't feel too badly."

Traevyn smiled. "Yes…speaking of which…" He cleared his throat and pointed to Talis. "I think someone here would probably like to see you."

She looked at Talis and sighed, then glanced back up at Traevyn, noticing for the first time that his usually immaculate black hair was pulled back into a disheveled pony tail and he had a good deal of black stubble peppering his defined jaw, not to mention dark circles under his eyes. She frowned. "You look terrible," she commented.

He rolled his eyes. "Yes, well. You try driving all night

long across two states and see how fantastic you look in the morning," he grumbled.

She smiled and forced herself to walk over to Talis. He still sat with his head down, and she took a seat next to him. Everything inside of her screamed to take him in her arms, hold him close, tell him she was sorry for being so stupid, but she couldn't. She didn't know how. She didn't know what he'd do. So she sat, and she sighed. "You really know how to make an entrance, Talis Whitelaw," she finally said with a small smile.

He slowly raised his head so that he could look at her. "You know something?" he mumbled. "At the beginning of the season, Ash was griping at me because he was forced to be the bad guy at the joust for the Arizona Renaissance Festival. He was being a baby because he said I always got to be the paladin and then Tempyst said that I couldn't help it because I *was* a paladin knight, or something like that." He met her eyes and narrowed his slightly. "Do you know what paladin means, Cadence? It means 'a paragon of chivalry, a knightly and heroic champion.'" He scowled. "I botched that one royally, didn't I?"

She gave him a sympathetic expression, even though she was trying not to giggle. "Well...you did come to rescue me."

He snorted. "Yeah, but instead of coming for you on the back of a noble, white steed I rode for ten hours in my brother's car with his pregnant wife in the back seat and Seth blasting metal music the entire way and belching. Not to mention, I was being followed by another carload full of rock stars and a rickety RV that I'm surprised even made it over the mountains without blowing up. Then, of course, when I finally did manage to find some sort of steed, I had to steal it, and it wound up being an old, tan mare." He rolled his eyes. "Oh yeah, and we can't forget the part where I crashed some poor guy's Twenty-first Century wedding by pulling a sword on him and humiliating myself right into the ground." He groaned. "That is so not how it goes in the movies."

She raised an eyebrow. "Not an epic romance, maybe... But it would work pretty well for a romantic comedy... Maybe one of those ones with Hugh Grant. We could get him to play you."

He scowled at her, clearly not amused.

She bit her bottom lip to keep from grinning. "Oh, come on, Talis. It kind of fits. I did, after all, meet you in a bathroom stall."

He retained his scowl. "No, you met me at a Bleeding Passion concert where I saved your butt and you promptly dissed me. If I'd had any idea that, for the next several months we would continue that pattern, I might have thought twice before pulling that fast one on you in the bathroom. I should have just let Lance have you. Maybe he would have beat some sense into you and I would have been saved one trip to the mental hospital."

She gave a soft sigh, preparing to speak, but he cut her off.

"Why did you run out on me, Cadence?" he blurted. "Why?"

She met his eyes. "Because I was scared," she replied sincerely. "I was scared of hurting you. I thought that I'd almost single-handedly killed your family and all I could hear was you telling me that Evie had pretty much saved your brother's life and that his family was all that mattered to him in the world. Traevyn had been so nice and welcoming to me and I couldn't deal with thinking that I had hurt them. All I could think of were all the horrible choices I've made in my life and how much I've hurt people I cared about. I didn't want to put you through that."

"But you did hurt me, Cadence!" he cried. "Don't you understand that?"

She glanced around the room and noticed that everyone had migrated to the far side in an attempt to give the two of them their privacy. "Talis, I was so afraid of being with you. Even though being with you was wonderful, I was terrified. I've been on my own my whole life. You blew into my life and took over. You re-routed my thinking and the way I live and managed to crawl right inside me without me even noticing. That's scary! You obliterated my world and everything I thought I knew about life and none of that really made sense to me until about two seconds ago when Danny told me that the present becomes the past so that we can have a future."

Talis frowned in confusion.

She waved it away. "Don't worry about it. Basically, I have a chance to make new choices, to make a better life for myself. I see that. I understand that now. It's what you've been trying to teach me all along, but I needed to hear it from him. I needed to have my bum of an ex-boyfriend stand before me on his wedding day, knowing that he had taken his sad excuse for a life and turned it around, and tell me that I could do the same. I could be better. I needed the proof, Talis. You couldn't give me that and that's why, no matter how hard you tried, I always ended up doubting myself. I needed to see it and hear it and know it from someone who has walked the same path as me, who came from my world."

He shook his head. "I would have spent my entire life reassuring you, Cadence, but you ripped that choice from me."

"It wasn't your choice to make, Talis. You can't fix me. Only I can fix me!"

"You ran out on me! You didn't even give me an option!" he cried, his voice full of pain and frustration.

"And you hunted me down!" she fired back. "You hunted me down when you swore you'd never come after me again! Why? Why did you do that?"

"Because I love you!" he shouted. The admission was ripped from his lips and his angry posture toward her seemed to dissolve. His shoulders slumped and he sighed, looking completely exhausted and unwilling to argue any more. "I love you, you stubborn, irritating, infuriating woman. You're the only woman I've ever wanted. I can't even take a full breath when you're not with me, and I'm sullen and brooding like my brother. I hate you for that."

She grinned and reached for his hand, needing to feel the solidness of him, needing to know he was really there with her. She had missed him so much, ached for him. Having him there was surprising, but the shock was wearing off. Now all she wanted was to feel his touch. "I wore your AFI shirt for a solid week and kept flipping through the same tattoo magazine just so I could pretend that you had done them all. Tawny started to fear for my sanity."

"Obviously. She called me, remember?"

Cadence rolled her eyes. "Yes, and between you and Ash, I believe she's done enough damage to merit me forbidding any lectures from her for the next year."

He glanced up at her and frowned. "You stole my shirt?"

She bit her bottom lip shyly. "Yeah."

"You run out on me and have the audacity to take my favorite shirt with you?"

She shrugged, liking that, even though his fierce scowl was still fixed on her, his banter was playful.

He shook his head and let out a ragged, weary sigh. "You're a piece of work, Cadence Lawson." he muttered.

"Don't I know it." She glanced down at their hands because she felt Talis begin to absently play with her fingers. She smiled and her heart skipped a beat. She closed her eyes and relished the simple touch for a moment, not realizing just how much she had come to crave the man in front of her.

She studied his profile and felt everything inside of her melt. He looked sad and confused, and she hated that she had caused that. He was being slightly playful and he was touching her with gentleness, but she knew the playfulness was just in his nature, and he touched her almost subconsciously, as if his hands were moving all on their own. His mind was in a different place and she couldn't stand to see him looking so lost. "Talis," she whispered.

He glanced up at her, exhaustion and fatigue etched into every line of his face.

"I'm sorry."

Her tone was soft and sincere, but he shook his head wearily. "I hear those words a lot from you, Cadence." He huffed. "My heart isn't a toy. You can't just take it out and play with it whenever you want and then throw it aside when you feel like it."

His words were like a slap in the face and she winced and averted her eyes. It was true. She'd spent the entire time she'd been with him insulting him, running out on him, doing stupid crap and then apologizing and swearing she wouldn't do it again only to turn around and do just that. Her issues had caused Talis pain and, through it all, he had been patient and forgiving, gently trying to reassure her and correct her wayward line of thinking. She'd repaid him by abandoning him. It was like betrayal, like repaying someone for their kindness by kicking them and walking away. She should be ashamed of herself.

She glanced at Talis as she contemplated what to say to him. Her first instinct was to get up and walk away, but she was through with running. Walking away from a difficult situation didn't solve anything. People just came after you with swords if you did.

She smirked to herself at the memory of Talis striding boldly through the room, sword drawn, looking like he'd stepped right out of a different time to come and rescue his lady. She would never forget that as long as she lived.

She tugged on his hand to get his attention and he looked up at her. She frowned in thought and chewed on her bottom lip. "You're right, Talis," she murmured. "I haven't really been all that great to you. I've been rude, selfish and pretty much insane. You should have just left me alone, but you didn't... Why?"

He shook his head. "Because you're the one, Cadence," he answered simply. "It's always been you. From the moment I saw you."

Time stopped for her in that moment. Time, her heart, and everything else that moved. Tears pooled in her eyes, but she blinked them away and shook her head, trying to look flip and indifferent. "You're silly, Talis," she said in a choked voice. She smirked. "Just a silly, medieval tattoo artist."

He arched an eyebrow and was silent for a long moment before he turned in his chair so he could face her completely. "You're right," he said. "That's all I am and all I'll ever be. A silly, medieval tattoo artist who happens to love a rude, stubborn and insane roadie/warrior/dancer who's going to be the death of me." He reached up and took her face in his hands, shaking her a little as if to drive home his point. "The death of me."

She grinned and met his eyes. "You were the death of me too, Talis. You and Raven and Traevyn, and all the others."

His smile was soft. "Do you see how many people are here right now? All of these people refused to let me come without them. Van and Kat said you were like a sister to them and one of the best members of their crew. Raven and the rest of the guys said that you were part of our band of brothers and that warriors didn't abandon each other. Since I met you, you've always acted like no one cared about you, like you were dispensable. Look how many people are here, Cadence. Look how many lives you've touched."

She couldn't stop the tears this time. They squeezed out of her eyes and cascaded down her cheeks.

"You didn't just abandon me," he continued. "You abandoned all of them too."

"I don't want to run anymore," she murmured. "I'm tired of running. I don't want to be alone anymore. I thought I was protecting all of you, but I realize that I only caused more pain. I should have stayed. I should have talked to you and Traevyn. I turned my back on everyone because I'm a coward." She shook her head. "I'm tired of being afraid, Talis. I'm tired of running away. All of you, you're the only family I've ever really known. I don't want to blow that." She looked up into his gorgeous eyes and sighed. "I don't want to lose any of you, but I especially don't want to lose you. You're the only one who's ever stuck by me, Talis, through all my insanity. It was torture being away from you. I've been such an idiot." More tears escaped her eyes and she couldn't help but notice the tender way he wiped at them.

Even when he was irritated at her and hurt because of her stupid actions, he stopped to take care of her. He was more than she deserved, more than she'd ever thought she would find. She couldn't believe she'd almost let him go. Thinking about it now, what she had done seemed immensely ridiculous, but then again, her hindsight had always been exceptionally good. "I love you, Talis," she whispered. "I'm so sorry."

He pulled her out of the chair and onto his lap, drawing her close to him. "You're going to make it up to me," he whispered over her lips.

She closed her eyes and shivered. She nodded. "I promise."

His arms tightened around her and he brought his mouth a mere inch from hers. "You're going to make it up to me over," —he kissed her very lightly, more a tease than anything else— "and over," —he did it again— "and over."

She shifted so the she could wrap her arms around his neck. "I'm going to spend my life making it up to you," she vowed. "I'm going to show you that I'll never run from you again. In fact, you're going to have a very difficult time getting rid of me."

He arched one eyebrow arrogantly. "That is, if I decide to take you back."

Her heart trembled at his words, even though she knew he was playing with her. The thought of not having Talis in her life was the most unbearable thing she'd ever considered. How she'd ever managed to leave him was beyond her. She shook her head. "I really am an amazing idiot."

His lips split into a stunning grin and his arms tightened around her. "Hmmm...I suppose that merits me giving you one more chance." He frowned. "One, mind you. I won't give you anymore. I refuse to chase after you again. I mean it this time."

She rolled her eyes. "Shut up, Talis." She brought her lips down on his with force and he groaned. He reached his hands up to tangle in her hair and her entire body lit on fire as she felt his tongue thrust into her mouth possessively. Her fingers bunched the front of his tunic and she kissed him back with an equal amount of passion. His lips... Good lord, how had she ever thought she could live without those lips?

"I'm not going to be able to carry you off into the sunset," he whispered as he trailed hot kisses along the line of her jaw and down her neck.

She shook her head. "That's okay," she replied breathlessly. "I'll take the rickety RV. I don't mind. You might want to return that horse, however, before you get arrested." She gasped as she felt his teeth nip her skin.

"I need to let my brother rest somewhere before we head back," he murmured, working his way around to her throat and across her collarbone.

She nodded, her mind struggling to stay on the conversation. "He looks like death."

"Hey, come on, you guys!" Seth's voice interrupted.

Talis raised his head from Cadence's throat and he glared at him over her shoulder.

"There are still people in the room," he continued. "Like, a lot of them."

Cadence glanced over at everyone and laughed at how awkward they all looked. Traevyn was scowling and covering Julia's eyes with his hand and Ash was leaning against the wall, whistling. She heard Talis chuckle also and she looked back at him. His eyes met hers and they were a warm, liquid blue that she adored. She smiled. "I love you, Talis."

He sighed and reached up to smooth her hair. "Try not to forget that, okay? I really don't want to have to do this again. It was embarrassing."

She giggled and nodded.

A sudden shout from Evie drew everyone's attention and Talis frowned as she put her hand over her stomach.

Her eyes widened and she looked up at Traevyn. "We need to find a hospital," she stated. "Now."

He blinked and his eyes bulged as realization dawned on him. "Now?" he rasped.

She nodded vigorously. "Now!"

There was a moment of complete, stunned shock, and then everyone exploded into activity. Cadence jumped off of Talis' lap and ran to Tawny. "Take Evie and Traevyn to the hospital," she commanded. "We'll be right behind you!"

Tawny hustled Evie and Traevyn out the door and Seth ran behind them, toting Julia like a sack of potatoes. Everyone else started to talk at once, trying to figure out what to do. Talis grabbed Cadence's hand and ran to Traevyn's car. Everyone else took their cue from him, and soon they were all peeling out of the parking lot and caravanning to the hospital.

Talis and Cadence entered right as they were putting Evie in a wheelchair and taking her to a room. She was glowering furiously and trying to breathe her way through a contraction. "I can't believe I'm doing this again," she bit out. "I hate you, Traevyn Whitelaw," she snarled. "I really, really do."

They started to wheel her down the hall and Traevyn ran a hand through his hair wearily. He looked back over his shoulder and gave Talis a pained expression before he followed after Evie.

Talis and Cadence exchanged glances, and both erupted into laughter.

"My poor brother," Talis chuckled.

Cadence grinned as she went into Talis' arms. She closed her eyes and snuggled against him, knowing that his arms would always be her haven and always be her home. It was the only place she ever wanted to be.

Cadence groaned and yawned as she and the rest of the posse trooped into Tawny's house. It was late at night and they were all far beyond exhausted.

Tawny flicked on a light and flung her keys onto the kitchen table. "Most of you are going to have to sleep on the floor," she said. "You'll have to draw straws for the couch. Talis gets the spare room. I think he earned it, and I totally owe him."

Talis chuckled and looped an arm around Cadence's waist. He pulled her to him and nuzzled her neck. "Stay with me?" he whispered.

She snorted. "Duh," she stated.

He grinned.

"Give Raven the couch," Draco yawned. "His rib's still jacked up. He shouldn't have to sleep on the floor."

As the rest of the guys shuffled around trying to find a spare patch of floor and Tawny rummaged through her closet trying to find adequate pillows and blankets for everyone, Talis and Cadence made their way toward the spare room.

Van, Lance and the rest of the rock star clan had gotten a hotel, but the rest of the guys would be calling Tawny's their home until Evie was released from the hospital.

They had all stayed in the waiting room until the doctor had given them the news that Brandon Talis Whitelaw had been brought into the world healthy, if not all that happy.

They had all taken their turn at seeing him and paying their respects to the exhausted parents. Afterwards, Traevyn had managed to crawl his towering frame into the hospital bed with Evie and fall asleep cradling her to his chest. Seth was still at the hospital with Julia, but would be coming to Tawny's shortly.

All in all, it had been an insane, chaotic, exhausting day with a very happy and satisfying ending.

Cadence flopped down on the edge of the bed and yawned, trying to will herself to take off the blue bridesmaid gown she still wore. She frowned in thought, wondering how Danny was doing. Poor guy. She hadn't even gotten to say congratulations. She hoped Olivia had recovered from the shock of her wedding day being obliterated and didn't have any hard feelings toward anyone.

She smiled as she felt gentle hands caress her shoulders and she looked behind her to see Talis completely shirtless, reclining on the bed beside her. She grinned and shook her head as the day's events replayed through her mind. "Why on earth do you love me, Talis?" she asked with a giggle.

He heaved a sigh. "Because you're nuts," he stated.

She laughed and turned to face him, lying down beside him so she could gaze up into his eyes. "I didn't know you went for the crazy ones," she teased.

He raised his eyebrows and shrugged. He traced a finger along her collarbone.

She smiled. "Why else?"

"Hmm... You're not bad to look at."

She laughed again and gave him a light shove. "Come on, I'm serious."

He grinned and sobered. He slipped an arm around her waist and pulled her full up against his body.

Her breath hitched in her throat and she closed her eyes as her heart started to pound.

"Because you're passion," he whispered seductively, "and chaos, and fire." He cupped her cheek in his palm and his eyes roamed over her for a long moment before his lips quirked devilishly. "And apparently I like to be tortured, which is interesting because I never considered myself much of a masochist." She burst out laughing, and he grinned.

"You're evil, Talis," she giggled.

He shook his head. "You have no idea. Now get out of that dress and come to bed. I want to sleep for about a century and I have no desire to do it without you in my arms."

She grinned and hurried to obey, wanting nothing more than to be beside him for all time. She threw her pajamas on and slipped into bed beside him, snuggling close and tracing her finger along the line of the dragon tattoo on his chest. He was warm and solid and perfect. His arms around her were heaven. "Talis?" she whispered.

"Yeah?" He had one hand buried in her soft hair and was relishing the feel of it. His blood was on fire at the sensation of her next to him. It had only been a week, but it felt like it had been an eternity since he had been close to her and touched her this way. He never wanted her away from him again, not so long as he lived and breathed.

"I was thinking of having you give me a tattoo," she said.

He smiled. "Oh yeah?"

She nodded.

"What were you thinking of getting?"

"On my lower back, under my dragon, I want a sword with a raven perched on the handle. And down the length of the blade I want your name in runes."

He blinked, taken aback by her request. "Are you sure?" he questioned. "Getting a name tattooed on you is danger-ous."

She shook her head. "It's symbolic, Talis. I want the sword because you and Raven taught me how to be a war-rior, which is why I want the raven on the handle. You both taught me how to fight, to not run away. I know that now. I'm done with running. I want your name on the blade to show my commitment to you is permanent. And, above the sword, right underneath where my other tattoo reads 'Katy-did,' I want it to say 'Cadeyrn.'"

He was quiet for a long moment, absently playing with her hair. Then, he turned and cradled her in his arms, gazing down into the only pair of eyes he ever wanted to look into for the rest of his life. "You sure?"

She smiled up at him. "Positive. Will you do it for me?"

He grinned. "Of course I will." He leaned in to kiss her and she whispered that she loved him. He caught the words in his mouth and savored their sweetness, believing her and knowing in his heart that she wouldn't run from him again. She was his, for all time. He would never let her go. He had fought for her, just like a knight of old, and he had proved himself worthy. Worthy of the beauty before him, worthy of her heart and her love. He'd won his Lady and he would love her until time stopped. For the rest of his days, he would be her champion and her paladin knight. He would bear that title proudly. Forever. He had definitely earned it.

EPILOGUE

One Year Later

The mountain air was cold and crisp as Cadence drew a great breath into her lungs and sighed. She could hear some of the other guys outside, already up and moving around. That was good. That meant that one of them would have gotten the fire going again. She glanced at Talis, who was still asleep next to her, and she smiled. His black hair had fallen across his forehead and one of the sleeves of his black thermal shirt had gotten pulled up, revealing all of the magnificent tattoos that she loved so much.

She reached out and gently pulled his sleeve back down, staring up at the tent ceiling while she woke up. Thank goodness they had a tent this year. As it was, Talis had only grudgingly agreed to it after she had threatened to withhold sex for the entire trip. It was one thing to have to sleep outside next to a fire when wild animals were prowling around and anything could come up and eat you, but to make love out in the open was a completely different matter. Any one of the guys could decide to take a leak and come out of their tent and get an eye full. It was just something she would not do. She was crazy and a bit wild sometimes, but she did have her dignity, and she did have her limits.

It was hard for her to believe that it had been a year since she had met Talis. It seemed like forever ago and yesterday all at the same time. She raised her left hand and studied her diamond engagement ring and her gold wedding band. She grinned. Life sure had changed since she had first camped up here.

A year ago, she had been a mess. Broken and careless

and half insane, on the verge of losing the only family she had. Now she was stable, married, on very good terms with her brother and had a happy life that she sometimes felt she didn't deserve.

She didn't know how she had ended up getting so very lucky, but she didn't like to second guess it. Talis had brought her happiness like she had never known and she didn't care why or how it had happened. She was just grateful that it had.

She sat up and started to unzip the tent, making to crawl out, but an arm around her waist halted her progress and pulled her back down. She giggled as Talis drew her back into his arms and started kissing along the back of her neck.

"Where are you going?" he purred.

She grinned and snuggled close to him. "Was going to see if one of the guys decided to make breakfast. Besides, Raven is supposed to get here this morning and I want to see him. I'm bummed he didn't get to come for the Arizona Renaissance Festival."

He shrugged. "Yeah, but he had to move so I guess that's a forgivable excuse."

Apparently, Raven had decided to move in with his brother in San Francisco. Seth and Raven had gotten to be very good friends over the past year and Seth was moving in with them also after he finished his last year of school. Because of relocating, Raven had been unable to attend the first event of the year, but he was due in at any moment to kick off the renfaire season proper with the annual camping trip in the Pinals.

Cadence snuggled closer to Talis, letting his body warm her and heat her blood. He tightened his arm around her and nipped her earlobe playfully.

"I have half a mind to not let you out of this tent," he said.

She grinned. "Didn't you get enough last night?"

He snorted and let his hand roam brazenly over her body for a moment. "I'll never get enough of you. Don't you know that by now?"

She savored his touch. It was the same for her. She always burned for Talis. The fire hadn't dimmed since marriage, hadn't cooled off at all. Her desire for him would never be sated. Her stomach growled suddenly and they both laughed. "Well," she said, "as much as the rest of me wants you, I think my stomach may have other ideas."

He chuckled softly. "Well, heaven forbid we deny your gut, baby."

He released his hold on her and Cadence crawled out of the tent, receiving a slap on the butt as she did so. She squeaked and shot a scowl over her shoulder at her husband, but he just grinned devilishly at her. She stood and stretched, shoving her feet in her shoes and starting over to the camp fire where Tempyst was making coffee. Talis followed behind her.

Ash glanced up at the two as they approached and rolled his eyes. "Good lord, when did you guys finally go to sleep?" he grumbled.

She frowned. "What do you mean?"

Draco and Ash exchanged a look. "Well, none of us slept until you guys finally did," he muttered.

She blinked and her cheeks flamed.

Talis chuckled and he wrapped his arms around her, pressing a kiss to her temple.

"Seriously," Ash continued. "The buying the tent thing to shield our eyes was a nice gesture, but next time maybe think of something you could do to shield our ears also."

Cadence's face was on fire, but Talis just laughed and shrugged nonchalantly. "Don't be pissed just because I'm getting some and you aren't. It's not my fault I have a hot wife."

If it was possible, Cadence's face got even hotter.

Suddenly, a car pulled up to the camp site and Raven leapt out, wearing his shades, his ebony hair longer than it had been the year before and flowing freely around his shoulders. He stood and faced everyone, holding his arms out flamboyantly. "Never fear, the party is here!" he shouted.

Cadence grinned and Talis chuckled. "Some things never change."

Her heart warmed at the sight of her dear friend. "Some things shouldn't," she said. She met Raven halfway across the camp site and he hoisted her off of the ground in a bear hug, making her squeal.

Talis smiled and he sat down across the fire from Ash and Draco while Tempyst and Devlyn started up breakfast.

"This is weird," Draco said. "It seems like just yesterday you brought her into our camp and she thought we were all a bunch of insane losers."

Talis grinned. "Yeah, I know. It's crazy how much can change in a year."

"Oh lord, they're at it already," Ash said, glancing over at Raven and Cadence.

Talis followed Ash's gaze and found Raven pulling a rattan sword out of his trunk and tossing it to Cadence. He shook his head. Cadence had been looking forward to sparring with Raven all year.

"No one would have ever convinced me she would come to mean so much to all of us," Draco continued. He shook his head. "Now she's like our little sister. All we want to do is watch out for and protect her."

Talis smiled. "Yeah except most of the time she ends up being the one protecting us."

Draco laughed.

"Come on, Cadence!" Raven's voice shouted. "What's wrong with you? Married life has made you old and slow!"

A sickening crack resounded through the camp, followed by Raven wailing like a baby. Talis chuckled to himself. Yes, certain things should never, ever change.

About the Author

If someone were to ask me what I am, it could be summed up in one, simple word: Dreamer. Ever since I was a small child my imagination has run wild. I have been telling stories for as long as I can remember, creating grand worlds in my head and going on adventures that were invisible to others around me. Am I eccentric? Yes. Am I proud of that? Absolutely.

I write about the things that inspire me, both in this world and in realms only seen with the imagination. My heroines are sassy and strong. My heroes are sometimes shy. I have an obsession with music (and musicians) and a fascination with wings. I believe true love does exist, and sometimes it is found in the strangest, most unexpected places. I also believe that family and close friends are the glue that hold people together.

Above all things, I believe in being true to yourself and seizing the day. Life is an amazing gift. Make your experience as beautiful as you possibly can.